"As fresh as a daisy, with a bouquet of irresistible characters."
—Elaine Viets, Author of the Dead-End Job Mysteries

Dearly
Depotted

Flower Shop
Mystery

Kate
Collins

Author of
Slay It with
Flowers

D0030945

C

SIGNET

| $7.99 | U.S. |
| $8.99 | CAN. |

ISBN 978-0-451-21585-7

5 0 7 9 9

EAN

Praise for *Mum's the Word,*
the first Flower Shop Mystery

"Kate Collins plants all the right seeds to grow a fertile garden of mystery. . . . Abby Knight is an Indiana florist who cannot keep her nose out of other people's business. She's rash, brash, and audacious. Move over, Stephanie Plum, Abby Knight has come to town."

  —Denise Swanson, author of the Scumble River mysteries

"An engaging debut planted with a spirited sleuth, quirky sidekicks, and page-turning action . . . delightfully addictive. . . . A charming addition to the cozy subgenre. Here's hoping we see more of intrepid florist Abby Knight and sexy restaurateur Marco Salvare."

  —Nancy J. Cohen, author of the Bad Hair Day mysteries

"Kate Collins's new flower shop mystery is fresh as a daisy, with a bouquet of irresistible characters and deep roots in the Indiana soil."   —Elaine Viets, author of the Dead-End Job mysteries

"A bountiful bouquet of clues, colorful characters, and tantalizing twists. . . . Kate Collins carefully cultivates clues, plants surprising suspects, and harvests a killer in this fresh and frolicsome new Flower Shop Mystery series."

  —Ellen Byerrum, author of the Crime of Fashion mysteries

"This amusing new author has devised an excellent cast of characters and thrown them in to a cleverly tumultuous plot. . . . Readers will savor Abby's courage. . . . The pacing is brisk, with parallel plots that intersect in interesting ways. A terrific debut!"   —*Romantic Times*

"This engaging read has a list of crazy characters that step off the pages to the delight of the reader. Don't miss this wanna-be sleuth's adventures."   —*Rendezvous*

"This story was cute and funny, had a good plot line which entwined a lot of interesting threads . . . an enjoyable read and a fine debut for this new mystery series."—Dangerously Curvy Novels

Other Flower Shop Mysteries

Dearly Depotted

A Flower Shop Mystery

Kate Collins

A SIGNET BOOK

SIGNET
Published by New American Library, a division of
Penguin Group (USA) Inc., 375 Hudson Street,
New York, New York 10014, USA
Penguin Group (Canada), 90 Eglinton Avenue East, Suite 700, Toronto,
Ontario M4P 2Y3, Canada (a division of Pearson Penguin Canada Inc.)
Penguin Books Ltd., 80 Strand, London WC2R 0RL, England
Penguin Ireland, 25 St. Stephen's Green, Dublin 2,
Ireland (a division of Penguin Books Ltd.)
Penguin Group (Australia), 250 Camberwell Road, Camberwell, Victoria 3124,
Australia (a division of Pearson Australia Group Pty. Ltd.)
Penguin Books India Pvt. Ltd., 11 Community Centre, Panchsheel Park,
New Delhi - 110 017, India
Penguin Group (NZ), 67 Apollo Drive, Rosedale, North Shore,
Auckland 1311, New Zealand (a division of Pearson New Zealand Ltd.)
Penguin Books (South Africa) (Pty.) Ltd., 24 Sturdee Avenue,
Rosebank, Johannesburg 2196, South Africa

Penguin Books Ltd., Registered Offices:
80 Strand, London WC2R 0RL, England

First published by Signet, an imprint of New American Library,
a division of Penguin Group (USA) Inc.

First Printing, July 2005
10 9 8

Copyright © Linda Tsoutsouris, 2005
All rights reserved

🄳 REGISTERED TRADEMARK—MARCA REGISTRADA

Printed in the United States of America

PUBLISHER'S NOTE
This is a work of fiction. Names, characters, places, and incidents either are
the product of the author's imagination or are used fictitiously, and any resem-
blance to actual persons, living or dead, business establishments, events, or
locales is entirely coincidental.

The publisher does not have any control over and does not assume any
responsibility for author or third-party Web sites or their content.

If you purchased this book without a cover you should be aware that this
book is stolen property. It was reported as "unsold and destroyed" to the
publisher and neither the author nor the publisher has received any payment
for this "stripped book."

ACKNOWLEDGMENTS

Writing this book has been a true labor of love—then again, after hours and days and months of pounding the keys, staring at the computer with glazed eyes, there were times when the love part was nowhere to be found. However, Abby and I both lived to see another day, thanks in large part to the following people:

My very wise, very supportive, always encouraging editor, Ellen Edwards.

My extremely knowledgeable, also supportive agent, Karen Solem.

My sweet and highly capable editor, Serena Jones, who has a keen ear for humor and can spot a flat line from a hundred yards.

Barb Ferrari, Mary Kennedy, and Cindy Winter, who have listened to me groan, whine, brag, shout for joy, and generally be annoying—and still let me be their friend.

Deanna, at Barry's Photography Studio, who was kind enough to give me a crash course in Videography for Dummies.

Phil Potempa, reporter extraordinaire, who has helped me many times over the years.

The girls at the T & B law office. (You really should put out a calendar, ladies.)

And could I not mention the unflagging support of my family? (Especially with my husband reading this over my shoulder?) Love you guys.

CHAPTER ONE

"Red, white, and blue carnations . . . That's what you ordered, right?"

"That's what I ordered," I assured my customer, a thirty-four-year-old, bubblegum-chewing, Barbie doll look-alike by the name of Trudee DeWitt. We were standing on the dew-coated front lawn of her sprawling house early on the Fourth of July; so early, in fact, that I was not fully awake—otherwise I would have caught the note of concern in her voice.

"Well, then," she said with a nervous giggle. "Oops."

Oops? I blinked hard as my sleepy brain scrambled into alert. "They're not red, white, and blue carnations?"

"Not exactly." Trudee motioned for me to follow, then started across the yard, wobbling unsteadily in her sequined red heels. In honor of the holiday she had donned a pair of extremely red, extremely short shorts and a tight, spangled T-shirt that looked like an explosion of fireworks across her bosom. Her shiny, silvery blond hair, pulled back in a loose, sexy braid tied with red, white, and blue ribbons, moved like a wiper blade across her back.

The DeWitts had hired me to provide floral decorations for their Fourth of July barbeque bash, culminating in a giant U.S. flag spread over the grass behind their house. It was one of two jobs I'd agreed to take on for the holiday; Bloomers was normally closed on Independence Day. The other job was an opulent evening wedding and reception for my cousin Jillian-the-drama-queen, which was stressful enough all by itself without adding an *oops* to it.

Trailing Trudee across the lawn were my helpers for the day, seventeen-year-old quadruplets Jimmy, Joey, Johnny, and Karl Dombowski, wearing unlaced Nikes, baggy jeans, and extra-large button-down shirts. The quads belonged to my assistant Lottie, who'd happily volunteered their services for the day to keep them out of trouble. I brought up the rear of our little parade, still trying to decipher what Trudee had meant by *Not exactly.* Not exactly carnations?

When Trudee came to a halt in front of an insulated trailer and opened the tailgate, the boys quickly formed a semicircle around her, unable to take their eyes off the spangles bouncing in front of their noses. I broke through the ranks and stepped up to the gate. In the cool, fragrant interior I saw three enormous bins, each filled with a different color of carnation: patriotic blue, paper white, and—petal pink?

"See what I mean?" Trudee asked, wrinkling her nose as if the pink flowers gave off an offensive odor.

"Not exactly red," I concurred.

"You can exchange them, can't you?"

On a holiday? Hours before her party? Was this her first visit to Earth?

I grabbed the arm of one of the quads—I wasn't sure which—slapped money into his palm, and said in his ear,

"Go to the hardware store and buy every can of fire-engine red spray paint you can find. Hurry!" Then I turned back to Trudee with a smile. "Don't worry. Everything will be fine."

It had to be fine. I needed that big fat fee Trudee had promised.

My cell phone rang. I pulled it out of my jeans pocket and read the message on the top. JILLIAN CALLING, it said, which could only have been worse if it had been Satan on the line.

"Excuse me a moment. I have to take this call," I told Trudee, opening the phone.

"That's okay. I need coffee. I'll be inside."

As she undulated toward her house I forced a note of cheer in my voice. "Happy wedding day, Jillian."

"It's off, Abby. The wedding is *off*. I can't go through with it."

"Jillian," I said through gritted teeth, "it's early. You don't get up until noon. Go back to bed for a few more hours and you'll feel like a new woman."

"I'm serious, Abby. I'm going to call Claymore right now and tell him."

I could tell by the determination in her voice that she meant it. "Hold on," I told her, then said to the boys, "Go mark off the flag in the backyard. The string and stakes are in my car."

As they shuffled off, grumpy now that Trudee and her spangles had gone, I put the phone to my ear once more. "Jillian, one crisis per morning is all I allow myself, and I've already had it, so pay attention. You cannot call off this wedding. Do you know how many flowers I've ordered? . . . Jillian, are you listening?"

She wasn't. "Claymore is such a jerk. What did I ever see in him? Tell me!"

What I wanted to tell her was *"I told you so."* Claymore Osborne was the younger brother of Pryce, the rat who'd dropped me because his parents couldn't live with the shame of my flunking out of law school. For the Osbornes it was all about appearances, and I had warned Jillian of that when she first showed me her three-carat diamond engagement ring. But when had she ever listened? Not when she'd gotten engaged to the Italian restaurant owner, the moody French artist, the English consulate, or the Greek plastic surgeon. In fact, not since she'd discovered boys.

Jillian was tall, gorgeous, and twenty-five. She'd graduated from Harvard, grown up in a big house, vacationed in exotic locales, and had a father who was a stockbroker and a mother who golfed. Because of all that, Jillian fit in with the Osbornes. I never had.

Besides not being able to cut it at law school, I was petite (the Osbornes liked statuesque women), I freckled rather than tanned, and I hated the country club scene. I'd gone to school on money from my grandfather's trust supplemented by summer jobs, and I had a father who was a retired cop and a mother who taught kindergarten and made weird clay sculptures.

The only reason the Osbornes hadn't objected to me at first was because my two older brothers, Jonathan and Jordan, were doctors. That, combined with their marrying fashionable wives and joining the country club, made them acceptable. Lucky them.

"Claymore adores you, Jillian," I assured my weeping cousin. "He would do anything for you. Why wouldn't you want to marry him?"

"Because he's an idiot. He has no taste. He *hates* the ascot I chose for him."

"Wait a minute. You're calling off the wedding because of a tie?"

She sighed dramatically. "It's an *ascot*, Abby."

"That is *not* reason enough to call off your wedding. But this isn't really about the ascot, is it? It's never about the ascot. You've got cold feet again."

"Don't be ridiculous. I'm marrying into one of the wealthiest families in New Chapel. Why would I have cold feet?"

"Because you like being pampered and courted, and you're afraid once you get married it will end. In other words, you don't want to grow up."

"You," she said, highly irritated, "are a snot." And she hung up.

She'd go through with it now just to prove me wrong.

With a quick glance at my watch, I dashed to the back-yard and found that the boys had outlined the flag. As we marked off the stripes, the fourth quad showed up with the paint, so we spread the pink carnations in the designated area and sprayed them red. I checked my watch. Half an hour lost.

"Won't that kill the grass?" Johnny asked me as we stepped back to study our handiwork.

"It'll grow back."

I left the quads filling in the blue and white parts of the flag and headed for the flower shop to pick up Trudee's indoor decorations. Because of all the street closings for the Fourth of July parade, I had to park blocks away from the town square, then weave through people who had already staked out their spots to watch the ten o'clock parade. Normally I wouldn't have minded the hike, but today I didn't have time to spare.

I unlocked Bloomers' bright yellow door and walked in to the sound of my assistant Grace humming as she ground coffee beans in the parlor, and my other assistant,

Lottie, singing along with her radio from the workshop in back. I inhaled the sweet fragrances of coffee, roses, lavender, and eucalyptus, and, for a brief moment, all was right with my world.

Then I thought of Jillian's wedding and got a headache.

Who held their nuptials on a Monday? Could she have chosen a Friday evening or Saturday afternoon like a normal person? Oh, no. Not Jillian. She had to have a Fourth of July spectacle. Her garden ceremony had been arranged to end just as the country club's big, splashy fireworks display was beginning, so the sky would explode as if the heavens themselves were giving her a standing ovation. My cousin was not a normal person.

If I were merely her florist, I could have shrugged off Jillian's eccentricities. Unfortunately, I was also one of her bridesmaids, and that meant suffering the company of my weasel of an ex-fiancé, the best man (as if!), who had dumped me two months before our own nuptials. Then there was my escort, deputy prosecutor Greg Morgan— New Chapel, Indiana's, answer to Brad Pitt—who was so self-absorbed he couldn't remember my being in the same high school with him.

I didn't even want to think about the bridesmaid's dress. Jillian had picked out a print that looked like a watercolor painting of white lilies swaying against an aquamarine sky—at least that's what it looked like on the bodies of the three willowy women who comprised the rest of the team. On my height-challenged form it looked like a clown suit.

As a final offense, there was the picky bride herself, Jillian Ophelia Knight, first cousin on my father's side, who had jilted four men already. If she made it through the wedding today, it would be a first. If I made it through the wedding without choking her, it would be a miracle.

Sadly, I had no one to blame for this situation but myself. Being the new owner of a floral shop, I had jumped at the chance to do the arrangements for Jillian's wedding. I needed the exposure, not to mention the business. I had agreed to be a bridesmaid because that was what one did for one's family. I hadn't factored in having to deal with an ugly dress, a hateful ex-fiancé, a Fourth of July party, and a cousin who attracted trouble like a magnet.

There was only one way to get through the wedding, and that was to look at it as a challenge. I'd never yet shied away from a challenge. Also, I'd never shied away from money, and this fee was going to be huge.

"Good morning, dear," Grace called from the parlor. "How are we this morning?"

"Wishing it were Tuesday," I answered.

"If wishes were horses, beggars would ride," she reminded me in her crisp British accent. Grace had a quote for everything. It came from working as a librarian, just one of the careers she'd held in her sixty-odd years. She was a legal secretary at a firm where I clerked during my year in law school and had retired just before I bought Bloomers, so I coaxed her to come work for me and put her in charge of the coffee and tea parlor. "Is the wedding on or off?" she asked.

"On."

"I wouldn't place any bets on it," Lottie said, coming through the curtain that separated the shop from the workroom. "Jillian's track record is zero for four."

Lottie Dombowski was a big-boned, big-hearted forty-five-year-old, with brassy curls, a laugh that could be heard across town, a gift for floral design, and more common sense than anyone I knew, other than Grace. Lottie had owned Bloomers for years, but then her husband's health problems had nearly forced them into bankruptcy and she had to sell. And there I was, freshly booted out of law school and desperate to support myself. I used the remainder of my grandfather's trust to make a down payment, and the rest was, well, hysteria.

"How did it go at Trudee's house, or should I be afraid to ask?" Lottie said over her shoulder as she weeded out the wilting flowers in our glass display case.

"The supplier sent pink carnations instead of red and I had to paint them."

"That would explain the condition of your fingers," Grace said, handing me a cup of coffee. I took a sip and savored the subtle touch of cinnamon that passed across my tongue. If there was one thing that always improved a situation, it was Grace's coffee.

"Fingernail polish remover," Lottie said, heading back to the workroom with her bundle of old flowers. "That'll take off the paint."

I parted the curtain and followed her into my favorite place in the whole world. Although our workroom was windowless, the abundance of blossoms and fragrances made it feel like a tropical garden. Pastel-colored wreaths and brightly hued swags hung on one ivory latticed wall. Vases of all sizes and containers of dried flowers filled shelves above the counter on another wall. A long, slate-covered worktable sat in the middle of the room. A stainless steel walk-in cooler occupied one side, and a desk holding my computer, telephone, and the normal assortment of items sat on the other side.

I printed out my list for the party, then opened the heavy cooler and stepped inside to check on the arrangements we'd done the evening before.

"Abby? Hello? Are you in there?"

I turned around, and there was the bride-to-be, searching the dim interior with a bewildered gaze. The cooler was such a riot of bright colors that I, with my red hair, yellow tank top, and black capris, blended into the background like a gigantic gerbera daisy.

Jillian was dressed in her usual chic style—mango-colored silk tee, ivory linen skirt, and sexy sandals that emphasized her long legs. Her copper-colored hair fell in shimmering waves around her shoulders, her perfect skin glowed with dewy freshness, and her golden eyes gazed out at the world with a look of keen intelligence, belying the SPACE FOR RENT sign behind them.

"Abs, we have a problem," she said, spotting me at last.

"*We* have a problem? If this doesn't concern flowers, I don't have a problem; you do."

Pushing out her lower lip like a wounded child, Jillian plucked a deep plum rose from a container and buried her nose in the fragrant petals. "But you always know what to do. And it's just an itty-bitty problem."

She knew how to yank those guilt strings. I guided her out of the cooler and we sat on stools at the worktable. "I'm sorry for snapping at you. I worked on your flowers until after midnight and I'm a little tired. Now, what's the problem?"

Jillian gave me a pained smile that told me that this was a whole lot bigger than itty-bitty. "Greg Morgan sprained his ankle playing tennis yesterday. You don't have an escort."

"If you're telling me I have to stand alone in that dress all evening," I managed to say through a clenched jaw, "you can find yourself another bridesmaid."

"I don't know what your problem is with that dress."

I eyed a pot of ivy within arm's reach, wondering whether I could use one of the trailing vines to choke her. "It's made for tall women, Jill. *Tall* women. Do I look at all tall to you?"

She leaned back to study me, as if it had never occurred to her that I only came up to her shoulder, then she sighed and said, "Okay."

"*Okay*? You don't care if I'm not in your wedding?"

"Of course I care, silly. I wouldn't want to get married without you there."

"Then why did you say 'okay'?"

"Because I understand how you feel. And because I know you'll find a replacement."

"Me?" I choked out.

She shrugged. "Unless you want to walk up the aisle alone. I mean, you don't honestly believe I have time to look, do you? And you can't possibly think Claymore can handle it. With his nerves?"

That trailing vine was so close . . .

Jillian slid off the stool and gave me a hug, pressing my face into the gold coin that hung from a chain around her neck. "I knew I could count on you." She hurried off, calling, "I'll have the tux sent over before noon."

The bell over the door jingled and she was gone. I glanced at Lottie, quietly snipping flowers, and she shook her head. "How many more fires are you going to have to put out before she says 'I do'?"

"Not a single one. Zip, zero, zilch. Not even if her head were to burst into flames."

The bell jingled again and seconds later Jillian swept back through the curtain. "One more thing. Claymore's grandmother is coming, and I need you to keep an eye on her during the reception. She tends to wander off looking for water."

There was absolute silence in the shop. Across the table Lottie continued to work, waiting to see what I'd do, and I was fairly certain Grace was hovering on the other side of the curtain, holding her breath.

I planted my hands on my hips and glared at my cousin. "Are you out of your mind? Don't you think I have enough responsibilities without adding a ninety-year-old woman to my list? If something happened to her, the Osbornes would roast me over live coals. Give her bottled water to keep in her purse."

"She won't remember it's there. *Puh-leeze,* Abby! You're the only one Grandma trusts. She'll be sitting with Claymore's parents for the dinner. You'll only have to keep an eye on her afterward, and she won't be staying long anyway." She folded her hands beseechingly and gave me that helpless little-girl gaze that always got to me. "Pretty please?"

"Are you sure I'm the *only* one Grandma trusts?"

"The *only* one. 'That Abby Knight is one sharp cookie,' she always says. 'Pryce, you were an ass to let her get away.' She likes you way more than she does Pryce or Claymore."

Two points in Grandma's favor. Truthfully, once the flowers were in place I wouldn't have all that much to do, and besides, I liked Pryce's grandmother. She wouldn't take guff from anyone, and she wasn't impressed by her children's expensive clothing, fancy cars, or country club memberships. The first time I met her, at one of the Osborne family dinners, she whispered in my ear, "Don't let their snobbish ways intimidate you. Pryce's great-grandfather made his living catching rats, and Pryce's father's nickname at school was Boogers. You figure out why."

"So are we good to go?" Jillian asked.

"Fine. I'll watch Grandma Osborne, but it had better be for a very short time, and even then, you'll owe me big-time."

Jillian gave me another hug, but this time I dodged the coin. "Thanks, Ab. I *wub* you."

I hated it when she started the baby talk. "I'll let you know how I feel about you after the reception."

I glanced at Lottie, who was trying not to laugh.

"*That* was the last fire," I told her after Jillian had gone.

Lottie's lips twitched as she stripped the thorns from a tall red rose with one smooth glide of her knife.

"You're right. Who am I kidding?" I said. "I should just walk down that wedding aisle carrying a hose and wearing a hard hat."

CHAPTER TWO

"I went through my entire phone book, and I can't find anyone who'll be a substitute groomsman," I complained as Lottie and I carried deep boxes filled with pots of flowers for Trudee's party to the alley, where a rental van was parked. Since Lottie's old station wagon wasn't big enough to carry everything, and I wasn't yet able to afford a company van, it was either rent one or make multiple trips. So we rented. "What is it with men and weddings?"

"What about Marco?" Lottie asked, sliding a box into the van.

"You've seen my dress. Would you want Marco to witness you in that getup?"

"Sweetie, with Marco, I wouldn't care if I'd been dunked in butter and coated with breadcrumbs. Call him, for heaven's sake."

Marco Salvare was the handsome hunk who owned the Down the Hatch Bar and Grill two doors north of my shop. He'd bought it around the same time I bought Bloomers, and we'd hit it off right away. He was a former

Army Ranger who'd tried life as a cop before finally settling in as a bar owner and part-time investigator. He was intelligent and forthright and didn't always play by the rules—all reasons we got along. Also, he excelled at untangling the messes into which I seemed to habitually entangle myself, and today was starting to look like one of those messes.

"Fine. I'll call."

Lottie went back inside the shop while I arranged the boxes to keep them from shifting. I heard a wolf whistle behind me, and, knowing the particular wolf it belonged to, I turned with a smile. "Hey," I said to Marco as he strode toward me, "your name just came up."

"I get nervous when you say that. Let me give you a hand."

I stepped back to give him room—actually to ogle him—as he hoisted the remaining carton onto his shoulder and deposited it in the van. Marco was in his usual outfit—a pair of scuffed black boots, formfitting blue jeans, and a T-shirt. I'd never seen him in a suit, let alone a tux, but I could certainly picture him in one. He was solid male sinew in a trim body topped off with a pair of shoulders that wouldn't quit. He had olive skin, dark hair, bedroom eyes, and a smile that would melt your mascara. He also had lightning-fast reflexes honed during his stint with the Rangers. I'd learned the hard way never to tap him on the shoulder without first letting him know I was there.

"How is your cousin holding up?" he asked. "Or should I ask, *where* is your cousin *holing* up?" Marco was well acquainted with Jillian's history.

"She gave me a moment of panic earlier, but she's okay now." I pointed toward the open back door of the shop. "Would you mind helping me load that palm tree?"

Marco glanced inside the door. "I don't see a palm tree."

"You're looking right at it."

What he was looking at was one of my mother's sculptures, a tall green tree with branches shaped to resemble bark-covered human arms. At the end of the arms were palms—the kind found on hands, not on trees—on which to hang coats. It was typical of the pieces she made, which ranged from the slightly eccentric to the extremely bizarre and had been known to send senior citizens into dead faints. She'd brought this one to the shop more than two weeks ago, and so far there had been no buyers, only a lot of chucklers and a few gaspers.

"You're kidding," Marco said, eyeing it guardedly.

"Sadly, no. My client wanted a tropical eye-catcher for her party today, and when she saw this tree she thought it would be perfect."

Marco fought his way through the branches to get his hands around the trunk without a finger jabbing him in the face. "If this doesn't catch people's eyes," he grumbled, "or blind them, nothing will." He shoved it all the way to the front of the van and shut the gate, leaving the top of the tree resting on the dashboard like a headless human holding on for dear life.

"Thanks," I said gratefully. "Now I have just one more favor to ask."

"I hope it's a quick one. The bar is going to be hopping today."

"How hopping?"

He came over to where I was leaning against the driver's door and tilted my chin up, his touch sending a tingle down my spine. "Why do I get the feeling you're about to ask me to do something I won't like?"

"Depends on your definition of *like*. Would you *like* to take a short walk with me this evening?"

He gave me a wary look. "Depends on your definition of *short*."

"Touché. How about from here to the garbage bin over there?"

Marco's lips twitched. "I'll probably regret this, but I'm going to say yes."

"Super. Next question. Would you like to eat, drink, and be merry with me? While wearing a tuxedo?"

His dark eyebrows came down to form a solid line of scowl. He was getting the idea.

"The thing is," I hastened to say, "one of the grooms-men—my escort, in fact—sprained his ankle, and I really, *really* don't want to be the only bridesmaid without an escort. Please do this for me, Marco. I'll be forever in your debt."

He folded his arms and gave me a stern look. "I hate tuxes."

"Trust me, you'll look great. It's top of the line. The women will drool over you." At least this one would.

"I don't like ceremonies either."

That wasn't good news. He and I had walked down the aisle many times in my dreams. "You'll like this one, I promise. It'll have fireworks in it."

"Is there a reception? I'm not fond of receptions." He was starting to soften.

"Think of it this way, you'll get to eat a gourmet meal, hear a live band, and have the privilege of dancing with me. Does it get any better than that? Besides, you've got capable staff at the bar. They can handle things for a couple of hours." I lowered my eyelids and tried to look irresistible. "What do you say? Will you help me out?"

He rubbed his jaw, as though calculating something. "How much will you be in my debt?"

I paused. Last time we had a wager he'd wanted roses for each one of his tables for a week. Luckily, he'd lost and had to provide me with a home-cooked dinner instead. "How about those roses for your tables?"

There was a devilish twinkle in his eye that told me he had something else in mind. "How about I let you know?"

Hey, whatever it took. "Sure thing. Now, about that tux. Jillian will have it here before noon, and I'll bring it to the bar so you can try it on. I think you and Greg are about the same size."

"Greg Morgan? That little runt? I'm at least four inches taller than he is."

More like one inch, but I wasn't in a position to burst his male ego. "I'll call the tuxedo shop and ask if they can send longer pants."

"You'd better hope they can. There's no way in hell I'd show up in one of those monkey suits with my socks exposed."

I wondered how he'd feel about showing up with a girl in a clown suit.

The Independence Day parade was in full swing as I pulled out of the alley with the fully loaded van, but all I caught was a glimpse of the high school marching band's blue uniforms and sweaty faces. When I got to Trudee's house I found three of the quads sprawled in lounge chairs on her back deck, icy colas at their sides.

"Okay, guys, let's get the van unloaded," I called, clapping my hands to snap them out of their daydreams. "Who's missing?"

"Karl," Johnny volunteered. "He's inside."

I peered through the sliding glass door and spotted the missing quad sitting at the kitchen counter having a

conversation with Trudee. Her seventeen-year-old daughter, Heather, was in the adjacent family room, flipping
through a magazine, ignoring both of them.

I'd encountered Heather several times before, and
none of those meetings had been pleasant. She was going
through a rebellious phase in which she despised her
mother's lifestyle, hairstyle, cooking, friends, TV shows,
and every word she uttered. Heather had dyed her short
hair shocking pink and wore beer-cap dangle earrings,
purple lipstick, and shiny black eyeshadow, a look that
Trudee, as a former makeup artist and hair stylist, could
barely tolerate—which was the whole point. Watching
her, I silently muttered a prayer of forgiveness for putting
my own mother through a similar hell.

"So, like, what's your favorite rock song?" Karl was
asking Trudee when I walked in.

I took him by the shoulders and turned him toward the
door. "Get moving. Time is money."

Once the van had been unloaded, I held open the front
door and guided the boys as they brought the palm tree
coatrack into Trudee's enormous foyer. In any other
home the coatrack would have looked ridiculous, but
since this entranceway already contained a waterfall with
accompanying jungle sounds, and wallpaper covered
with giant parrots, lizards, and other flora and fauna of
the tropics, the palm tree had no trouble fitting in.

While the boys were busy setting pots of flowers along
the paths and on the back deck, I decorated the foyer,
where I arranged bushy ferns and half a dozen white or-
chids around the waterfall pool.

"What's that?" Heather called, leaning over the banis-
ter at the top of the curving staircase and pointing to my
mother's palm tree.

"A coatrack."

"It's gross. Where did you find it?" she asked, coming down the steps. "The junkyard?"

"Yes," I said dryly as I stepped back to study the orchid arrangement. "I found it at the junkyard and brought it to your house."

"Shut *up*. Why are those creeps all over the backyard?"

"They're my helpers."

"You know they're, like, total losers, right? I mean, who else takes the bus to school? And look where they work. Burger King. What's that about?"

At that moment the front door opened and one of the so-called losers—who, it turned out, was Karl—stuck his head in. He saw Heather and smiled. Rolling her eyes, she marched back upstairs looking very put out.

"All done?" I asked Karl.

"Um, well, about that," he said, scratching his neck. "We ran into a minor problem."

"Karl, unless this is a *major* problem, I don't have time for it."

He thought for a moment, then said, "It's a major problem."

I pushed him outside so Trudee wouldn't hear. "Okay, spill it."

"There was this gigantic hornets' nest under the deck, see, and—"

"Bottom line, Karl," I said, checking the time, "who got stung?"

"My brothers."

"*All* of them? Where are they?"

"In the van. They're not feeling well. Yeah, you might want to stop by the hospital on your way back to the shop."

I glanced back at the house to see Heather in the doorway holding her hand to her forehead to form a big letter L.

*   *   *

Fortunately, none of the hornets' victims required emergency care. Back at Bloomers, Lottie iced their stings, doused them with calamine lotion, and drove them home, while I took the tuxedo my aunt had dropped off to Down the Hatch. Marco was eating a sandwich at the sleek black desk in his office, and he didn't look extremely happy to see me.

"Here it is," I said, putting lots of enthusiasm in my voice. "Your tuxedo."

"Did you get longer pants?"

Did I want to tell him I forgot? "They'll fit," I assured him.

He took the black suit, hung it on the back of the door, and removed the pants from the hanger. He pulled off his white socks, started to unbutton his jeans, then stopped and eyed me.

"Are you really going to ask me to turn around and close my eyes?" I asked. Then I caught his devilish gaze and my cheeks grew hot. I turned after all.

"Too short," he announced moments later.

I stared at his ankles in dismay. It wasn't that there was anything wrong with them; it was just that they were, well, ankles. Not quite the formal look Jillian would want. Obviously, Marco had been right about being taller than Morgan, although it was more like two inches, not four. But was I going to argue the point?

I knelt down for a better look. "I have an idea."

"You have red fingers."

"I know that. It's part of being a florist—like having a green thumb, only redder and more of them."

"Looks to me like you were into red paint."

"Are you going to take off those pants?"

"I thought you'd never ask."

Fifteen minutes, a pair of scissors, and a roll of duct

tape later, I had let out the hems and turned the raw edges inside. It wasn't the neatest job in the world but, after all, who'd be looking at Marco's ankles? Not me. There were other, more intriguing areas that had my eye.

"I'll pick you up at seven fifteen," I told him and took off. Another problem solved.

After a stop at the deli to eat a turkey sandwich, which took way longer than expected because of the hordes of people in town, Lottie and I loaded the van with the wedding decorations and raced over to the banquet center.

The Garden of Eden Banquet Center was an annex of the New Chapel Country Club, which made it an acceptable place to hold an Osborne wedding. The center had a grand ballroom, a fully equipped kitchen, a coatroom, dressing rooms, a posh reception area inside the glassed front entrance, and a large, shrub-enclosed garden with a gazebo for outside events. Everything about the banquet center was deluxe, down to the waiters' short white jackets with tails, gold vests, black pants, and black and gold berets. However, the main reason Jillian had selected the center was because the nearby country club had a fantastic fireworks display.

The garden where Jillian's ceremony would take place was a large square of plush Kentucky bluegrass enclosed by red rose shrubs and accessible through a white trellised archway. It had a redbrick center aisle, rows of white chairs, and a large, lattice-sided gazebo, open in front, with two wide steps leading up to a red cedar pulpit. Inside the gazebo were four chairs for a string quartet and electrical outlets for video equipment, a consideration for Jillian since she had hired a media team of two videographers and two photographers.

It took an hour to decorate the ballroom, then we turned our attention to the gazebo, which we draped with white gauze, peach satin ribbon, and cascades of climbing roses. As I positioned vases of white and peach-colored blossoms on risers beside the last row of seats, I noticed that the turf was damp, as though it had recently been sprinkled.

"The sun will dry it," Lottie said. "Not a problem." I left her fastening big satin bows on the end chairs, while I carried stacks of boxes filled with boutonnieres and bouquets to the kitchen, where preparations were already under way for the wedding feast. I gave wide berth to the team carving ice sculptures and carried my load to the industrial-sized coolers lining one wall. The only problem with that plan was that once I got there I couldn't open a door without toppling the boxes.

"Excuse me," I said to a scruffy guy in a stained white jacket washing dishes at a nearby sink, "will you open one of the coolers for me, please?"

"Why? What do you need?"

I peered around my tower of white cardboard to see whether he was serious. He was.

"Gunther, you blockhead," one of the female employees snapped as she pulverized a mound of vanilla beans with a marble pestle, "open the . . . Oh, for pity's sake, I'll do it myself."

She put the heavy pestle down with a thunk, then stalked over and pulled open one of the massive doors, letting out a cloud of frosty air. "Slacker," she muttered, casting the dishwasher a glare. She was a tall, thin-faced, droopy-eyed woman, probably in her late thirties, and definitely a candidate for *What Not to Wear*. Her white kitchen coat hung open, revealing a teal tank top paired with red spandex pants and navy sneakers.

She took half my load and set it in the cooler, and I followed with the other half. "Thanks," I said. "Sorry for the interruption."

She gave me a quick once-over. "Don't I know you from someplace?"

"Possibly from my flower shop, Bloomers." I stuck out my hand. "Abby Knight."

A big smile spread across her face as she shook my hand. "Sheila Sackowitz. Sure, I've been to your shop—gosh, it's been months—but as I remember, it was a nice little place."

I dug in my purse for one of the coupons I'd had printed. When it came to promoting Bloomers I was unabashedly forward. "Here's a reason to come again."

"Well, isn't that sweet? Thanks, I will."

"Gunther! Telephone," someone called from the hallway.

Dripping soapy water, the dishwasher rushed past me and nearly bowled over Lottie, who was just coming to get me. As we left the banquet center, we saw him in the reception area with his face tucked into the marble phone niche, having a hushed conversation. At that moment my cell phone rang. I checked the screen, saw JILLIAN CALLING, and started to put it back.

"Aren't you going to answer it?" Lottie asked.

I showed her the screen. "Good choice," she said.

We made a quick stop at Trudee's, where I was relieved to see that the flowers, even the painted ones, were holding up. I misted them, and we made it back to Bloomers by five o'clock, just as Grace was getting ready to leave. "Jillian's been calling every fifteen minutes," she told us. "That can't be good."

"It's just nerves," I said. "She wouldn't call off the wedding this late. Even Jillian wouldn't be that brazen."

The phone rang, as if on cue. Grace and Lottie

exchanged glances, then Lottie patted my shoulder. "Good luck," she said; then she and Grace fled.

I picked up the phone and heard noisy sobs on the other end. "What is it now, Jill?"

"You were right, Abby. I've got cold feet. I can't marry Claymore."

"Jillian, listen to me. The flowers are in place. The food is simmering. The quartet is probably tuning up this very minute. Two hundred people are putting on their dress clothes and combing their hair in preparation to see you march up that aisle. You *have* to marry Claymore. Now, put your mother on the phone. I need to talk to her." I'd have to alert Aunt Corrine that Jillian was a flight risk so she could block the exits.

"You can't talk to her because I'm not at home. I *left* home and I'm never going back."

CHAPTER THREE

I glanced at my watch and did a quick calculation. Since I'd last seen my cold-footed cousin, she'd had ample time to drive clear across the state and head off in any direction she chose. That was what she'd done before the last four weddings. "Where are you, Jill?"

"In my car."

"So help me, Jillian, if you don't come back this instant I will hunt you down and—"

"I'm in the alley behind Bloomers."

"Behind *my* Bloomers?" I slapped the phone into the cradle, ran to the back exit, pushed open the heavy door, and there she was in her gold Volvo, the cell phone to her ear, her forehead against the steering wheel. I nearly collapsed in relief.

"You almost gave me a heart attack, do you know that?" I asked, sliding into the passenger side. "Get a grip, Jillian. You're not Julia Roberts in *Runaway Bride*. People will not be amused if you cancel this wedding." When she didn't say anything, I let my head drop against the back of the seat. "What are you going to do?"

"I wish I knew," she said in her little-girl voice.

"Do you love Claymore?"

"Uh-huh."

Good sign. She hadn't said that about the last four grooms. "Does he love you?"

"Yes."

"But you don't want to marry him."

"I'm afraid he'll change."

"You'll change, too. The trick is to change together."

"What if he gets fat and bald?"

"You'll have to get fat and bald with him."

She snorted back a laugh. "Yeah, like that would ever happen."

"So you'll exercise together and get hair plugs. Should I bother listing all of Claymore's good qualities?"

"What good qualities?"

"How about this? Do you love that three-carat honker of a ring on your hand? Because if you call off this wedding, the ring goes back."

Her head came up and she stared at the diamond. "Claymore bought me matching stud earrings as a wedding gift."

"Also going back."

"He said I'd get the pendant on our honeymoon."

"Back."

As she gazed lovingly at the rock on her finger, I saw her lips press together and a steely look come into her eyes. She muttered something that sounded like, "I'll do it."

"Would you repeat that, please?"

"I'll do it. I'm going to marry Claymore." With a slightly hysterical laugh, she lunged across the console and squeezed me tight, rocking us back and forth. "Thank you, Abs. Thank you, thank you, thank you. I wub—"

I freed myself in time to clap my hand over her mouth. "You're getting married today. Time to get over the baby talk."

"Well I do love you," she said, taking my hand away.

I studied that face I knew so well, remembering everything we'd been through together—good vacations, bad holiday parties, first bras, painful sunburns . . . Her getting married was sad in a way—the end of an old chapter and the beginning of a new one—but certainly nothing to get all weepy about. So why were my eyelids suddenly scratchy?

Enough of that nonsense. "Jillian, rest assured that to my dying day I will never forget that you forced me to wear a ridiculous bridesmaid gown at your wedding."

She laughed, then I laughed, and our mushy moment was over. "Silly," she said. "The dress is only ridiculous on you. On everyone else it's darling. Now scoot, scoot, or I'll never make it by eight o'clock."

I glanced at my watch in dismay. Jillian wasn't the only one pressed for time. I had less than an hour to whip my hair into some kind of shape, don the ugly dress, and return for Marco.

At seven fifteen Marco came striding out of Down the Hatch looking like an understudy for Pierce Brosnan in a James Bond movie. His black hair had been combed back, setting off his angular face, which, even shaved, still showed traces of five o'clock shadow. The black tux only further emphasized his dark eyebrows, and the cut of the suit on his torso made my stomach go marshmallowy. He slid into the passenger side and all I could do was gawk at him.

"Don't say anything," he grumbled, misreading my look. "I told you I hated these monkey suits."

"Honestly, Marco, when I saw you come out of the bar, a monkey was the farthest thing from my mind. At the risk of inflating your ego, I have to say you look like a movie star."

"Groucho Marx was a movie star."

I was searching for a comeback when suddenly he gave me that little Marco grin, a slight, almost imperceptible upturn of his mouth that stirred my heart into a strawberry fondant. Then, as if he'd just noticed, he took a long look at my outfit. I braced myself for a wisecrack.

"Pretty hot, sunshine."

Fearing I was having one of those weird dreams where I forgot to put on clothes, I quickly glanced down at the dress. Whew. It was still there. "You actually like it?"

"I like *you* in it," he said in a throaty male purr, his gaze lingering on the V-cut neckline.

Wow. Maybe I wouldn't have to join the circus after all. I fingered a strand of hair that my roommate Nikki had arranged to hang *artfully* (her word) in front of my right ear, hoping to look even hotter. "Thanks."

"I like your hair up, too," he added.

Now my whole body was blushing, melting that clown image into a puddle of red rubber noses. I was *hot*. I was so hot I was sizzling.

"Dying your fingers to match your hair is a little over the top, though."

My sizzle fizzled. Damn. Nikki's extra-gentle fingernail polish remover hadn't worked, and there hadn't been time to buy anything stronger. Too bad the outfit hadn't included gloves.

As we headed west on the highway I filled Marco in on what to expect at the wedding, including my grandma-tending duties. Over the past few months Marco had become acquainted with the members of my slightly eccentric family, which made it even more amazing that he'd agreed to help out. "I really appreciate your stepping in at the last minute," I told him.

His mouth curved up playfully. "You know what they say. Paybacks are murder."

At the word *murder* a shiver raced up my spine. If I were superstitious I would have thought it was an omen. "Let's not talk about murder. Tonight I intend to let my hair down and have fun. You dance, don't you?"

"A little."

"Good enough." In that tux Marco could stand stone-still on the dance floor and I wouldn't mind. As long as he put his arms around me I'd do the dancing for both of us.

At the Garden of Eden we were directed by Claymore's father to an alcove on our right, where the groomsmen were cooling their heels. I introduced Marco to Bertie and Flip—both Claymore's former fraternity brothers—and Pryce, who let me know by his expression that he wasn't pleased I'd brought a stranger into their midst. Jillian's younger brother, Kevin, was there, too, in his role as usher, being his usual disinterested self.

I did a final check on the garden arrangements, then distributed the boutonnieres and corsages before finally being able to join the bridesmaids for last-minute primping in the dressing room. The room had marble counters and sinks, mirrored walls, upholstered settees, and lockers for storing belongings. I put my purse in a locker, slipped the key in my bra, then took a seat with the others to wait for the star of the show to arrive.

I'd met Jillian's sorority sisters—Onora, Ursula, and Sabina—three weeks earlier, when they'd flown in from New York for prewedding festivities. I wasn't thrilled about having to walk up the aisle behind the five feet-nine, model-perfect beauties. Topping off at a mere five feet four inches in heels, I'd look more like the flower girl. But now that I thought about it, that was probably Jillian's plan, since she had opted out of having a real flower girl. She didn't want any little cherub stealing *her* show.

Glancing at their tense faces, I could see they were expecting to discover that the bride had changed her mind, sticking them with dresses they'd never wear again. So when Jillian breezed in at last—wearing her off-the-shoulder, pearl-studded designer gown and fingertip-length veil over an elaborate updo held in place with pearl-tipped bobby pins—we let out such huge sighs of relief that toilet paper rustled in the stalls. She'd made it. We were home free. Then we took a look at her face.

Ursula tossed aside the magazine she'd been reading. "I knew it. You've called off the wedding."

"I didn't call it off," Jillian said, twisting her fingers together, as if afraid someone would rip the diamond from her hand. "But I might have to." Her chin trembled. "Claymore is gone."

"I'll be damned," Onora said with a snicker. "The *groom* got cold feet."

"You don't understand," Jillian said, growing hysterical. "Claymore didn't leave me—he'd never do that. He loves me to distraction. Claymore is *missing*! He's not even answering his cell phone. I'm supposed to march up the aisle in two minutes. What am I going to do?"

At that the girls crowded around her for a group hug. I decided my time would be better spent tracking down the groom, so I slipped out to the reception area and found Claymore's father pacing in front of the glass doors. Claymore's mother was sitting on a small sofa, fanning her face with a program, and Pryce was standing outside the door talking on his cell phone. The other groomsmen just looked perturbed.

I walked over to Marco. "What's going on?"

"Claymore was supposed to pick up his grandmother on his way here, but no one has been able to reach him or his grandmother to find out why they haven't arrived."

"I'm missing something here. Why would they have the *groom* pick up his grandmother? Isn't he a bit busy?"

Marco nodded toward Pryce. "Your ex-boyfriend was supposed to do it, but a client called with an emergency, and his parents had already left to come here."

I turned to glare at the man I'd once foolishly wanted to marry. "Pryce is a corporate lawyer. What kind of emergency could he have? A client's check bounced too high?"

Marco began to massage the back of my neck. He knew how Pryce set my teeth on edge. "Calm down, sunshine. I'm just reporting what I heard."

At the touch of his fingers on my nape I closed my eyes and sighed, feeling my irritation drain away. With Marco so near, I couldn't even remember why I'd been angry.

At that moment Pryce ended his call, conferred with his father, then headed in our direction. Grudgingly, I had to admit he looked good—in a plastic, store mannequin kind of way. His light brown hair was perfectly cut, his fingernails manicured, and his shoes impeccably shined. I immediately stuck my red-tinted hands behind my back.

"Claymore will be here in a few moments," Pryce announced to the groomsmen. "He didn't realize he'd turned off his cell phone. It seems my grandmother left her handbag in her room at the retirement village, necessitating a trip back to get it."

Only Pryce would call a purse a handbag. I saw him glance at Marco, whose hand was still on my neck, then at me, as if calculating the distance between us and what it signified.

"I suppose I should report back to Jillian," I told Marco. "She's hyperventilating in the dressing room."

"I'll finish your massage later," he murmured in my ear, sending little shockwaves of excitement straight into my brain. He removed his fingers, leaving my nape to fend for itself.

"Here's another thought for later," I said, turning to run my palms down his lapels. "I'll take a turn as masseuse and repay the debt I owe you."

Marco's gaze grew warm. "I like your thinking."

"Claymore is on his way," I announced to the frantic foursome in the restroom. The three bridesmaids gave each other high fives. Jillian clasped her fingers around the diamond studs on her earlobes and dropped to her knees in prayer.

There was a knock on the door, then my uncle called, "Jillian, a word, please?"

"What is it, Daddy?" Jillian asked, stepping into the hall. A moment later I heard her shriek, "No! They can't be here. They didn't RSVP. You have to make them leave before the Osbornes see them."

"I can't do that, Jill," my uncle said. "I told you only to prepare you."

A moment later Jillian barreled inside and grabbed my shoulders, her eyes wide and desperate. "My uncle Josiah and cousin Melanie are here. We have to get rid of them."

"There you go with that *we* thing," I said, pushing off her hands. "Be happy they're here. You never see your mother's side of the family."

Her mouth dropped open. "Are you brain-dead? Picture Uncle Josiah, with his scowling face, hooked nose, and dirty farmer overalls. What if he *wore* his overalls, Abby? What if Melanie wore one of her dowdy flowered dresses? Or brought her baby? You *do* remember Melanie had a baby last year, don't you?"

"So she's a single mom. I still don't see the problem."

Jillian bent to stare me in the eye. "She had a baby with *Jack Snyder*—remember Jack? Arsonist, thief, felon—sent to prison for selling drugs?"

"All very interesting, but not relevant. Your uncle and cousin are here, Jill. Suck it up."

"Come on, Abby, you know how particular Claymore's parents are. Can you imagine what they'll think of me after meeting Melanie and Uncle Josiah?"

I didn't know Melanie and Josiah very well—they were related to Jillian on her mother's side—but I did know that Aunt Corrine had never liked her sister Roxanne's choice of a husband. Roxanne died from a sudden stroke eight years ago, and Josiah had grown overly protective of his only child, Melanie. Since then, there'd been little contact between the families. The Turners had been invited to the wedding as a courtesy. No one had expected them to come.

"Look at it this way, Jill. You're poised and polished. The Osbornes will take one look at them and you'll shine by comparison. They'll appreciate you even more than they do now."

Jillian blinked rapidly, digesting the information, but it didn't take her long to see the advantages of her position. "You're absolutely right." She heaved a sigh of relief. "Thanks, Abs. Flunking out of law school didn't damage those little brain cells of yours one iota."

*   *   *

At ten minutes past eight o'clock that evening, with the sun low on the horizon, the groomsmen in place, the guests facing the rear, and the video cameras rolling, I marched through the arch behind the other bridesmaids to the strains of Pachelbel's Canon, with Jillian and her father steps behind. I glanced back just to make sure the bride hadn't bolted. Of course, it didn't hurt that her father had her arm in a viselike grip.

Occupying the first three rows on the left was the Knight clan, with Grace and her new beau, Richard Davis, seated behind them. Richard looked very Texan in an ivory linen suit, a tan shirt, and a brown string tie, had his arm around Grace and was murmuring something in her ear that was causing her to glow. In the very last row on the left were Jillian's cousin Melanie and uncle Josiah, who had mercifully not worn his bib overalls, but had instead donned a coal black suit that looked more suitable for a funeral. Lottie and her husband had opted to stay home and enjoy the holiday with their family.

On the right, Claymore's parents were sitting like bookends with his grandmother pinned between. Grandma Osborne was a small woman with silver hair, a tremble in her voice, and an iron will. She'd always been the matriarch of the Osborne family and still considered herself so, despite occasional memory lapses and a physical decline that gave her a slightly shuffling gait.

Ahead, I could see the groomsmen standing on the grass with their backs to the gazebo. Marco was definitely the hunkiest man there, although the whole lineup looked like they could have stepped out of the pages of *GQ*. My gaze met Marco's, and after that I barely noticed anything else, not even my mother's incessant picture taking, although the little green halos from her flashbulb did make it difficult to focus. I took my place next to

Sabina on the far left, then leaned back, trying to catch another glimpse of Marco. Pryce must have noticed, because he gave me a frown and stepped back to block my view.

Once the bride had been handed off by her relieved father, the service ran without a hitch until the reverend asked if anyone had a reason why the couple shouldn't be united—a line I'd begged Jillian to leave out, but once again, when had she ever listened to me?

Grandma Osborne had a reason. "There's insect spray on this grass," she clamored, rising from her chair. "Claymore, you know strong smells make me vomit. Someone get me a paper bag." She was immediately shushed by Claymore's embarrassed parents and lowered to her seat, where she was given a piece of hard candy to settle her stomach.

Once the service resumed I decided to give the eye contact thing with Marco another try, but when I went to step back I found that my right stiletto had sunk into the damp earth. I tried to dislodge it but succeeded in freeing only my foot. In a panic, I slipped my toes inside the shoe and pulled up on it as hard as I could. It came loose with a loud *thwuck,* causing me to lurch forward, then backward, in an effort to compensate. My bouquet flew out of my hands as I windmilled my arms, then grasped the nearest object, to save myself from a fall.

The only problem with that plan was that the object turned out to be Sabina's arm, and since she wasn't expecting it, we both went down. I grabbed the bouquet and scrambled to my feet, whispering apologies to her, mortified beyond belief, only to discover that no one was looking at us. They were staring at something in the back row that was causing my beautiful floral arrangements to teeter.

The first thing that came to mind was that Jillian had used my fall as a diversion to make a mad dash for freedom, and some of the guests had tackled her before she could escape. But there she stood on the steps of the gazebo, next to Claymore, her palms pressed against the sides of her face, her mouth open in shock.

From the back I heard grunts, and punches being thrown, and fists hitting flesh. Then I heard a woman scream, "Stop it! You'll kill him!"

At that moment my arrangements started to topple. I hitched up my skirt and sprinted down the aisle to rescue them, grabbing the risers just before they fell onto the two men wrestling on the ground. As I stood with an arm slung around each vase, Marco and Bertie pulled the men apart, affording me and the videographers—who were capturing the event for posterity—a view of their faces.

There on the ground, his coal black suit askew and his nose dripping blood, was none other than Josiah Turner. His sparring partner, who was now being helped to his feet, was the infamous arsonist, thief, felon, and, now, wedding crasher—Jack Snyder.

CHAPTER FOUR

Seeing that the danger was over, Pryce stepped forward to take command, directing Marco and Bertie to take Jack off the premises and the guests to resume their seats. As Jack was being led away, Josiah shook his fist at him, thundering, "Sinner, ye shall be damned for all eternity for what ye have done!" He attempted another lunge and was instantly strong-armed into the building, while Aunt Corrine edged through the crowd to comfort a sobbing Melanie.

After order had been restored, we returned to our positions so the embattled bride and groom could get hitched. Unfortunately, the brawl had delayed the ceremony long enough to cause one more problem. As the anxious couple recited their handwritten pledges of devotion, the fireworks display roared into the night sky, exploding into loud, splashy waterfalls of color, then spiraled down with shrieks and hisses—completely obliterating their words.

"You were right. That certainly was different," Marco said as we took our place in the reception line inside the banquet center. "I've seen a lot of bar fights, but this is the first fight I've ever seen during a wedding ceremony."

I paused to shake a guest's hand, then whispered, "Could you tell who started it?"

"The big guy in the black suit."

"That was Josiah Turner, Jillian's uncle. The other one was Jack Snyder."

"Apparently, Turner saw Snyder come through that arched thing and take a seat in the back row on the groom's side, and the next thing I know the big guy—"

"Josiah."

With a look that asked, *Is it important to fill in the names right now?* (men don't understand our need for details), Marco finished, "Okay, *Josiah* took Snyder down."

"Wow. I knew Jillian's uncle hated Jack, but I had no idea his hatred was that strong."

At that moment I caught sight of Grace outside the glass doors, talking to Richard, her hand on his arm. He bent to give her a kiss, then, after a lingering look between them, he turned and strode away. Clearly they were much closer than Grace had let on. I was delighted for her.

Moments later, Grace came down the line, looking her usual dignified self in a pale blue silk suit and matching pillbox hat that covered her neatly layered gray hair. "Lovely ceremony, dear," she said, then leaned close to whisper, "I doubt anyone will notice the grass stain on the back of your gown. It blends rather well with the print."

"Thanks—I think. Where did Richard go?"

"Something came up at work that needed immediate attention. He'll be back shortly."

Grace moved on and other guests followed, congratulating the groom, hugging the bride, and nodding politely at the rest of us.

"Why do we have to stand here?" Marco whispered in

my ear after several people shook his hand. "I didn't do anything except show up in a monkey suit."

"It's custom," I whispered back. "Haven't you ever been to a wedding before?"

"Yeah, but I skipped out right after the last 'I do.'"

"I hope you weren't the groom."

He paused as more people came past, then he leaned toward me to whisper, "I'd elope before I'd go through something like this."

Elopement. There was a new fantasy to add to my list. I imagined Marco and myself on a tropical island, standing barefoot on the white sand of a pristine beach, flowers woven through my hair, a boom box blaring the wedding march, and a sea captain with a neatly trimmed beard saying, "Do you take this man to be your lawfully wedded husband?"

"I do."

"You do what?" Marco asked, jolting me out of my daydream.

"I do—think you're right about that elopement."

After all the guests had gone through the line, the members of the bridal party were herded back to the gazebo for more photographs before finally being allowed to join the guests in the ballroom. We took our places at the head table, decorated with my four-foot-long arrangement of callas, roses, and baby's breath, then Pryce rose to give the toast. He lifted his glass of champagne and the guests followed suit, ready to clink rims and get to the food.

After ten minutes of Pryce's droning voice, their joy had dissolved and their arms wavered as they struggled to keep their glasses aloft. The only one who seemed to be enjoying herself was Grandma Osborne, planted firmly between Claymore's parents at a table right up front.

Grandma had polished off her champagne and was contentedly munching a roll.

I gave up, too, set my glass on the table, and propped my chin in my hand, letting my mind tiptoe down the table to Marco, who looked so dashing in his black tux that I wanted to nibble his sleeve and work my way up from there. I sighed, happily ensconced in my tropical island daydream, only to have Sabina nudge me with her elbow. I sat up with a start, grabbed my glass and hoisted it, sloshing some bubbly on my hand, ready to toast the newlyweds.

"He already gave the toast," Sabina whispered. "Now he's doing introductions. Where have you been?"

In a much happier place. I glanced at Pryce, who was shooting daggers at me with his eyes as he said, "And on the end we have Abigail Knight, cousin of the bride, who did all the beautiful flowers here today."

My face filled with heat at the applause, most of it coming from the Knight table, specifically from my mother, who was giving me a standing ovation. The Osborne section was much quieter. Actually, *muted.*

After the food had been consumed, the cake cut and distributed, and the tables cleared, the fun finally began. The room had a great dance floor, and Jillian had hired an enthusiastic rock band with amps loud enough to shatter eardrums, so I was ready to kick off my heels and get down, when the band launched into a sedate waltz. Marco and I watched from the sidelines as the bride and groom took the floor for the traditional "Let Me Call You Sweetheart."

"If they do the Hokey-Pokey," Marco said, "I'm out of here."

I decided not to tell him about the Chicken Dance. As Jillian and Claymore swept past, I said, "You have to admit it's romantic."

"A moonlit beach, a sky full of stars, a bottle of champagne—that's romantic. Dancing in the middle of a room with hundreds of eyeballs watching every step you take—not romantic."

"Tell me more about this moonlit beach," I said, seeing the opening scene of a new fantasy begin to play in my mind: *Dancing on the Dunes*, starring Abby Knight and Marco Salvare, Hollywood's hottest duo.

Seeing Claymore's parents take to the dance floor suddenly reminded me that I was supposed to be watching Grandma Osborne. I glanced toward their table, now pushed to the side of the room, but she wasn't there, nor was she in the surrounding area.

"I'll be back in a moment," I whispered to Marco, then quickly wove through the tables, searching all the silver heads, until I finally spotted Grandma soliciting guests with a bread basket.

"Save the platypuses," she cried, shaking the basket. Coins rattled inside. People had actually donated money.

"Grandma, I think you should do that some other time," I said quietly.

"You've got those sturdy, childbearing hips, don't you?" she announced. "Not like those skinny minxes Pryce has been seeing. That boy never did know what was good for him. Do you know where I can get some water?"

I steered her across the room. "There's a big pitcher at your table."

"It's not icy, is it? Ice hurts my tongue."

I poured her a glass of ice-free water, seated her next to Claymore's aunt, and asked her to stay put until I returned. Then as the bridal party merged onto the floor for a slow number, I grabbed Marco's wrist and pulled him into the center. He put one hand on the small of my back and took my other hand in his, as if he actually knew what he was doing. I smiled into his eyes, content to stay in one spot and sway with him. What did it matter as long as his arms were around me?

Without warning, his grip tightened and away we went. "You told me you only danced a little," I said in surprise as he led me into a turn.

"This is it: the only two steps I remember. Forward and turn."

"You're very smooth."

"My dancing isn't bad either." He arched an eyebrow, giving me a look that made my ribs tingle. Or was it that someone had just jabbed me in the side?

I looked over my shoulder in time to see Pryce glide by with Onora. Her face was expressionless—the result of her Botox treatments. His face was hostile—the result of being a class-A jerk. In the spirit of the day, I dismissed the jab as an accident and turned my attention back to the extremely good-looking man holding me in his arms.

"What are you doing after the reception?" Marco asked. He gave me that lazy smile that made me forget everything but him. Then I got another jab, this time in my arm. I stopped and turned, ready to let loose with a few uncharitable remarks, only to find that it was Jillian and Claymore, not Pryce, doing the jabbing.

"You're supposed to be watching Grandma Osborne," Jillian hissed.

"I *am* watching her. She's right over . . ." I pointed to where I had put her minutes before, but the seat was empty. "I'll find her," I assured them. "Keep dancing."

Marco and I split up to circle the room, threading our way through chattering guests. We met at the exit. "Maybe she went to the restroom," I suggested.

"You check the ladies' room. I'll check the men's."

Except for a waitress who'd sneaked in for a smoke, the ladies' room was empty. So were the dressing room and coatroom. The kitchen staff hadn't seen her either.

I met Marco in the reception area. In the distance the pops of firecrackers could be heard. "She might have gone outside for some air," Marco said.

I didn't like the image that sprang to mind: an elderly woman stumbling around in the dark, growing disoriented and frightened, all because I hadn't done my duty. "I'll take the garden; you scout the parking lot."

With my heart in my throat I exited the building, then hurried up the sidewalk, through the arch, and into the garden area—unlit now except for the light that spilled out of the huge windows of the ballroom. I was halfway up the aisle when a small figure suddenly appeared at the top of the gazebo steps. I knew by the faint glint of silver that it was Grandma.

"Are you okay?" I called as she made her way down the steps.

"I found water." She held up a glass. "It was sitting on a shelf behind the pulpit."

"You came all the way out here for water?" I asked, taking her arm to escort her back.

"No, it was too noisy inside. Noise makes me jumpy."

"Let's find you a clean glass, okay? That one was probably the minister's."

She gave me a puzzled look. "He didn't look like the minister."

"Who didn't?"

She stopped to point a shaky finger toward the gazebo. "That man behind the pulpit."

"There's a man back there?"

"Yes, but don't disturb him. He's napping. He probably had too much to drink."

Napping? I didn't like the sound of that. I left Grandma on the path, climbed the steps to the gazebo, and moved cautiously around the right side of the podium, squinting to see in the dim light. I stopped suddenly when I saw a pair of legs clad in black trousers lying on the floor. "Hey," I said, touching an ankle with the tip of my shoe. "Wake up."

No answer or movement. I crouched beside the legs. "Hey, are you hurt?"

Still no response, just an eerie silence that was giving me a really bad feeling.

"Abby?" Marco called. "Where are you?"

"Behind the pulpit. Call 911. There's someone up here and I think he's unconscious."

I could hear Marco's phone buttons beeping as I searched for a pulse. I found the wrist and knew by the coarse hair and thickness of the bone that it belonged to a male. I also knew the male wasn't unconscious. He was dead.

CHAPTER FIVE

I wasn't normally a squeamish person, but I did manage to put some distance between myself and the body in under two seconds, about the same amount of time it took Marco to come up the steps. "D-dead man," I whispered, pointing to the pulpit behind me. "No pulse."

Marco stepped around to the back of the podium and clicked the penlight he kept on his key ring. I heard him let out a low whistle of exclamation, then he said quietly, "Come take a look at his face and tell me if you recognize him."

"Did the man wake up?" Grandma called.

"I'll let you know in a minute," I said, trying to keep a lightness in my voice. "Stay right there." I peered around Marco as he shined his light over the body of a man wearing a short white jacket with tails, and a gold vest. A beret lay beside his head, which was turned to one side.

"Looks like a waiter," Marco said, crouching beside the body.

"Marco, that's Jack Snyder!"

"He hasn't been dead long. He's still warm." Marco

checked his watch. "It's ten o'clock. This must have happened within the last hour." He shined the light on Jack's bloody face. "Look there, on his jaw. See that mark? That's from his fight with Turner." Marco moved the light up, illuminating a deep indentation in Jack's forehead. "And that's probably the blow that killed him. It's recent."

The shock of finding a dead body was still settling over me, but my first thought was a scary one—that Jillian's uncle Josiah had somehow managed to finish the fight he'd started earlier. "Is there any chance Jack hit his head on a corner of the pulpit?"

Marco shined his light along the top edge of the wooden stand. "This isn't the best light to work with, but I don't see any blood." He swept the small light around the gazebo, but we didn't find any obvious weapon, either. "We'd better back out of here so we don't taint the crime scene any more than we already have."

"What are you two doing?" Grandma asked, coming to peer between us. She took one look and fell back, clutching her chest. "Oh, my word!"

"Let's go back to the building, Grandma," I said putting my arm around her to lead her down the steps.

"We have to get help," she said in a quivering voice.

"I've already called for help," Marco said and helped me guide her down the steps. "Hear those sirens? They'll be here in just a few moments."

"Oh, my word," she muttered over and over, shaking her head in disbelief as Marco and I ushered her up the aisle. "All that blood."

Just as we came through the arch, the banquet center doors opened and Pryce and his parents rushed out of the building. "Mother," Mr. Osborne cried, "we've been looking everywhere for you. What are you doing out here?" All three shot me reproving glances.

"All that blood," the elderly woman kept murmuring.

"Blood?" Mrs. Osborne said, her face draining of color. "What are you talking about?"

I signaled for them to wait a moment, then said quietly to Pryce, "Why don't you see your grandmother inside?"

"Here we go, Grandmother," Pryce said, trying to take her arm.

She shoved his hand away, suddenly finding her bearings. "Don't fuss over me, Pryce. Can't you see I'm upset? Now, stand back. This able fellow here will help me." She looked up at Marco and he obliged with a masculine gallantry that put a skip in Grandma's step.

As soon as she was out of earshot I said to the Osbornes in a rush of breath, "There's been an accident in the gazebo and we've already called for help so there's no need to panic."

"An accident?" Mrs. Osborne asked, panicking anyway. "What kind of accident?"

There was no point in beating around the bush: the police were moments away. "Jack Snyder is dead. Grandma Osborne found him behind the pulpit."

Mr. Osborne muttered an oath I wouldn't have thought he knew, and Mrs. Osborne's mouth opened but no sound came out. Then Pryce pointed to my fingers and in a voice dripping with suspicion asked, "Is that blood on your hands?"

At that, Mrs. Osborne fainted dead away, straight into her husband's arms. I gave Pryce an icy glare. "It's red paint. I had to dye a load of carnations this morning."

He had enough sense to look embarrassed as he crouched down beside his father. The two men patted Mrs. Osborne's cheeks and rubbed her arms until her eyelids fluttered open, then Mr. Osborne said to her, "Let's get you up now and back into the center for something cool to drink."

"I'll handle everything out here," Pryce assured him.

His parents had barely reached the sidewalk in front of the doors when four police cars sped into the parking lot and screeched to a stop, unloading a dozen blue-shirts. An ambulance arrived next and two medics got out, just as curious guests began to pour out of the center.

"This way!" I called to the cops, waving them toward me as I backed up the path.

"I'll take it from here," Pryce said, trying his best to look masterful. He strode up to the gazebo and turned to face the police brigade streaming toward us.

The police had divided into two groups, half remaining behind to keep the guests at bay, the other half heading toward the gazebo to secure the murder scene. Fronting the group coming up the aisle was Sergeant Sean Reilly, a good-looking, dedicated, forty-year-old cop I'd come to know pretty well over the last two months, not in the most pleasurable of circumstances. Behind him was Marco.

It didn't surprise me to see that Reilly had let Marco join the troops. The two had worked together during Marco's stint on the force and had maintained a casual friendship ever since.

"Officers," Pryce said, using his officious voice, "we have a body up here."

Reilly glanced around at Marco with a slight lift of his eyebrows, as if to say, *What's with this jackass?* Then he turned and saw me.

"Hello again," I said with a little wave.

He planted his hands on his waist. "You'd think I'd be surprised to find you at another murder scene—what's it been since the last one, three, maybe four, weeks?—but, no. Why is that, do you suppose?"

"Probably because you . . ."

Behind Reilly's back, Marco drew his finger across his throat, as if to say, *Don't even think about making a joke at his expense*, so I let the rest of the sentence go. Reilly wasn't paying attention anyway. He was giving instructions to his men, who then started up the steps, their wide-beamed flashlights throwing light everywhere. Pryce tagged along behind.

"Sir, you'll need to step down from there," Reilly called to him. "It's a crime scene."

Pryce's face was red as he joined us, but he covered his embarrassment by taking out a white handkerchief and mopping his neck. "Muggy evening," he remarked.

"Is anyone else hurt?" Reilly asked us, pulling out his little notepad.

"Not that we've seen," Marco said.

"Who found the body?" Reilly's gaze lit on me. "Never mind. I already know the answer."

"Wrong," I retorted. "I was the second one here. Pryce's grandmother found him."

"I'll have to interview your grandmother," Reilly said to Pryce, writing it down.

"She's inside. Just bear in mind she's ninety years old and isn't always lucid. And her memory isn't what it used to be, either."

Reilly made a note of it, then said to me, "So you were the *second* one to see the body. Please tell me you didn't disturb it and that isn't blood on your hands."

I should have worn a sign around my neck that said, IT'S RED PAINT BUT THANKS FOR ASKING. "I had to dye flowers this morning. The only thing I touched was a wrist when I took his pulse. Actually, there wasn't any pulse to take, which is how I knew—"

"Did you see anyone leave the area?" Reilly asked the three of us, cutting me off. I'd forgotten he didn't care for long explanations. We shook our heads no, then had to step out of the way to let the crime scene investigators through.

"Let's start with you," Reilly said to Pryce. "What do you know about the victim?"

"His name is Jack Snyder, he's from New Chapel, he's twenty-eight years old, and he wasn't invited to the wedding. That about sums it up, other than that he got into a fight with another guest during the ceremony."

"Jack Snyder? Bill and Norma's oldest kid?" Reilly asked, looking suddenly less like a cop and more like someone's next-door neighbor. "He just got out of prison about a month ago."

"That's him," Pryce answered.

Reilly shook his head as he wrote it all down. "I knew Jack's father. He owned acreage south of town where the new shopping mall sits now. He made a lot of money on that deal but never lived to enjoy it. Got up one morning and dropped dead. Now I hear that Jack's mother has terminal cancer. Can you beat that for luck?"

He gave a heavy sigh, no doubt pondering the ironies of life, then became the cop once again. "Okay, you said Jack got into a fight during the ceremony. Who else was involved in the fight?"

"A man named Josiah Turner. Abigail can tell you more about him," Pryce said.

"Where can I find this Abigail?"

"Here," I said, holding up my hand.

"Okay, *Abigail*," Reilly said, "your turn."

I ignored his little snicker of amusement and said, "Josiah Turner is my cousin Jillian's uncle. No relation to me."

"Turner," Reilly mused. "Does he have a farm out on Route Two? Big, sour-faced guy? Looks like that painting of the farmer holding a pitchfork?"

"American Gothic," I said before Pryce could get the words out. He wasn't the only one who'd ever cracked an art book. "Yep, that's Josiah."

"Do you know what the fight was about?" Reilly asked me.

"No, but if I had to guess, I'd say it was about Josiah's daughter, Melanie. She had a baby with Jack, and he refused to acknowledge the child. Josiah supports Melanie and the baby now."

"What happened after the fight?" Reilly asked.

"We took Turner into the banquet center for medical aid," Pryce said, craning his neck to watch Reilly jot it down. "He had a bloody nose and some cuts on his hand. Mr. Salvare here escorted the victim to his car."

"Jack wasn't a victim yet, Pryce," I said.

"Technically," Pryce replied in his know-it-all tone, "he was the victim of assault."

I glared. "You can call Jack by his name."

"I hate to interrupt," Reilly said acidly, "but did any of you see Josiah Turner leave the reception at any time this evening?" At our *nos* he said, "Are you aware of anyone else here tonight who might have had a beef with the victim?"

"Melanie Turner," Pryce said.

I scoffed at him. "Melanie? She wouldn't hurt a fly."

"She had to have abandonment issues," Pryce retorted.

He wanted to talk about abandonment issues?

"You might want to check out Vince Vogel, too," Pryce told Reilly. "Vince is a friend of my brother's. He and the victim grew up next door to each other and there's been bad blood between them for years."

"Did you see any interaction between Jack Snyder and Vince Vogel this evening?" Reilly asked Pryce.

"There wasn't time. The victim came in, the fight

started, and the victim was taken out. I didn't see Vince or the victim after that."

"Would you stop saying *victim*?" I snapped. "You're not a cop and you're not in court."

"It's the way I talk," Pryce muttered.

I rolled my eyes. We both knew he was trying to impress Reilly.

"Any reason I need to stick around?" Marco asked Reilly. I gazed at him in surprise. He was deserting me?

"Not unless you have something to add. One thing you can do for me," Reilly said, "is to take a look in the parking lot to see if Jack's car is there and if you can tell whether it's been moved since you last saw it. Benson, go with him," he said to a cop standing nearby.

"Okay if I use your car?" Marco asked me, dangling the car key he'd stowed in his pocket.

I took him by the arm and led him a few yards away. I didn't want Pryce to overhear. "You're leaving me here?" I whispered.

He nodded toward Pryce, who was talking to Reilly. "You'll be in good hands."

"That's not even remotely funny."

"In case you haven't noticed, Pryce still has a crush on you."

I scoffed. "Yeah, right. Like a shoe on a bug."

Marco touched a finger to the tip of my nose. "You're cute when you pout. I won't be gone long. I just want to check in at the bar to see how things are going—you know, make sure no one burned it down during my absence—then I'll come back. Okay?"

"Okay," I said slowly. "You take my car and we'll call my debt repaid."

He merely grinned, then he turned and strode toward the parking lot, his sexy saunter looking even sexier in that black tux. "Fine," I called. "At least leave the tux on."

"Abby!" I heard my cousin wail. I turned just as Jillian dodged the cops and came sailing toward me, her veil flying behind her like a pennant in the wind. On her heels was one of her videographers, a camera in his hands.

"Abby, everyone left the ballroom. My reception is a flop!"

I turned her around so her back was to the camera and whispered, "Look around you, Jillian. What do you see? Cops? Aren't you at all curious as to what the cops are doing here? They're here because Jack Snyder is dead, so stop whining about your reception."

Her eyes widened in surprise. "Are you serious? Jack is dead? What was it, a drug overdose? Seizure? Heart attack?"

"None of the above."

"Then what happened?" She studied me a moment, then her eyes got even bigger. "Don't tell me someone killed him."

"Sh-h! Keep your voice down. Do you want to start a panic?" I noticed the cameraman filming me over Jillian's shoulder and put my fingers over the lens. "Would you turn that off, please?"

He immediately pivoted to film the action at the gazebo, where investigators were busy taking pictures, measuring distances, and dusting for prints.

Jillian grabbed my wrist. "Is that blood on your fingers?"

"No, but I can remedy that."

"Get that camera out of my face!" Reilly barked.

Jillian twirled around and saw her videographer filming the police. "What are you doing? You're supposed to be making a movie of my wedding!"

He shrugged, then began filming her. "Not now!" she cried. "Go back to the ballroom. Film my ice sculptures before they melt away entirely."

"No one's in the ballroom," he told her, "but, hey, you're the boss."

As the man schlepped up the aisle with his equipment, Reilly yelled, "You, with the camera. I'm going to need that tape—disk—whatever the hell it's called."

Jillian turned toward Reilly with a gasp. "You're confiscating my wedding video?"

"Video, still shots—anything filmed here today," Reilly said.

"You can't do that," Jillian cried, her voice a notch below a shriek.

"Calm down," I said as her cameraman handed the memory cards to Reilly. "You'll get it all back."

"When will that be?" she asked Reilly.

"When we're finished with them." Reilly handed the cards to another cop, who dropped them into an envelope.

"You don't understand," Jillian said, folding her hands together as if she were begging. "My parents are throwing a party for us when we return from our honeymoon, and my wedding video is the entertainment. That means I need them back right away so they can be put on a DVD."

He narrowed his eyes at her and I could almost hear his jaws clanging together. "You'll get them back when we're *finished* with them."

"Jillian, drop it," I said quietly. "You won't change his mind. Besides, the cops might find something helpful on that video."

"Well, isn't that special? A murderer on my wedding video. You know what? I've had it." She started yanking the pearl-tipped pins out of her hair. "This whole day has been one big catastrophe. I knew I shouldn't have let you talk me into going through with this marriage. I could have been halfway to Florida by now."

"Hey!" I cried, trying to catch her flying pins. "Your veil will fall off."

"I don't care. I'm leaving. Let the cops try to stop me."

"Jillian," I said, yanking her hands away from her head, "this isn't third-grade recess. You're married now. You have a husband. You can't have a tantrum and run away."

"Watch me."

"Darling?" Claymore called from behind the police lines. "Is everything all right? Did you find out what happened?"

I turned her around, forcing her to face the groom. "Will you look at Claymore standing there waiting for you—his beloved bride? How can you turn your back on him?"

She stared at him for a long moment, her nostrils flaring, her hands clenching and unclenching; then her anger dissipated; and finally, she let her arms flop down at her sides. "You're right. I can't act like the child I was"—she paused to check her slender, pearl-encrusted bracelet watch—"three hours and fourteen minutes ago."

"There you go. Now straighten your shoulders and show your husband what Knights are made of."

She tucked her loose locks behind her ears, moistened her lips, and adjusted her gown. "I can handle this."

"Sure you can."

"Besides, the cops don't know there's another videographer"—she pulled me close to hiss—"and don't you dare tell them. I know too many of your secrets."

"You wouldn't," I breathed.

"Oh, yes, I would."

Oh, yes, she would. I gave her an outraged look, but she merely turned to Claymore and called in a dulcet voice, "It's worse than we thought, lambkins. Jack Snyder is—"

I clapped my hand over her mouth. "Think of Melanie, for heaven's sake. Is that any way for her to find out the father of her baby is dead?"

She pushed my hand away. "Melanie left a long time ago, and Uncle Josiah, too, thank God. What a grouch. He was pulling the whole room down."

"Did I hear you say Josiah Turner left?" Reilly asked, coming toward us.

"Yes," Jillian replied frostily, "when the music started."

"When was that?" Reilly asked.

She shrugged. "Nine thirty, I guess." To me she said, "Uncle Josiah said Melanie's baby was sick, but I think they left because he doesn't approve of dancing. Heaven forbid Melanie should have fun."

Reilly started to say something else to Jillian, then noticed that Pryce was behind him, sticking to him like glue. "You can join the guests inside the building now, Mr. Osborne."

"The building is empty," Jillian remarked unhappily. "Everyone is out here."

Reilly glanced over our heads and saw the crowd gathered on the wide sidewalk in front of the doors. "Why are those people outside?" he called to the cops forming a barricade. "Get them in and start processing them!"

Jillian watched Pryce head up the aisle, then turned back to Reilly. "Can Claymore and I leave? Our limo is waiting."

"You have to be ID'd like everyone else."

"But my honeymoon!" Jillian cried. Reilly ignored her and started back to the gazebo.

The indignant bride spun on her heel and flounced up the path in the opposite direction. I followed Reilly.

"Why aren't the detectives here?" Reilly snarled. "Did anyone think to call them, or is that asking too much?"

"Lt. Corbison is away at a conference," one investigator reported. "Lt. Williams should be on his way."

"Sergeant?" Officer Benson called, striding up the path behind us. Reilly stopped so abruptly I almost ran into him.

He glowered at me, fists planted at his waist. "Where do you think you're going?"

"Up to the gazebo with you."

By the expression on his face I could tell that my answer wasn't working for him. Luckily, I had the power of female persuasion on my side, and since he liked quick, clear, logical answers, that's what I gave him. "The way I see it, Reilly, you've already got my fingerprints on file, and you know who I am, so why should I sit inside and stare at the walls when I might be of assistance out here?"

He turned me to face the building and gave me a gentle push. "If I need your help I'll ask for it."

I wouldn't hold my breath waiting for *that* to happen.

The young cop stepped aside to allow me to pass, but since I didn't want to miss hearing what Benson had to report about Jack's car, I went about two yards up the path, stopped, took off my left shoe and pretended to shake a pebble out of it.

"What did you find out?" Reilly asked the young cop.

"The victim's vehicle had been moved from its original parking space, Sergeant."

I stopped shaking my shoe and stood there balancing on one foot, thinking about the timing. Jack had been escorted to his car around eight twenty. Sometime between then and when Grandma Osborne found his body, he'd moved his car, had donned a waiter's uniform, and was killed.

Reilly spotted me and crossed his arms over his chest. "Forget your way to the building?"

"Had a pebble," I said, holding up the offending heel. He didn't look convinced, so I put on my shoe and left, still mulling over the information. Jack must have known Josiah would still be gunning for him, so why had he come back? Was it to even the score?

CHAPTER SIX

I entered the glass doors and found the reception area empty, so I walked up the hallway past the coatroom and the restrooms, opened one of the ballroom doors, and was promptly met by two policemen standing guard. "Reilly sent me," I told them, trying to look official.

One of the cops held up his walkie-talkie and said with a dry smile, "Yeah, we heard you were coming."

Ignoring their snickers, I stepped inside and glanced around. The guests had been divided into four groups and were talking among themselves in hushed voices, while police officers diligently collected pertinent information. Across the dance floor, the musicians were packing up their instruments, the bored photographers were snapping anything that moved, and the banquet's cleaning crew was gathering dirty linen, folding tables for storage, and lining chairs along the walls. The videographers were gone, and I was fairly certain Jillian had managed to smuggle them and the second video out of the building. She wasn't about to let the cops confiscate her party entertainment.

"Abigail," my mother called, holding up a hand so I could find her in the crowd. She was sitting beside my father in a group that contained all the Knights and the Osbornes, so I motioned for her to come to me so we wouldn't be overheard. She guided my father's wheelchair toward the two folding chairs I had moved to one side.

My dad is a paraplegic, the result of a stroke suffered during an operation to remove a bullet from his thigh. He'd been caught in an ambush while chasing a drug dealer. Amazingly, he'd never had regrets, nor had he allowed himself any self-pity. He'd done his duty. That was what cops did. I was still in awe of his courage.

"Is there any more news?" my mother asked quietly. "We've heard only sketchy details."

"I keep telling you, Maureen, it's too early for more news," my father said. "But why would you listen to me? I was only on the force for twenty years."

"I believe you, Jeff," my mom assured him, patting his knee. "I merely wanted to know if it was true that Pryce's grandmother found the body, since the Osbornes are being so tight-lipped about it. I've been telling everyone that it couldn't possibly be so, because Abby was keeping an eye on the woman and would never have let her wander outside alone in the dark." She turned her gaze on me and smiled proudly.

Rather than burst her bubble I changed the subject. "Haven't they cleared you to leave yet?" I asked my dad. Being a former cop, he usually got preferential treatment.

"They cleared us. Ask your mother why we're still here."

"We're here," she said tolerantly, "because I was waiting for a good time to give Jillian and Claymore their wedding sculpture." She looked around and spotted the newlyweds. "They don't seem to be busy now."

I had to think fast. At Bloomers my mom's sculptures could affront only a small number of people. Here she had hundreds to offend. The mood in the room was already tense; I didn't want to see it turn ugly.

"With so much going on right now, Mom, it would probably be best to wait until later to give them your gift—like when they return from their honeymoon."

She fixed me with the look mothers have perfected—the one that says, *I spent twenty-seven hours in labor with you, and now you cut my heart out?* "What are you trying to say, Abigail?"

"I'm trying to say"—What *was* I trying to say? Better yet, what was I *thinking*?—"that given the circumstances, I doubt Jillian would be able to fully appreciate all the effort you put into your sculpture. I mean, look at her over there, pacing and fretting, her mouth going a mile a minute. If she were wound up any tighter her brain would squeak."

At that moment Jillian spotted me and came barreling over, her arms flapping in exasperation against the full skirt of her beaded gown, a photographer on her heels. "It's almost eleven o'clock. We're supposed to be on our way to Chicago right now. *Right now!*"

I saw the photographer aim his lens at my boobs, so I bent my knees to bring my face into focus. "Heads up, lowlife. I'm wearing heels that will break the bones of your insteps."

"Don't worry," he said with a wink. "The cops took my film."

At my steely look, the man shrugged and moved on.

"I don't understand what the problem is," Jillian said, scowling at a cop standing a few yards away. "They can't possibly think Claymore or I killed Jack. The whole room can vouch for our whereabouts."

"Jillian," I said, "show a little respect. A man is dead."

"I understand a man is dead," Jillian ground out, "but this is my wedding night. I'm supposed to be on my way to Hawaii, not stuck here in Stalag Thirteen."

"I'll see if I can do something about it, Jillian," my dad said and wheeled toward the door guards, my mother right behind.

"Thank you, Uncle Jeff," Jillian called. She shot another sullen look at the cops nearby, then turned with a sharp sigh. "This is totally ridiculous. If you were in charge of this investigation, Abby, would you make me stay?"

"Not on your life. I'd be glad to get rid of you."

"Then why don't you?"

"Let you leave? Because I don't have the authority."

"No, silly. I mean why don't you investigate? You're a natural snoop."

"Two reasons. First, if Reilly found out, he'd lock me in the county jail and swallow the key. Second, I do have a flower shop to run."

"You always say that." She flounced down into the folding chair my mother had deserted, skirts billowing around her. No charm school had ever held Jillian for more than two days. "I'm bored stiff. Tell me what you'd do if this were your case."

An armchair detective game. I could handle that. "If this were my case," I said, enjoying the mental exercise, "the first item of business would be to find out why Jack returned to the banquet center."

"Jack Snyder—what a loser," Jillian said as Claymore joined us. "He always was the bad acorn of that family. Wasn't his brother Rick in school with you,

Abs? Now *he* was a real brainiac. Oh, sorry. You probably didn't know him."

What would it take, I wondered, to collapse her chair? A little nudge with the toe of my shoe? "I knew Rick, Jillian. And the expression is bad *apple,* not acorn."

"Not in Jack's case. He was definitely a member of the nut family. Who else would be crazy enough to fool around with Uncle Josiah's daughter, and then refuse to acknowledge his own kid or pay child support? Who else would get out of jail and immediately take up with a woman old enough to be his mother? God only knows what Melanie saw in Jack, unless she was hoping to escape the clutches of her father. Now she *and* the baby are stuck living with that maniac. I can't imagine how she stands it."

"Perhaps she has nowhere else to go," Claymore suggested.

"Well, it's her fault for falling for Jack." Jillian gave an indignant huff. "I could just kill Jack for ruining my reception." She caught Claymore's appalled look and said, "Well, I could."

"So who would your suspect be, Abby?" Claymore asked, clearly embarrassed by his new wife's lack of sensitivity.

"That's a no-brainer," Jillian said, rolling her eyes as though she couldn't believe the man she had married could be so dense. "Uncle Josiah."

"I was asking Abby," Claymore said coolly.

"I knew that," she retorted.

Fearing I would be caught in their crossfire, I said quickly, "Josiah had a motive. Plus he left the reception before Jack's body was found, so he had the opportunity."

"It had to be Uncle Josiah," Jillian said. "He hated Jack with a passion."

"Hating Jack is one thing," Claymore said; "killing him is another. Josiah isn't a stupid man. He had to realize that murdering Jack would be counterproductive to his daughter getting any support money. What he should have done was to have Melanie go after Jack in the courts."

"Don't think she hasn't tried," Jillian said. "The first time Jack left town and the second time he went to prison. How do you make a prison inmate pay support?"

"Why doesn't Melanie move out?" I asked.

"She doesn't have a college degree or any skills other than cooking and cleaning, so what can she earn, maybe ten bucks an hour? Where can she live on that income and pay for child care?"

"There's your second suspect," Claymore said. "Melanie. She certainly had a motive—and the opportunity."

"I don't know Melanie very well," I said, "but she doesn't seem like the killer type. A lot of women get dumped. They don't commit murder because of it."

"*You* didn't," Jillian pointed out, in case I'd forgotten what Pryce had done. "Maybe living with her crazy father drove Melanie over the edge. It might have been a crime of passion. She saw Jack in the gazebo and pleaded with him to pay child support. He laughed in her face— *hahahahaha*—and she clobbered him."

I grabbed her hand before she could demonstrate on Claymore's head. "What was her weapon? The gouge on Jack's forehead was deep."

"Did you get a look at those combat boots she had on?" Jillian rolled her eyes. "Have you ever seen a chunkier heel? Where are the fashion police when you need them?"

"But why was Jack in the gazebo?" I put to them. "In my opinion, this whole case rests on Jack's purpose for coming back. Was it for revenge, or was he supposed to meet someone there? What about your friend Vince Vogel?" I asked Claymore. "Pryce mentioned that he had a long-standing feud with Jack."

Claymore scoffed. "That happened a long time ago."

"Four years isn't that long," Jillian said, leaning back in her chair, "and Jack did ruin Vince's dream of getting into the FBI. The poor guy was devastated."

I smelled a motive. "Tell me about their feud."

"It happened during my junior year down at IU Bloomington," Claymore explained. "Vince blackballed Jack to keep him out of our fraternity, so Jack stole a professor's car, set it on fire, and made it look like Vince did it. Vince spent a week in jail and was nearly convicted. He was eventually cleared of the charges, but the arrest was enough to disqualify him for any government job."

"Jack is four years older than you," I said. "Why was he at IU at the same time?"

"He'd go a year, drop out a year, switch to a different school, change majors—"

"You know how that goes," Jillian said helpfully.

One little push against the hinge of that chair leg . . . "I only changed majors once, Jill, and I never dropped out of college." I turned back to Claymore. "Did Jack ever finish school?"

"Up here, at the extension."

"Has Vince ever said anything more about the incident?" I asked Claymore.

"Not to me. Vince is happily married now and working as head butcher at the Meat Market."

Jillian instantly shushed him. "Keep your voice down. My mother is a member of PETA. Besides, how can someone be happy when all they do is chop up dead animals?"

"He makes a good living," Claymore said patiently. "He doesn't need to be happy."

That was typical Osborne thinking. "Does Vince strike you as a killer?" I asked him.

"Absolutely not," Claymore said.

"But he does have a bad temper," Jill reminded him.

"He keeps it under control," Claymore countered.

She glared at him. "Usually."

"So a couple of times down at school Vince got a little carried away," Claymore said. "He was drunk, and some people are mean when they're drunk."

"Are you mean when you're drunk?" Jillian asked, her hackles all set to rise.

"As you know, dearest, I don't get drunk. I've never been so much as tipsy a day in my life."

Jillian beamed at me as she slipped her arm through Claymore's and gave it an affectionate squeeze. "Isn't he priceless?"

I smiled back, wishing my life had been Pryce-less.

"I'll point Vince out," Jillian said and turned to look around the room.

"He left after the ceremony," Claymore reminded her. "Don't you remember? He came through the receiving line and said he had to go home to check on his wife. She had a migraine."

At that moment, my parents returned and my father said to the newlyweds, "You're all set."

Jillian clapped. "Super! Thank you, Uncle Jeff."

"Jillian, do you have two minutes?" my mother asked hopefully. "I want to give you and Claymore your gift."

"Not now, Mom," I said. "They have a plane to catch."

"I'm truly sorry we can't stay," Claymore said. "We'll

open our presents as soon as we get back from Hawaii. As it is now, we'll just make our flight."

"Let's not be too hasty," Jillian said, smiling at my mother. She never could turn down a present.

"I promise this will only take a moment," my mother told them, motioning frantically to my brother Jordan, who had been trying in vain to hide behind his wife, Kathy. He carried over a three-foot-tall, foil-wrapped box and set it on the floor in front of them. The rest of the Knight clan gathered to watch, and all those bright red heads drew the Osbornes like moths to lit matches. By the time my cousin had ripped off the ribbon and torn her way through the wrapping paper, most of the people in the room had gathered around her.

The moment Jillian lifted the top off the box I scrunched my eyes shut. Around me, guests gasped, and a woman nearby whispered, "Look at that!"

I knew I'd have to look eventually, so I opened my eyes just a little and saw Claymore. He hadn't fainted—that was a good sign—so I shifted to Jillian, whose mouth was open, but not in horror. More like *Wow!*

Holding my breath, I took the plunge and looked straight at it. What I saw was—a vase. Not an ordinary vase, naturally—this was my mother's creation, after all—but a two-foot-tall vase that curved and swayed in graceful motion like a wet manicotti noodle. My mother had painted the clay in soft pastel colors, then heated it somehow so that the colors ran and bled into each other, forming a hazy aura that was actually rather attractive—in an offbeat kind of way. Just the thing Jillian would go for. I let out my breath in a *whoosh*. I'd been holding it so long I might have blacked out for a second.

"Let me through," Grandma Osborne called, jabbing people with her bony elbows. She pushed her little gray head between two people, fixed her gaze on the gift, and said, "What the hell is that?"

"Aunt Maureen, it's beautiful," Jillian exclaimed, ignoring the outburst. She knelt beside the vase and stroked a hand lovingly down its curves. "Isn't it beautiful, Claymore?"

"Yes. Lovely," he said, rather stiffly. But at least he was being a sport about it, which is more than Pryce would have been.

I glanced in Pryce's direction and could see the snicker building behind those taut lips, so I flashed him a look that said, *Don't you dare make fun of my mother. I'm the only one allowed to do that.*

"Dearest," Claymore said quietly, "we really must be going."

Jillian jumped up, threw her arms around my mother, then bent to hug my dad. She turned, saw me, and rushed over to crush my head against her pearl-studded bodice. "Little Abs."

"I know," I said, trying to untangle my hair pins from her dress, "you wub me."

"Actually, I'm so beyond the *wub* thing now." She squeezed my head between her hands, pressed a kiss on my forehead, and dashed off, pulling Claymore by his sleeve.

"Well, Abigail?" my mother said as I scrubbed lipstick off my forehead. "What do you think of my sculpture?"

"Mom, you couldn't have made anything more perfect or beautiful." And I meant every word.

She sighed, very pleased with herself. "My work here is done. Jeff, let's go home."

"When can we leave?" my brother Jonathan asked, indicating the other family members, who were standing around forlornly, looking like cast members from some long-forgotten *Survivor* episode.

"Have you all been fingerprinted?" my father asked.

"An hour ago."

"Come with us," my mother said. "Your father will spring you."

At a tap on my shoulder I turned, and there was Grace. "May I have a moment, dear?"

We moved to a quiet spot where Grace said softly, "I'm worried about Richard."

I glanced beyond her and saw Richard chatting amicably with some of the other guests. He certainly didn't seem worried, but that was in keeping with his character. Richard Davis was a throwback to the rootin'-tootin' cowboy of old—a shade on the aggressive side and always in charge, which seemed at odds with Grace's quiet, refined ways. I was surprised when they started seeing each other. Until two months ago, Grace had maintained that she was beyond needing a man's companionship. Yet they seemed to adore each other, so who was I to say they weren't a good match?

Richard had moved to town from Austin, Texas, shortly after his wife had died three years ago. His only son had attended the university here, then married a local girl and settled down to raise a family. Deciding he was ready to retire and be a grandpa, Richard had sold his hugely popular roadhouse and landholdings in Texas, packed up his belongings, and headed to Indiana. Within a year he'd purchased a bowling alley and miniature golf course and had built a recreation center. Now he had a sporting empire that employed more than one hundred people.

The only negative I'd ever heard about Richard was

that he had a quick temper—any employee who didn't get with his program was canned on the spot, and any customer who didn't behave respectfully was shown the door—yet he was reported to be fair and generous to a fault. What really sold me on his character, though, was his car, a 1971 fire-engine red Cadillac Eldorado Biarritz convertible with monster fins on the back. Anyone who drove a car like that was okay by me.

"Why are you worried?" I asked her.

"As you know, the police are asking for the names of anyone who left the banquet center after the wedding. In addition they're asking for the names of anyone who knew Jack Snyder previously. Unfortunately, Richard falls into both categories."

"He knew Jack?"

"It seems Jack worked for Richard at the sports center about a year and a half ago, in his accounting department. Then Richard discovered that Jack had been embezzling funds—over twenty-five thousand dollars in all—but Jack fled the country before the police could arrest him. The money has never been recovered."

"It would be a stretch to pin the murder on Richard for that reason," I assured her. "Jack has probably bilked other people, too. And I'm sure Richard will have witnesses who can verify his whereabouts this evening."

Grace twisted her fingers together. "There's more, dear. At the time of the theft, Richard told a newspaper reporter that if he ever got his hands on the varmint— those are his words, not mine—Jack's goose would be cooked—also his words—which, if one didn't know Richard, might be construed as a death threat. I felt it best for him to be forthcoming with this information before the police uncovered it themselves—so they don't think he's trying to hide it—but he's adamantly opposed to the idea. He said what's in the past is in the past, and that we should let sleeping dogs lie."

"I know what Dave Hammond would say," I told her, referring to the lawyer for whom we'd both worked. "Don't give the cops more information than they ask for. Besides, they have enough on Josiah Turner to make him their prime suspect."

Grace thought it over, then smiled in relief. "Thank you. I feel much better. As the old saying goes, one should never borrow trouble. I must remember that."

"Let me out of here, you overgrown Neanderthals!" I heard a warbling voice cry. I turned around and saw Grandma Osborne trying to dodge the policemen who were determined to keep her from leaving the ballroom. "I'm an old lady. Have some respect."

"Our orders are to keep everyone inside the room, ma'am," one of the exasperated officers explained, side-stepping a kick.

"Thugs! Haven't you ever heard of the Geneva Convention?"

"You're not a prisoner of war, ma'am," the other cop said, dodging a swinging purse.

"Tell that to the commandant who interrogated me!"

Mr. Osborne and Pryce tried to grab her swinging arms from behind. "Mother, please!" Mr. Osborne said. "You're causing a scene."

"The police have promised me that we'll be able to leave in half an hour, Grandmother," Pryce assured her, "then we'll take you straight home."

"Half an hour? Why don't they just dig a grave for me right here?"

"Grandma Osborne?" I called cheerily. "Do you need water?"

"Now here's someone with a little horse sense," she

said, shaking off their grips. "The way they hoard water around here you'd think we were crossing the Sahara."

I walked over to the cops guarding the swinging doors between the ballroom and kitchen and said quietly, "Is it okay if I get her a glass of water?"

The cops exchanged glances, then one of them opened the door wide enough for me to get through.

"I'll get your water, Grandma," I called. "Have a seat. I'll be right back."

I stepped into the kitchen and looked around for help. The staff had already been fingerprinted; now they were bustling about, trying to clean up and get out of there. I approached the man who seemed to be in charge. He was wearing a chef's toque, a day's growth of beard, a sheen of perspiration, and a scowl.

"I'm sorry to interrupt," I said as sweetly as possible, "but could I trouble you for a glass of water?"

"Gunther!" he called over his shoulder. "Get a glass of water for this lady."

Lady? When had I crossed the line into ladyhood? I wanted to grab something reflective and check for wrinkles.

"Gunther isn't here, Anthony," one of the employees called.

"What do you mean Gunther isn't here?" Anthony bellowed. "No one leaves before the work is done."

As Anthony continued his diatribe, a quiet voice behind me said, "Excuse me, *señorita*."

I turned as an olive-skinned teenaged boy in an oversized white jacket handed me a glass of water. "Here is your *agua*."

"Thank you. *Muchas gracias*." I took the glass and he backed away, smiling shyly.

As I headed for the door, a waiter rushed in, dropped

off a load of soiled tablecloths, then headed out again. Seeing his white-tailed coat I asked myself again, why had Jack wanted to disguise himself as a waiter? Was it to keep Josiah from spotting him? Why had he come back at all? And where had he gotten the uniform?

I noticed Sheila Sackowitz unloading piles of soiled napkins from a stainless steel cart, so I walked over to her, hoping to have at least one answer before I left.

"Hey," she said, pushing a lock of hair away from her face. "What's up?" She looked frazzled, so I decided to keep it short.

"Sheila, do you know if a man by the name of Jack Snyder ever worked here?"

"Not that I know of, but I haven't been here that long. Ask Anthony."

I glanced over at Anthony, saw him scolding one of the cooks, and decided against it. "Do the waiters buy their outfits?" I asked her instead.

"Pants and shirts," she said. "The banquet center supplies the rest."

"Let's get moving, people," Anthony barked, clapping his hands. I had a feeling he was directing his comment toward me, so I thanked Sheila and left.

As soon as I stepped back into the ballroom, Grandma Osborne yelled, "Abby! Here I am." She was seated in a chair along the wall on the far side of the dance floor, guarded by her son and grandson. I started across the floor only to have Pryce jump up and come to meet me. Astoundingly, there was a cordial expression on his face. It made him look almost—oh, I don't know—sane.

"I'll take the water to her," he said. "You've got better things to do."

I wasn't sure whether to thank him or take his temperature—he did look somewhat fevered—so I simply handed him the glass.

His gaze moved to my hair, which by that time had slipped some of its pins, rendering it more windswept than upswept, then traveled the length of my gown and up again. "I meant to tell you earlier; you look stunning in that dress."

Now he was scaring me. We both knew I didn't look stunning; Pryce hated large prints on me, and I wasn't particularly fond of them either. So why was he lying?

Marco's words whispered hauntingly in my head: *"In case you haven't noticed, Pryce still has a crush on you."*

No way. Pryce had dumped *me*, not the other way around. It didn't make sense that he would suddenly find me desirable, or even socially acceptable. He must have had too much champagne. So why was he gazing at me like that? Was he waiting for a return compliment?

Standing there in the middle of the room, my stained fingers clasped behind my back, feeling like every eyeball in the place was focused on me, all I could think to say was, "And you look good in your tux, as well." I cringed inwardly. How lame was that?

"Are you going to bring that water over here or leave me to melt in this chair?" Grandma Osborne called. I wondered whether she'd noticed me—red-faced and starting to sweat—and had taken pity on me.

"I have half a mind to let her melt," Pryce muttered. "She hasn't liked me since the day we broke up." He pivoted on the heels of his shiny black shoes and strode away.

Since the day we broke up? I had to clamp my jaw shut to keep from yelling: *It wasn't we who broke us up, you disloyal, egotistical moron. It was* you. *You not only broke us up, you stamped on us until we were ground into sawdust.* Instead, I pasted a smile on my face and walked in the opposite direction, just in case anyone (my mother) was observing us.

I spotted Reilly in a discussion with one of the cops who'd been interviewing the guests, and since I hadn't seen him come in, I strolled over to see what he was up to. He stopped talking and looked around at me. "What?"

"Just wondering if you had any leads. Did the detective ever show up?"

Reilly glared at me for a good thirty seconds, then turned back to the cop and said, "I told you to clear her so she could leave."

"She did leave, Sergeant." The cop gave me an icy look. "Then she came back."

"I had to go to the kitchen to get a glass of water for Grandma Osborne," I explained.

"Does she have her water now?" Reilly asked, trying to maintain a pleasant demeanor.

"Yes, she does."

"Good. Then you can go home."

"I can't go home until Marco brings back my car. Geez, Reilly. Why are you in such a hurry to get rid of me?"

"Because if I let you stay, you'll try to take over my job."

"I have a job, thanks."

Reilly folded his arms across his chest. "Really? Then who was it that said, 'If this were my case, my first question would be, why did Jack return to the banquet center?' "

There were spies in the ballroom. I pointed toward the door. "I'll just wait for Marco outside."

"Good idea."

I was on my way up the hallway when I heard Reilly say, "Hey, Abby, hold up for a moment. I forgot to ask you something."

I turned as he strode up to me, his notepad open. "Grace Bingham works for you, right?"

"Right," I said slowly, trying to figure out where this was leading.

"Do you know her boyfriend, Richard Davis?"

Because of what Grace had just told me, I was immediately cautious. "I wouldn't use the word *boyfriend* where Grace is concerned, but yes, I know Richard, in the sense that everyone in town knows who he is."

"Were you aware he left the banquet center after the wedding?"

"Grace mentioned he had some kind of business matter to attend to, which he did, then he came right back."

"Define *right back.*"

That was a problem, because I hadn't seen Richard leave or return. Since I didn't want to incriminate Grace's beau by way of a bad definition, I had no choice but to fudge it. "By right back," I said, drawing out the words until my brain was up to speed, "I mean that he left right after the wedding and was back during the reception."

"But you don't know what time he returned."

"No, but Grace would."

He checked his notes. "She said she couldn't be sure." The way Reilly put it I knew he didn't believe her.

"So what are you implying? That Richard Davis killed Jack?"

"I didn't imply anything," he said irritably. "All I did was ask a simple question."

"You asked"—I held up the appropriate number of fingers—"three questions. One question is simple. Three—complex." I grinned, but he didn't grin back.

"What's your point?" Reilly snapped.

"That you should be focusing on the most logical suspect—Josiah Turner—not a reputable businessman and model citizen like Richard Davis."

A flicker in his eyes betrayed his thoughts. Reilly knew something about Richard that he wasn't sharing with me.

"Are you saying he's not a model citizen?" I asked.

Reilly underlined a note he'd written on his pad. "Let's just say, as of this moment, he's a person of interest."

CHAPTER SEVEN

A person of interest? That wasn't good. I hurried after Reilly, who was headed back up the hallway toward the ballroom. "Come on, Reilly. You don't honestly think Richard had anything to do with this murder, do you?" He ignored me, so I said, "Okay, we'll discuss this later."

He stopped at the door long enough to say, "*We* don't need to discuss anything." Then he stepped inside and was instantly mobbed by cranky wedding guests who'd had enough. Reilly finally grabbed a chair and stood on it. "Okay, folks, I know you want to get home, so listen up. Everyone who's been ID'd and fingerprinted, form a line right here in front this officer holding the clipboard. If your name is on the list, you can go home."

"It's about time," I heard Grandma Osborne say.

There was no sense hanging around—Reilly wasn't going to give me any more information—so I hustled to the dressing room to retrieve my purse before the mob came charging through the hall in their hurry to exit the building. I located the key I'd tucked in my bra, opened the locker, and was about to remove my purse when my cell phone rang. I stuck my hand inside the bag and groped blindly, discovering my wallet, a tube of lip gloss, a travel pack of tissues, two packs of cinnamon-flavored sugarless gum, and a lint-covered cough drop before finally finding the phone. By that time it had stopped ringing, so I checked for missed calls and saw Marco's number pop up. I punched in his speed dial number, then, holding the phone between my shoulder and ear, I took off my heels and flexed my cramped toes. Much better.

As soon as I heard his voice, I said, "Where are you? I'm ready to leave."

"I'm standing outside the building, in front of the doors."

At that moment I heard what sounded like a stampede in the hallway. "You might want to move back," I told him. "There's a herd of grumpy people headed your way."

"I'll wait around the corner."

I applied lip gloss and tried to repair my loose locks, giving the crowd ample time to exit the building, then I stuffed the stilettos in my purse and walked barefoot through the reception area, holding the hem of the skirt so it wouldn't drag. I was about to push open the exit door when I heard someone say, "Abigail, wait up."

I turned around as Pryce strode up the hall toward me. He opened his mouth to say something, then glanced down at my feet and announced, "You're not wearing shoes." Leave it to him to state the obvious.

"My toes held an uprising and I was overpowered. What are you still doing here?"

"I told Claymore I'd stick around to make sure everyone had gone." He shrugged nonchalantly. "Just to ease his mind. It was a rough evening for them."

"That was thoughtful of you." I didn't know what to

say next, so I hitched a thumb over my shoulder in the direction of the door. "I was about to leave myself."

"Let me get that for you." He strode ahead of me and opened the door. I walked under his arm into the muggy night air and looked around for my old yellow Vette and Marco.

"Here's a crazy idea," Pryce said with a forced chuckle. "Why don't we go get a cup of coffee somewhere?"

He had the crazy part right.

At that moment Marco stepped out of the shadows, saving me from having to come up with an excuse. Despite my earlier request, Marco had changed out of the tux and was in his usual jeans and T-shirt, which still looked better on him than on any man I'd ever met. Behind me I heard Pryce mutter something under his breath that sounded like *bastard*.

"Ready?" Marco said, making it a point to ignore Pryce.

I turned around to thank Pryce for the coffee offer, but he was already striding toward the east end of the parking lot.

"What was that about?" Marco asked, leading the way to my Corvette.

"I'm not sure."

"Yes, you are. He was flirting with you."

"No."

"Yes."

"Okay, yes, and it's creeping me out. Three months ago he couldn't stand to be in the same room with me. Now, suddenly, he wants to go for coffee."

"He could be a grass-is-greener-on-the-other-side-of-the-fence kind of guy. He wants what he doesn't have, then once he gets it—"

"He drops it into the nearest manhole, replaces the

cover, and walks away, brushing any remaining traces off his hands," I finished for him.

"I was going to say he doesn't want it anymore."

"I prefer a more graphic interpretation. Want to hear my interpretation of what happens to him after he walks away from that manhole?"

"Does it involve a heavy object falling from a roof?"

I swatted a mosquito away from my face. "No, but I could work it in. Pryce can flirt with me all he wants, but he had his chance to marry me and chose to walk away from it. Correction. His parents chose."

"And there's your answer to his renewed interest—his parents. Now that you own your own business, you meet their standards for a daughter-in-law."

"So all it takes to make Pryce interested in me again is the Osborne seal of approval? I have two words for that. No thanks."

"I see everyone left but the police," he said, nodding toward the garden, where evidence was still being collected. "How did it go inside?"

"Not good. Reilly has started calling Richard Davis a person of interest."

"You're right. That's not good." Marco glanced at my feet. "Did they confiscate your shoes as evidence?" He was so much more creative than Pryce.

"They should have," I replied. "Those heels were killers."

He groaned. "That was bad."

"Sorry," I said with a weary shrug. "It's been a long day."

Marco put his arm around my shoulders as we walked along. "You're quite a trooper, sunshine, you know that?"

I beamed up at him. I was a trooper. Not as good as hot, but still admirable, especially when Marco was doing the admiring. "Thanks."

"Why don't I drive? Your toes might not be up to operating the pedals." He opened the passenger door for me, and with a grateful sigh I slid in.

As I buckled up and settled against the seat, Marco shut his door and turned the key, and the engine roared to life. I reached over to stroke the steering wheel of my sleek yellow baby. "Did you miss me?" I cooed. "Was Marco good to you?"

"I treated her like the hot stuff she is—with gentle hands, as is my style." He lifted an eyebrow, and all I could think about was the touch of those gentle hands on my nape—and that massage he'd promised to finish.

"Should I forgive you for changing out of the tux?" I asked playfully.

"I can explain."

"Over coffee at my place?"

"I was thinking of a special bottle of chilled white wine I have tucked away at the bar."

I liked the way he thought. I glanced at my watch. It was twelve thirty in the morning, I was still wearing the ugly dress, my feet hurt, my hair was a mess, and my eyes felt like sandpaper, but would I turn down a chance to get cozy with Marco? I wasn't that tired.

As if to prove me wrong, I was overtaken by a rogue yawn. Another followed. I rubbed my eyes, blinked hard, and decided I'd better keep talking if I wanted to stay awake, so I told him about my conversation with Jillian and Claymore, the new information on Vince Vogel, and the reason for Reilly's interest in Richard Davis.

"But none of that matters, does it, since the police are handling it." Marco gave me a pointed look as we sailed along deserted roads.

"I hear you loud and clear. And even though I'm a little concerned about Richard, I'm keeping my nose out of it."

"Thank you. And just so you know, I had to change out of the tux because a water pipe broke in the bar's kitchen and I didn't want to ruin your fancy hem work by wading through water. I've got the suit on a hanger. I'll drop it off tomorrow."

"That's the problem with those old buildings. Something is always going wrong." But right then everything was going right, so I sat back and put my mind on cruise control, letting my gaze drift over to the man-licious hunk beside me, who would soon be pouring glasses of crisp white wine and getting cozy. Was there any better end to an evening?

We pulled up across the street from the Down the Hatch Bar and Grill and Marco shut off the engine and unbuckled his seat belt. "I'll be back in a second," he promised. "Then we'll talk about that debt you owe me."

Ah. Payback time. With all sorts of wicked thoughts in mind, I leaned my head against the seat back and watched Marco jog across the street and into the bar. Then I fell asleep.

Slumbering soundly, I dreamed that Marco, wearing his black tux, of course, was carrying me up a grand, curving staircase into a gauzy, candlelit boudoir, easing me onto a big, soft bed, and bending over me like a prince preparing to awaken his princess with a tender smooch. "Ready to hit the sack?" my dream prince asked in a husky whisper.

Wow. Nothing like being blunt. "Don't I get a kiss first?" I murmured.

"Sure."

It wasn't quite the romantic answer I expected, but, hey, it was the best my sleepy brain could do. I curled my toes and puckered up expectantly.

He gave me a peck on the forehead.

My pucker froze in place and my eyes flew open as the real Marco pulled a sheet over my prone body and tucked it gently under my chin. I gazed around in confusion, my groggy mind struggling to make sense of my surroundings. Wasn't that my U2 poster on the wall? Was I at home?

"I'll stick the wine in your fridge," he said. "You get some sleep. I'm going back to the bar to take care of the plumbing problem. That floor isn't going to mop itself."

I was at home. Marco had carried me all the way up to the apartment. Damn. A real-life fantasy, and I'd been too exhausted to enjoy it. "What about my debt?" I managed to mutter.

"We'll work something out." With a cryptic smile, he closed the door and was gone.

I let my lids flutter shut, then spent the rest of the night dreaming about the kiss-that-might-have-been, only in my version it had a completely different ending.

When the alarm clock went off the next morning, I groped for the Off button, pulled myself to a sitting position, and struggled to lift my eyelids beyond a slit. I peered down at Simon, who was sitting next to, not on, the green throw rug beside my bed, keeping one eye on it in case it should attack without warning. He had a dire fear of throw rugs.

As soon as I threw back the sheet, Simon began to meow. I shushed him so he wouldn't awaken Nikki, sleeping in her room across the hall. To retaliate, he gave me that helpless expression cats are so good at—head cocked to one side, eyes wide and innocent. At his feet was an object I took to be a piece of an old felt mouse he'd found behind the sofa.

"Sorry, buddy," I said, patting his head. "I'm really tired. We can play later."

Simon gazed down at the object, then up at me again, tilting his head like he didn't get it.

I sighed. There was no way I could win against that look. I picked up the toy to toss it, then realized it was a dead bumblebee, partly chewed, missing its legs. I immediately dropped it, shuddering, then had to scramble for Simon before he finished it off.

"What's going on?" Nikki said from the doorway, yawning. Her short hair was sticking up all over and her pink Tinkerbell pjs were askew. I'd known her since third grade. I'd moved in with her after graduating from Indiana University and enrolling at New Chapel University Law School. I'd planned to live there only until I married Pryce and moved into his condo. Since neither of those events had happened, I was still there, like an ink stain on a cuff.

Since she was already awake, I thrust the cat into her arms. "Simon ate the legs off a bee. When was the last time you fed him?"

"My, aren't we grouchy this morning?" Nikki said, following as I stumbled to the kitchen for a glass of orange juice.

"Five hours of sleep," I groused, "and a missed chance at romance."

"Late nights are murder on you, aren't they?"

I stopped pouring the juice and glanced around at her.

"What did I say?" Her eyes got wide in mock alarm. "Omigod, Jillian finally pushed you over the edge and you did away with her. How did you do it? Did you hold her face under the frosting of her cake?"

"No, but that's a good idea. I wish I'd thought of that last night."

Between gulps of juice and mouthfuls of toast, I gave Nikki the rundown on the entire previous evening, including Jack's fistfight, return to the banquet center, and murder. I also mentioned Jack's disguise and the cops' interest in Grace's beau. Then I tossed in the part about Marco tucking me in, and Nikki nearly had a seizure.

"You slept through that?" she kept saying, until finally I threw on my workout clothes and headed for the park to escape her. Then I plodded around the track like an elephant slogging through wet cement. Five hours' sleep was not enough for this sleeping beauty.

When I dragged myself into the shop at eight o'clock, Grace didn't come out of the parlor as she usually did, ready to greet me with a cup of coffee and her chipper, "Good morning, dear. How are we today?" In fact, she didn't come out of the parlor at all, so I peered in at her and smiled. "Good morning."

There were circles beneath her eyes and her hair wasn't as neatly styled as it usually was. "Oh, good morning, dear," she said, trying to put cheer in her voice. "I didn't hear the bell. Let me get a cup of coffee for you."

"I'll do it," I said, but she was already pouring, so I took a seat at the coffee bar. On the counter was a copy of the *New Chapel News*, open to the front page, where a headline blared: MURDERER ON THE LOOSE. Underneath it was an article and a photo of Jack Snyder. I turned it over so Grace wouldn't have to look at it. "You're exhausted, Grace. Why don't you take the day off?"

"I'd only sit and fret. The police questioned Richard extensively last night, and I'm afraid they're not done with him. They've asked him not to leave town."

"That's standard procedure. I wouldn't worry."

"It's not that I want to worry, dear, but they didn't ask *me* not to leave town."

She had a point.

"And one more thing," Grace said. "It appears Richard doesn't have anyone who can verify his movements after he left the banquet hall after all."

"No one at the sports center saw him?"

"No one. He used the back entrance and went directly upstairs to his office. At that time of evening he has a manager on the main floor, but the second floor is empty."

"Tell me again why he had to leave."

She poured herself a cup of tea and joined me at the counter. "All I know is that it was a business matter. I didn't ask for specifics because I didn't really feel it was my place. I've only known him a short while."

"Let's look at this from the police's viewpoint. What would Richard's motive be?"

"I suppose they could say he did it out of revenge, but I tell you, Abby, Richard is a kind, decent man. He would never stoop to such a level." She set her cup into the saucer with a clatter.

"Are you sure about him, Grace? As you said, you haven't known him that long."

She struck a pose, a sure sign a quote was on its way. "As Josiah Gilbert Holland wrote, 'The time demands strong minds, great hearts, true faith, and willing hands.' I can't think of a more apt description of Richard, and as you know, I'm an excellent judge of character."

"You didn't trust Marco when you first met him."

"I still don't, but it has nothing to do with his integrity and everything to do with his devil-may-care attitude. I worry about you when it comes to matters of your heart. I know how shattered you were after Pryce broke your engagement."

"Yes, but didn't *that* turn out to be a blessing in disguise."

She picked up her cup and sipped quietly, her gaze straying to the bay window. "When my husband died, I didn't think I'd ever meet another man who had as much integrity and charm as he had, and I certainly wasn't about to settle for less. When I met Richard I felt a new glimmer of hope that perhaps I wasn't destined to live the rest of my life alone. Yet for months I resisted his offer of friendship, fearing I'd be disappointed. But he's a persistent man, so I finally let him into my life. Now I can't help but think it was a mistake. Look what has happened to him because of me."

Grace looked so racked with guilt and sadness that my heart ached for her. How many times had she consoled me, and there I was without even one good quote to cheer her up. The best I could come up with was, "You can't blame yourself for this."

"But you *can* ask Abby for help," Lottie said. She was standing in the doorway, a shrewd gleam in her eye. No one could raise four boys without gaining a little shrewdness. Obviously Grace had filled her in on the events of the night before.

"I'll bet you any money that Abby can figure out who killed Jack Snyder," she said.

I glanced at Grace, preparing myself for her resounding *"Absolutely not."* She hated when I poked around in police business. To my astonishment she lifted an eyebrow, as if she were actually considering it.

One thing I've learned about Grace: if I wanted to convince her to do something, I had to take the opposite stance. "I'm not sure I'd be of much help," I said to Lottie. "Reilly won't tell me a thing anymore. He gets feisty when I ask him questions."

"Forget Reilly," Lottie said, playing along. "You've got a better source—that hottie Greg Morgan in the prosecutor's office. He owes you for standing you up at the wedding."

Morgan hadn't actually stood me up, but her point was well taken. Not only did he have access to police records, but he had also developed an interest in me that I milked whenever I could. It was payback for all those snubs I'd gotten from him in high school.

I looked at Grace to see how our ploy was working and thought I detected a glint of hope in her eyes. It was time to toss more fuel into the fire. "There was another person at the wedding who Jack had wronged and, as it happens, he left early, too. He's a butcher at the Meat Market. It wouldn't be hard to check out his story."

"And since you're practically family, you can pay a visit to Jillian's uncle Josiah to fish around there," Lottie added.

I didn't rush to agree. It would take a better sportsman than me to pull a tuna out of that pond.

Grace finished her tea and took her cup to the sink behind the bar. She was humming a flat tune, which meant she was doing some serious deliberating. The more carefree Grace felt, the livelier her tunes became. Lottie gave me an encouraging wink.

The phone rang in the shop and Lottie went to answer it. "Abby, it's Trudee DeWitt," she called a moment later.

Oh, no. I'd forgotten to make arrangements to have the carnations removed from her backyard. I jumped up and ran to the other room. "Trudee? Hi. I'm so sorry I didn't call you."

"That's okay," she said in her perky voice. "I just wanted to let you know that your cute little helpers are here."

"My cute little helpers are at your house?" I said, glancing at Lottie for confirmation, but she shrugged, as if it was news to her.

"They're loading a pickup truck now. They want to know where to dump the flowers."

I was amazed the quads had thought to do that all on their own. "Tell them to take the flowers to the park department's recycling center. How was your party?"

I heard the pop of bubblegum and couldn't help but wonder if Trudee suffered from jaw pain from all that chewing she did. "The party was super," she said. "We had only one mishap when someone stumbled into the flag, but Karl came right over to fix it. He's such a cutie-pie. I just want to pinch his cheek. Do you want me to send your check with him?"

"Thanks, but I'll pick it up when I come to get my decorations in"—I checked my watch—"about an hour, okay?"

"Okay. See you then."

I hung up and let out a loud, "Woo-hoo!" as I danced around the shop. I gave Lottie a high five. "Bring on the bills. I'm picking up Trudee's check in an hour, and I'm taking you and Grace out for a celebration dinner—my treat."

"Sweetie, that's kind of you, but you don't need to waste your hard-earned money on us," Lottie said.

"I made you a promise when I took that job, and a promise is a promise. Are you with me?"

"Are you kidding?" She reached for the phone. "I'll call Herman and let him know he and the boys are on their own tonight."

Grace was being rather quiet, so I returned to the parlor to see why, claiming I needed a refill on my coffee. She was setting out bud vases and filling them with white daisies, a worried frown on her face, but when she heard me come in, she turned with a smile. "Congratulations on the check, dear. That's wonderful news."

"Thanks," I said as I filled up the cup with her fragrant brew. "You'll be able to join us for dinner tonight, won't you?"

"I wouldn't miss it." She put out the last vase, stuck two flowers in it, then said, "If the offer of help is still open, I'd like to take you up on it. Mind, now, I'm not entirely happy about encouraging your inquisitive nature, but desperate times call for desperate measures."

I nodded soberly. "I understand."

She heaved a sigh, as if she were resigning herself to the inevitable. "I suppose you'll want to get started on it right away. What will you do first?"

"Interview you. Have a seat, Grace."

CHAPTER EIGHT

I grabbed a tablet and a pen from under the counter and took a seat at one of the white wrought iron tables in front of the bay window. Fortunately, the shop didn't open for another half hour, so I had some leeway. Grace poured herself another cup of tea and sat down beside me, and we began.

"First of all, what time did Richard leave the banquet hall?"

She raised her cup to her lips and took a sip, pondering my question. "He received a message on his phone as soon as he turned it back on, which would have been immediately after the ceremony as we were leaving the garden area and walking toward the building."

I wrote it down. "What did the message say?"

"I didn't hear it. Richard listened to it, then put the phone in his coat pocket and said a problem had come up that needed his attention. He told me he'd take care of it and join me as soon as he could. Then he started toward the parking lot and I went inside the building."

"What time did he come back?"

"I didn't check my watch, but it was after the police arrived."

"Let's make a timeline," I said, drawing a line across the page. "The wedding started at eight ten and ended right after the fireworks show, so he would have left about eight forty-five." I marked the line accordingly. "The reception started at nine sixteen, because that's when Pryce began the world's longest, dullest toast. And it was around ten o'clock that Grandma Osborne found Jack's body."

Grace thought a moment, then said, "I remember following everyone out of the ballroom to see what all the sirens were for, and as I stood behind the police barricade Richard came up to ask what had happened."

"That would make it about ten fifteen, give or take a few minutes. Did he say anything about what the problem was or whether he'd solved it?"

"The only thing he said was that he had taken care of business."

I wrote it down and looked over my notes. There was an hour and a half of time Richard would have to explain, but would he explain it to me? "Grace, what would Richard say if he knew you'd asked me to investigate?"

"Possibly something to the effect of, 'Is that little lady at it again?' "

"That was a remarkable Texas accent, Grace."

"Thank you, dear. I do have quite an ear for languages." She leaned closer to say, "Listening to Lottie all day doesn't hurt, either."

"I heard that," Lottie called from the other room. She didn't like to be reminded of her Kentucky twang. To her ear, we were the ones who talked funny.

"Would you call Richard and ask if I can stop by to see him after I make my deliveries today?" I asked.

Grace rose and took her cup to the sink behind the counter. "I'll do it right now."

I cut the photo of Jack Snyder from the front page and tucked it in my purse, just in case I needed it later. Then, with my coffee cup refilled, I went to the workroom to look over the new orders: four arrangements for a funeral at the Happy Dreams Funeral Home, an anniversary bouquet, a basket arrangement for a woman's thirty-fifth birthday, a dozen roses for another birthday, and a door wreath. I'd have time to do the basket arrangement before I left for Trudee's house and deliver it on the way.

I took a basket made of woven reed off a shelf and put it on the worktable in front of me, then went to the cooler to select the flowers: a mixture of bright orange gerberas, yellow button spray chrysanthemums, deep pink roses, and the reddish-orange *Hypericum* berries. The round basket had a high handle, which I wrapped with tangerine-colored ribbon that I tied in a bow on one side. Into the plastic liner went green foam that had been soaked in water, followed by the flowers, forming a mound of bright colors, sweet scents, and varied textures. I wrapped it in bright birthday paper, stapled it at the top, attached a gift card, and voila! My design was done.

Lottie had already finished the anniversary bouquet, so I loaded it and the basket in her station wagon and took off. Delivering flowers was one of the high points of my job. I got a new thrill each time I saw the happiness in people's faces when they opened their doors and found me standing there, a wrapped surprise in my arms. Today was no exception.

At my first stop, a thirtysomething woman answered the door, a fussing infant in her arms and a whining toddler hanging on a leg. I could tell she was ready to brush off whoever was complicating her life further, but as soon as she saw the wrapped bouquet, her expression changed.

"Happy anniversary!" I cried.

"Oh, my goodness!" She opened the door wider. "Would you mind bringing it in?"

I stepped inside and found myself in the compact, cluttered living room of a small ranch house. I looked around for a place to set the bouquet, but every surface was covered with plastic toys. "Would you like me to hold the baby while you—?"

I hadn't even finished the sentence when I suddenly found myself holding a small, diaper-encased bundle of arms and legs and big eyes that didn't know what to make of the sudden change of scenery. I was feeling the same way.

"Oh! It's beautiful, just beautiful," she cried, holding up the bouquet of pink and purple carnations, yellow narcissi, and white roses. "I thought he forgot." She burst into tears, startling the baby, who screwed up his little face and began to wail, which changed the toddler's whines to shrieks of terror.

"I'm sorry," the woman said, laughing through her tears. "I'll take the baby. Thank you so much. This has really made my day."

I was more than happy to hand the child back and escape to the outdoors, where even the neighbor's lawnmower sounded peaceful by comparison. One thing the visit proved: I wasn't ready to have children.

My second stop was much quieter but no less thrilling. The wedding basket was for a summer school teacher at the high school. I took the package to the office, explained my mission, and waited as the secretary used the intercom. I was surprised when the teacher turned out to be male, which just proved that women weren't the only ones who could receive romantic gifts.

Next stop was Trudee's upscale subdivision. I pulled up in front of her house and saw that my risers and other paraphernalia had been grouped outside her front door. I walked around to the backyard and found that the masses of carnations and the string borders had been removed from her lawn. Not only that, but the lawn where we'd spread out the flag had been freshly mowed.

I walked across the deck to a sliding glass door, peered through the screen, and saw one of Lottie's quads standing with his back to the door—a bare back, actually. The rest of him was covered by long, baggy shorts and flip-flops, and by all the posturing going on, I had a strong hunch the quad in question was Karl.

He was jabbering to Trudee, who had perched on a stool at the counter and crossed one long leg over the other, her big doe eyes fixed on him as she listened intently. Trudee wore a tight, scoop-necked T-shirt—more scoop than shirt—in turquoise blue, with matching turquoise hoop earrings and a pair of white short-shorts.

"Hello," I called through the screen.

"Abby! Come in!" Trudee said, hopping off the stool to greet me, while her guest turned in surprise, holding a glass of something cold in his hand.

"Karl was just telling me about football practice," Trudee said, as if this were a special treat. "Did you know the coach makes them do drills in this heat?"

"We put all your stuff out front," Karl immediately offered, sensing I wasn't too pleased to find him bending Trudee's ear, "and we cleaned up the backyard."

"Karl even mowed the grass for me. Isn't he a cutie-pie?" Trudee wrinkled her nose at him as she pinched the firm flesh of his cheek.

"Yes, he certainly is." I patted his other cheek smartly.

As Karl scowled at me and rubbed his cheek, Trudee clicked her way across the kitchen in her high-heeled mules to a built-in desk, opened a drawer, and pulled out a check. I glanced at Karl and saw his eyes bulge as he watched her lean over to sign the check. I elbowed him in the side and hissed, "Stop it."

The phone rang and Trudee answered it, then clicked out of the room to the staircase to yell, "Hea-a-ther. Pho-o-ne!"

I massaged my ear canals. No intercom needed in that house. Trudee knew how to make her voice carry. She clicked back and handed me the check. "Here you go, Abby. Thanks for everything. Your flowers were super."

I tucked her payment in the pocket of my navy capris. There was something I was dying to know, yet I was almost fearful to ask. I took a breath and decided to go for it. "How did the coatrack go over?"

"It blew everyone away," she gushed. "I could tell by the looks on their faces."

I'll bet it had.

"You don't want it back, do you?" she asked.

"Oh, no," I said quickly. "It suits your decor to a *T*. I wouldn't dream of moving it anywhere else."

She smiled and blew a big bubble with her pink gum.

"Okay, Karl," I said, "let's go."

"Now? Why? I don't have to be anywhere."

Karl didn't seem to realize he was overstaying his welcome. No one needed a hormonally charged teenager hanging around, drooling all over the floor. "I need your help, that's why."

"I'm not finished with my water," he protested, holding up the sweating glass.

"I'll buy you a bottle," I told him and grabbed an earlobe to drag him out the sliding door.

He yanked his head away, rubbing his lobe. "All right! You don't have to rip my ear off." He snatched his shirt from a lawn chair as we crossed the deck, and I could hear him grumbling as we walked around the house to the front yard. As soon as we were in his mother's car I said, "What's up with you?"

"What do you mean?"

"I mean it's pretty obvious you have a crush on Mrs. DeWitt."

"You're insane," he said and slumped down in the passenger seat.

"How were you going to get home?"

"I figured Trudee would give me a lift."

"It's Mrs. DeWitt, not Trudee," I reminded him.

"Whatever. You can drop me at the sports center."

My ears perked up. "Mini-World sports center?"

"Yeah, why? Is that off-limits?"

I pulled off the road to call the shop. Grace answered on the second ring. "Have you talked to Richard yet?" I asked.

"Yes, dear. He said you're welcome to stop by anytime."

"I'm on my way there now. Any messages?"

"Just your mother, reminding you—"

"—about Friday-night dinner," I finished with her. "Got it. I should be back at the shop in an hour. Tell Lottie that Karl is with me and I'll explain why later."

"Thanks a lot," he muttered, shooting me murderous looks. "Like you never had a crush on anyone."

Here was my chance to talk some sense into him. "I've had many crushes, and that's why I'm doing you this favor now."

He sat up, taking new interest in me.

"In high school," I told him, "I was crazy about my biology teacher, and in college it was my speech professor, who used to let me hold his watch and time the other students' speeches. I was sure that watch symbolized something. And then there was a mailman . . ."

He chortled. "A mailman?"

"Don't laugh. I was only eleven years old. Besides, he was very charming, and he had nice legs. Mail carriers wear shorts in the summer. I remember following him down the block on my pink Rollerblades. I thought I was really hot stuff in those blades."

That made Karl laugh so hard the car rocked as he slammed his body against the seat.

We pulled into the sports complex's huge blacktop parking lot and parked near the main entrance. Karl got out of the car and started for the building, with me right behind.

"You're not going to follow me around, are you?" he asked.

"Not even if someone paid me to do it. I have to see a man about a body."

We walked up to the entrance where wide, glass doors slid open to admit us, letting out a blast of ice-cold air. Inside, I looked around, trying to decide which way to go. The huge, open room ahead of me looked like the lobby of an enormous hotel. There was a reception counter to my left, a sandwich shop to my right, a brightly patterned carpet on the floor, and a room straight ahead that extended as far as the eye could see, where the beeps, buzzes, and bells of video games could be heard.

Karl started off in the direction of the arcade, so I called, "Thanks for helping with the flowers today."

"That's cool," he called over his shoulder.

"Are you staying here or coming back to the shop with me?"

"Staying. I'll have one of my brothers pick me up later."

I walked up to the semicircular counter, where a smiling girl greeted me with a cheery "How can I help you?"

"I'd like to speak with Richard Davis. My name is Abby Knight."

She picked up a phone, made a call, and told me to take the elevator to the second floor. I found the stairs and used them instead. That container of Chunky Monkey ice cream in the freezer was just waiting for someone with a negative calorie count to dig into it.

At the top of the stairs I went through more glass doors into a reception area that was tastefully decorated in muted colors and artwork. A neatly dressed woman about fifty years old came out from behind a counter to usher me down a quiet hallway to an office at the far end. She opened the door and we both stepped inside, breathing in the tangy aroma of men's cologne.

I gazed around the room in awe. Not only was the office itself gigantic, but so were the windows, the highly polished wood table that served as a desk, the leather chairs, the sofa, the floor-to-ceiling bookcase jammed with books, a bronze sculpture of a horse, and the paintings on the walls, all scenes of the Old West. Oddly, as big as it was, it still had a comfortable, cozy, denlike atmosphere that made me want to curl up with a good book and a cup of coffee.

"Abby Knight is here, Mr. Davis," the woman said softly.

A burgundy leather chair behind the enormous desk rotated, and Richard Davis jumped up, striding around the desk to greet me, his hand outstretched. He had on a brown, Western-style shirt, string tie, and tan slacks, all of which set off his white hair, blue eyes, and tanned skin. I almost expected to see a ten-gallon hat parked nearby.

"Well, hello, little lady!" he said, clasping my hand hard enough to make me wince. It didn't help that he had on a big silver and turquoise ring that dug into the tender flesh below my pinkie. "Great to see you again, although I wish it was under better circumstances. Sit down and take a load off. Adele, would you see what she'd like to drink, please?"

"Would you care for coffee, tea, iced tea, or a lemon-lime drink?" Adele asked with a pleasant smile.

"Iced tea would be great. Thanks." I sank into one of a pair of buttery-soft, caramel-colored leather chairs opposite his desk. Richard took the other one, exuding confidence and charm. I could see why Grace found him attractive.

"I understand you have some questions for me about last night."

"I do." I dug through my purse and pulled out a tattered notebook and pen.

He leaned forward, pinning me in place with a commanding look. "Before we get started I want you to know something. I'm a private person and I don't normally discuss my business with anyone but a few carefully chosen people. I'm doing this for Grace's sake because I think the world of her and I understand her concern for my well-being. If it were just me, I'd tell the cops to take a long walk off a short pier. But I want to ease Grace's mind, so I'm putting myself at your disposal." He leaned back, elbows on the arms of the chair, hands folded on his stomach, and waited.

If he was the killer, he certainly knew how to put on a good front.

"We have a common purpose," I told him. "I'm doing this for Grace's sake, too, so let's start by reviewing what I know about your movements yesterday evening." I read from my notes. "You left the banquet center immediately after the ceremony, around eight forty-five, and used the back stairs to come up to your office; no one was here to verify either your arrival or your departure."

"That's right."

"Why did you use the back entrance?"

"It's easier and quicker."

"What was your reason for coming here?"

"Business."

I thanked Adele for the iced tea, then said to Richard, "Could you be more specific?"

"I had a big deal in the works and it was in danger of falling through. I had to come back here to handle it because this is where I keep all my information."

I wrote it down, with a note to ask Adele what she knew about the deal. Richard hadn't waited until she left the room to talk, so obviously she was one of those carefully selected confidants. "Grace said you'd received a call on your cell phone. To whom did you speak?"

"It wasn't a call; it was a voice-mail message. I had to come here to check data on the computer and make a decision, which I did; then I sent out an encrypted file over the Internet."

"What time was that?"

He got up and typed something into his computer. "Nine twenty-three p.m."

"You returned to the banquet center then around ten fifteen?"

"That sounds about right."

"Does anyone else have access to your computer?"

"Adele does."

Then Richard wouldn't be able to prove he'd been the actual one to do the sending.

This wasn't looking good. No one had seen him in the building, he hadn't spoken to anyone on the phone, and he'd been gone over an hour, which left him plenty of time to kill Jack, conduct his business at the sports center, and return to the reception. "Jack Snyder used to work for you, right?"

"He worked in the accounting department."

"How did you come to hire him?"

"I did it as a favor for his pa, who was one of the most upstanding men I've ever met. He introduced me to the right people in town so I could get the center built. I owed him for that, so I agreed to hire his son, who'd just graduated from college with a business degree. With a pa like that I never would have guessed him to be a low-down thief and liar."

"How did you catch him?"

Richard shook his head, as if he still couldn't get over it. "Jack was wily. He never took a vacation day and always insisted on staying late to finish up. One day Adele mentioned to me that she had a bad feeling about him, and I always trust Adele's instincts, so I ordered a surprise audit. That's when we discovered he'd siphoned off over twenty-five thousand dollars." Richard pounded his fists on the arms of his chair. "The dirty varmint had devised a scheme to defraud my company!

"I called the police and filed charges, but Jack was long gone by then, probably hiding down in Mexico. The next thing I heard was that he was doing time in prison. I felt sorry for his pa, but Jack deserved that jail time." Richard leaned forward, his blue eyes blazing with anger.

"If I'd gotten my hands on him first, he'd have gotten a whole lot worse than a prison sentence."

I watched him carefully, wondering if there was an even darker side lurking beneath that tanned face. "Like maybe a death sentence?" I asked.

CHAPTER NINE

"A death sentence." Richard threw back his head and let loose with a Texas-sized laugh. "I like you, girl. You're not afraid of the tough questions. No, I wouldn't have killed the varmint, but I'd have taught him a lesson he wouldn't soon forget."

"I hope you didn't say that to the cops. They tend to misinterpret statements like that."

"They can misinterpret all they want. That doesn't mean they can prove I did anything wrong."

"They don't always have to prove it to put someone behind bars. People are convicted on circumstantial evidence every day," I reminded him.

He drummed the fingers of both hands on the arms of the chair as he considered my advice. "You're right. I shouldn't be so bumptious. I forget people in these parts don't always understand my ways."

"Oddly, I find that applies to me, too." I finished my iced tea and put away my notebook. "That's all I have for now, but if you don't mind, I'd like to ask Adele a few questions."

"Be my guest. I don't have anything to hide." Richard took my glass and rose to see me to the door. "I appreciate your help, Abby. You're a kindhearted little lady. A man can't go wrong with you on his side."

I wasn't on his side—I wasn't on anyone's side until I had more information—but I didn't want to risk losing Richard's cooperation, so I said nothing.

I stopped at Adele's desk to ask her what she knew about the emergency Richard had come back to the office to handle. She told me the name of the company it concerned and verified that he'd been working on the deal for months.

"It almost fell through, but he managed to salvage it by the sheer force of his personality," she explained. "Naturally he'd have to come back to his office so he'd have his financial data handy."

"Is it typical for him to come here in the evenings?"

"For something like this, absolutely."

"Have you ever sent anything over the Internet from his computer?"

"Yes, I have, on his authority."

I studied Adele as she spoke. She seemed very certain of her answers, didn't fidget, and maintained eye contact with me throughout our conversation, which meant that she was either honest or a very cool liar. My instincts told me she was honest.

I left the sports center feeling better about Richard's character but still uneasy about the case the police could potentially build against him. I buckled my seat belt, then decided to call Reilly before heading back to Bloomers, hoping I'd catch him in a good moment and he'd tell me what evidence they'd collected.

"Is this the phenomenal Sgt. Sean Reilly?" I asked when he picked up the phone.

"What do you need?" he replied with a sigh.

"Nothing much. Just wanted to see how your day was going and if you had any strong leads on the murder investigation."

"Detective Williams is in charge of the case now, so you can go pester the hell out of him."

I wasn't thrilled to hear that. Detective Williams was a brusque, unfriendly man who made Reilly look like Santa Claus. "So you're not working on the murder at all? You're not even collecting evidence?"

There was a pause, then he said, "You have evidence?"

"I'd prefer to call it information."

"And that information would be?"

"Available in trade."

"See, this is why I'm happy that Williams is on the case. You want to bargain? Go bargain with him. I don't have time for games."

"Okay, but can I ask you just one quick question?"

The line went dead. So much for jolly old Saint Nick.

I knew Reilly was counting on Williams's unpleasant personality to deter me, but he didn't understand my determination to help Grace. I called the dispatch operator and asked for Williams, and when he came on the line I said in my most professional voice, "Detective Williams, my name is Abby Knight. My father is Sgt. Jeffrey Knight. I'm sure you remember him. Anyway, I was at the banquet center the night of—"

"Get to the point."

"I'm trying to get a little information on the murder case. I just spoke with—"

"Read the newspaper." There was a click and he was gone.

I was frustrated, but not defeated. I had other resources, like Marco—if I could talk him into helping me—and Greg Morgan, and even my dad, who still had a little clout. I could get around Williams. No, make that I *would* get around Williams.

I drove back to Bloomers with Lottie's car windows down and the radio blaring Christina Aguilera. It was a normal July day—temperature in the mid-eighties, with the smell of freshly mown grass in the air and a few fluffy white clouds in the sky—the kind of day that made me wish I were in my convertible zipping along an open road, singing at the top of my lungs. That always boosted my spirits. Then again, so did seeing the pretty redbrick front of my flower shop, with its cheery yellow door in the middle, and pots of colorful geraniums and petunias on the sidewalk in front of the two bay windows.

A car was pulling out of a parking space across the street from Bloomers, on the courthouse side, so I nabbed the spot. I loved having a shop on the town square, where something was always happening. Today, all four streets around the square were crowded with shoppers who'd come out for the annual post-holiday sidewalk sales.

I got out of the car, slung my purse over my shoulder, and heard a male voice say, "Well, if it isn't New Chapel's hottest petal pusher."

I looked around and there, like an angel from heaven, was Greg Morgan, who prided himself on being on top of every big case. As usual, he had on an ultrahip suit, probably Hugo Boss, with a crisp white shirt, paisley silk tie—my gaze dropped to his feet—and black sandals? Not quite a fit with his wholesome, boy-next-door image.

"If it isn't New Chapel's handsomest deputy prosecutor," I responded, "and if you don't believe me, ask him."

"I hadn't heard you'd turned into a stand-up comedian." Morgan snapped his fingers. "I know what it is. You're sore because I couldn't be your escort for the wedding."

"More than sore. I'm crushed. I may never recover. Cool sandals, by the way."

"I thought they'd go well with the ankle wrap." He lifted a pant leg to show me a thick Ace bandage wound around his lower limb. Two women walking past nearly dropped their shopping bags twirling around for a glimpse.

"I'll bet you'll start a fashion trend," I said.

"Hey, I'm sorry I couldn't make it to the wedding. I hear I missed a real firecracker of a reception." Morgan chuckled, impressed with his own cleverness.

"Was that supposed to be a pun?"

"Only if you thought it was funny."

"I'm not really a fan of murder-based humor."

Morgan shrugged. "It was worth a try. Too bad the reception was ruined. Your cousin Jillian must have been beside herself."

"She'll recover. So, Greg," I said sweetly, "what do you hear on the police investigation of the case?"

"Nothing yet," he said, a calculating twinkle in his eye, "but possibly by six o'clock this evening I'll know something. What do you say I make it up to you for missing the wedding by taking you to a fine Chicago restaurant?"

Time out. I'd suffered through a horrendous dinner with Morgan once before, and I wasn't in a hurry to repeat the experience. However, he did have access to information I needed, so I decided lunch would be tolerable. But first I had to steer him away from that dinner date. "I've got a really heavy schedule and I'd hate to put you off, so why don't we do lunch instead, like, say, today?"

"I can't." He checked his watch. "I have a trial starting in fifteen minutes and it'll probably run late."

"How about tomorrow?" I hated to sound desperate, but when it came to helping Grace I was willing to make sacrifices.

"That'll work. Call my secretary and have her put you down for tomorrow." Morgan liked to pretend he had his own staff, when actually all five deputy prosecutors shared one rather uppity and not-very-efficient receptionist-typist.

"One o'clock at Rosie's?" I asked as he backed toward the courthouse.

"Should be fine. I'll see you then."

"Take care of your ankle," I called. "I couldn't survive being stood up twice." Snickering to myself, I turned around and there was Marco.

He had parked his car by Lottie's station wagon and was leaning against the hood, arms folded across his chest, watching me with an inscrutable look. I was certain he'd heard the last part of my conversation with Morgan, but I couldn't tell what he thought of it. My face was burning as I joined him for the walk across the street. It was embarrassing to be caught groveling.

"Pumping him for information?" Marco asked.

"No. I was—flirting."

"Tell the truth."

"I *was* flirting," I said, "so I could pump him." We stopped in the middle of the street to let a van pass, then continued across. "It's not like I'd flirt with Morgan for any other reason."

"Didn't you have a crush on him in high school?"

"Yeah, but I was young and stupid back then."

Marco didn't say a word.

I stopped on the sidewalk in front of Down the Hatch and said, "Okay, this is where you're supposed to say 'What do you mean, you were young *then*? You're young *now*.'"

"I need to tell you that?"

"Be honest," I said, looking him straight in the eye. "Do I look older than twenty-six going on twenty-seven?"

"There is no safe way to answer that question."

Marco was right. There were more important matters at hand, anyway, such as convincing him to give me ideas on the quickest way to find Jack's killer. I decided to start with the famous beating-around-the-bush strategy. "I had a fascinating interview with Richard Davis this morning."

"For the purpose of?"

I blinked several times, my little brain cells trying to catch up with him. He was supposed to have let me rattle on for five minutes, telling him all about this fascinating interview so I could gradually work up to the purpose. Now that he had cut to the chase I had no choice but to ditch my not-so-clever strategy.

"For the purpose of finding out who killed Jack Snyder. And before you start lecturing me about the dangers of poking my nose into a murder investigation, Grace asked for my help, and when she asks for *my* help, you know it's serious. But even if she hadn't asked, I would still look into it just so I know Grace isn't dating an ax murderer." Having made my case, I folded my arms, pushed out my lower lip, and waited for his rebuttal.

Marco studied me, shaking his head. "You just can't help yourself, can you?"

"Not really, no."

"I suppose you'll need my help."

"I'm sorry; I think I'm going deaf. Did you just offer to help?"

"After a fashion."

"This is a trick, isn't it?"

A group of restaurant patrons came out, laughing and talking, so we stepped aside. As soon as they'd passed, Marco said, "The way I look at it, trying to talk you out of getting involved would be a waste of time, and since I don't want to see Grace hurt either, if you want my input I'm available."

"Does this go on my payback list?"

I'll make it a freebie."

"In that case, wow. I don't know what to say except, sure, I'd love some help."

Marco glanced at his watch. "Have you eaten lunch?"

"Not yet."

"Good. Why don't we meet here for a sandwich at one o'clock and you can tell me what your interview turned up."

"It's a deal." I turned away smiling and practically skipped up the sidewalk.

Not a bad start for an abbreviated workweek: a fat check from Trudee, a payment due for Jillian's wedding flowers, a lunch date with Marco, a dinner date with Lottie and Grace, and lunch tomorrow with Greg Morgan. Not a frozen pizza in sight. Life was good.

When I returned to Bloomers, Grace was busy with customers in the coffee parlor and Lottie was hard at work in back, so I tucked Trudee's check in the cash drawer, made dinner reservations at Café Solé for the three of us, then called Greg Morgan's number. The nasal-toned secretary answered on the fifth ring with her abrupt "Prosecutors' office."

"This is Abby Knight. Mr. Morgan wanted me to ask you to put a lunch meeting on his calendar."

"Are you a lawyer?"

This was a ritual we went through every time I called. "No, I'm the florist, remember?"

"If I had remembered, I wouldn't have asked," she replied in a snippy tone.

Being the polite person my mother had raised me to be (regardless of what she said about my teenage years), I overlooked the attitude and said calmly, "Would you check his calendar for tomorrow at one o'clock?"

"He has a lunch meeting at one o'clock."

"What about Thursday?"

"Golf outing."

"Friday?"

"Jury trial."

"Here's a thought. Why don't you tell me what day he's free?"

There was a long pause, then she said, "Oh, wait a minute. I was looking at last week's calendar. What day did you want?"

I started from the beginning, and—surprise—Wednesday was free. Muttering unkind thoughts, I hung up with Miss Sweetness and went back to join Lottie in the workroom, where I saw that six orders had come in during my absence: an arrangement for a kitchen table, a birthday bouquet of roses, and four flower baskets for Jack Snyder's funeral, which were needed for an evening viewing at the Happy Dreams Funeral Home.

Lottie had finished three of the funeral flower baskets and had started the fourth, so I pulled supplies for the table arrangement and set to work. After all the red-white-and-blue themes I'd done over the past month, I was in the mood for something different, something yummy that would be perfect for a kitchen setting. I started with a papier-mâché pot, glued cinnamon sticks around it in vertical layers, put wet foam inside, then filled the pot with chocolate cosmos, black-eyed Susans, orange dahlias, and purple artichokes. Perfect.

I was just putting on the finishing touches when Grace poked her head through the curtain and asked anxiously, "Did you speak with Richard?"

"I sure did. He was very forthcoming."

"Should we be worried about him?"

"No, you shouldn't. I'd hate to second-guess the prosecutor before I have more information, but the case against Richard would be too circumstantial to make sense. I'll know more after my lunch meeting with Greg Morgan tomorrow."

"Thank you, dear. I feel much better."

The doorbell jingled, announcing new customers, so Grace went out to take care of them.

"So you've got a date with our courthouse cutie," Lottie said, her eyes twinkling with excitement.

"Not a date, just an informational meeting." I had to be careful what I said to her about Morgan. Lottie had a crazy notion that he and I were meant for each other, and to prove her point she was always looking for ways to throw us together, certain that eventually we'd stick. Somehow it had escaped her attention that Morgan was already stuck on himself.

The phone rang and I heard Grace pick it up at the front counter. She hung up and came back to the workroom to say, "That was Richard. The police have just called him back for more questioning."

"Routine procedure," I assured her, crossing my fingers behind my back.

*　　　　*　　　　*

At one o'clock I slid into the last booth at Down the Hatch, and a few minutes later Marco joined me. We ordered sandwiches, then got down to business. Marco was in his serious PI mode, taking notes and asking questions as I filled him in on everything I had learned from my conversation with Richard. I even had my timeline with me, written across a sheet of yellow legal paper, a reminder of that nightmare year in law school.

He looked at it and said, "Did Richard give you these times?"

I leaned over and tapped one of the lines. "He gave me this one—the exact moment he sent the file over the Internet."

"What about these?" Marco pointed out the time Richard had left and returned.

"Those are from Grace, but Richard confirmed them."

Marco gazed at me as if he couldn't believe what I'd just said.

"What?"

"It doesn't work if *you* supply the times for the person you're questioning. You should let him do it. But that's okay," he quickly added, sensing my chagrin. "You're new at this. You'll learn."

Damn right I'd learn. I wouldn't make that mistake twice. I waited until our sandwiches and fries had been delivered, then, as I picked through the steaming mound of fries, looking for the crispiest ones, I said, "We have to find a way to verify Richard's alibi."

"Are you one hundred percent sure he didn't do it?"

I jabbed a fry in the ketchup and popped it in my mouth, savoring the burst of tangy flavor as I thought about his question.

"If you have to think about it," Marco said, picking up his sandwich, "you're not sure."

"I'm not one hundred percent sure, no."

"Then he stays on your suspect list."

"Fine, but I still say Josiah Turner is the most likely killer."

"When are you going to go see him?"

I thought about the chilly reception I'd get when I showed up on his front steps. Family connections or not, he wouldn't welcome me with open arms. Open fire, maybe. "I might just question Melanie instead. She'll be able to give me the details."

"Even if those details incriminate her father, the man who's supporting her and her baby? I don't think so."

"You never know. She might be glad to get rid of the old coot. In fact," I said, thinking out loud, "if he were convicted of murder, Melanie would have that farm all to herself, wouldn't she?"

Marco took a swig of his cola. "So she murders her ex-boyfriend, pins it on her father, and gets rid of two problems at once. Interesting theory. How well do you know Melanie?"

"Not very well. The only times I ever saw her were at Jillian's birthday parties when we were kids." I paused to take a bite of my BLT. "The problem with that theory is, Melanie just doesn't strike me as the murdering type."

"Which means you've got to find a way to get her father to talk to you. I'll check police records to see if anything turns up about him there."

"Don't you think the key to solving the case is to find out why Jack came back to the banquet center? And why he had on a waiter's outfit? Someone who was there Monday night has to know."

"Yeah, his killer. That's why you need to be smart when you talk to these people. Remember, you're just trying to get a little information to help a friend. You're not out to bag a murderer. And no interviews without witnesses around. Got it?"

I saluted him. "Yes, sir."

"Anyone else on your list?"

"Vince Vogel."

"What about Jack's brother? He might have some answers as to why Jack went back."

I was a little squeamish about questioning Rick so soon after he'd lost his brother, but I didn't want to tell Marco that. Private investigators, even amateur ones, shouldn't let a little squeamishness stop them. I borrowed his pen, turned my timeline over, and wrote *Rick Snyder* on the back.

"Have you interviewed the staff at the banquet center to see if anyone noticed a new face among the waiters?"

I added that to the paper, too. I had to make a trip there anyway to pick up my vases and risers.

"Why don't you try talking to Claymore's grandmother again?" Marco suggested. "With some gentle probing you might get her to remember more details of what she saw that night."

I wrote it down.

Marco read over his own notes. "It would help to have the autopsy report, but that probably won't be available for a few days. In the meantime, you can be working down your list of names, and I'll pay a visit to the boys in blue and see what I can shake out there."

"Sounds like a plan."

He put aside his pen, picked up what was left of his sandwich, and smoothly engulfed it. I stared in amazement. His throat muscles had barely moved.

"What?" he mumbled.

"How do you eat like that?"

"Like what?"

"Like a pelican swallowing a fish. Never mind. I'll try to get out to see Grandma Osborne today. Shall we meet at nineteen hundred hours to review our information?" At Marco's frown I said, "Didn't I say that right?"

"Yes, if you were in the army."

"Fine. I'll drop by here tonight at seven o'clock."

He checked his watch and slid out of the booth. "How about I'll call you instead? Lunch is on the house." He stopped to talk to the bartender, then strode out the door.

That was a brush-off if I'd ever heard one. I glowered at the empty spot across from me. Why the sudden rush? And why didn't he want me to drop by the bar? Did he have a hot date planned for tonight and didn't want me to know?

Still stewing, I finished my sandwich and headed back to Bloomers, where I knew there were several dozen roses waiting to have their thorns stripped. At the moment it was sounding like good therapy.

I was dethorning those very roses—and enjoying every minute of it—when I heard the bell over the door. Since Grace had gone to lunch and Lottie was busy manning the parlor, I went up front to see whether I was needed. There stood Trudee DeWitt's husband, Don, all six feet five inches of him, and after taking in the disgruntled look on his face, I immediately started calculating how much grass seed it would take to fill in those red stripes of lawn.

Don was a large man in his early forties, long-faced and starting to go bald on top. As the owner of the De-Witt Bottling Company, he was a wealthy man, yet he still drove a beat-up pickup truck and wore the same outfit every day: old work boots, faded jeans, and a light blue, long-sleeved cotton shirt with a company logo on the pocket. He was a shy, soft-spoken man, which sometimes gave people the notion that he was a pushover. He wasn't.

Several years back, a new employee at his bottling plant, hired on as a delivery man, had made the mistake of mocking Don, imitating his lumbering walk and rough-edged speech, not realizing his boss was standing nearby. Don let it go on for a few minutes, and when the man continued to ridicule him, he stepped up behind him and lifted him over his head as if he were nothing more than a rag doll. Everyone thought Don was about to heave the frightened man across the room. Instead, after a few nerve-wracking minutes, he set him on his feet, said quietly, "Don't ever do that again," then walked off. The man quit the same day, and the story became part of the town lore.

"Don, I'm really, *really* sorry about the red paint," I said to mollify him. "I'll deduct the cost of new seed from your bill."

"Red paint?" For a moment he looked stymied, then his face cleared and he said, "I didn't come here about the grass—it'll grow back. There's something else I have to talk to you about." He glanced over his shoulder toward the coffee parlor, then added, "In private."

I was startled. I'd met him on only two prior occasions, and then only for business purposes. Lottie and Herman were the ones who'd known him for a long time.

Feeling a little anxious, I led Don back to the work-room, where he stood scrunching his cap in his big hands and shifting from foot to foot, as if he could barely contain his distress.

"Okay, Don," I said, perching on a stool to give me some height, "let's talk."

"One of your helpers," he said gravely, "is annoying me."

There was no way I could avoid it. I took a breath, smiled, and said, "Which helper would that be?"

"Karl."

Why was I not surprised?

CHAPTER TEN

K arl had always been the black sheep of the family, and after seeing how he'd drooled over Trudee, I was almost afraid to ask what had caused Don's concern. I pulled out a stool for him, but he shook his head, preferring to stand.

"So," I said, trying to look so helpful and sweet that he wouldn't have the heart to sue me, "what's the problem?"

Don put his cap on the table and started to say something, only to hesitate, scratch his ear, rub his palms against his hips, glance over his shoulder, and finally blurt, "I can't stand the way that young pup hangs around our house. I've seen the way he stares at my wife, and you know Trudee—she's an eyeful. I can't honestly fault the boy for gawking . . . It's just that, well, I think she *likes* it—maybe she even likes the boy—and I don't know what to do about it. I'm a good deal older than she is—and I sure ain't much in the looks department—so I can't blame her for being attracted to a young buck like that."

I wanted to laugh at the image of Trudee with gangly,

shaggy-haired Karl, but I couldn't—not when this poor man was in turmoil. "Don, do you genuinely believe Trudee would fall for a boy your daughter's age?"

"I don't like to think so. Still, this kid shouldn't be hanging around our house all the time. I'd say something myself, but I don't want my wife to think I'm jealous of a teenager, and I don't want to offend Lottie and Herman, either."

"Trust me; Karl isn't a threat. He's just got that teenage hormonal thing going on. You remember how that is, don't you? Think back to when you were his age. I'll bet you had a crush on an older woman who didn't even know you existed."

He shook his head. No crush. Time for the straightforward approach. "I'll make sure Karl stays away from your house. And just so you know, I saw Karl admire your wife a time or two, but she was completely oblivious to it. She loves you, Don."

His chest swelled with relief. He put on his cap and held out his hand, pumping my arm up and down so hard I thought I'd inflate. "Thanks. I really appreciate it."

"No problem. Just keep having those big parties—with lots of flowers."

Five minutes later, I was arranging the bouquet of roses when Lottie came in and began to jabber. "Whew. Thank goodness the lunch rush is finally over. We had quite a crowd. Putting in that coffee shop was a stroke of genius. I even got two flower orders from it. My, Don DeWitt sure seemed worked up over something, didn't he?"

That was her roundabout way of asking me what was going on with him.

I didn't want to tell her about Karl's crush on Trudee because I knew it was a harmless stage he had to go through. Besides, Lottie would be upset and get on his case; then he'd be angry at me for ratting him out. I was better off handling the matter by myself. "Don's fine," I told her. "It must be tough being an insecure man married to a gorgeous woman."

"Yeah, Herman has the same problem." With a guffaw, Lottie went to the cooler to pull flowers for her orders.

I finished the bouquet and wrote out the gift card, then noticed the address on the order: 403 Freeburg Road. Grandma Osborne lived a block away, which meant I could drop off the roses and visit her on the same trip. The bell over the door jingled, so I got up to see who it was. I parted the curtain, and there was Grace tucking her purse behind the counter.

"Any word on Richard?" I asked.

"When I checked a little while ago he was still being interviewed." She gave the clock on the wall a worried glance. "He'd been there for two hours already."

"The police are just trying to be thorough," I assured her. "I'll bet he'll be calling any minute to say he's heading back to the sports center."

The phone rang almost on cue. Grace started toward the counter, but then we heard Lottie pick it up in the workroom, singing out in her firm voice, "Bloomers."

For a moment she was silent; then I heard her say, "Why are you at the DeWitts' house? Didn't you finish up there this morning?"

Grace and I exchanged looks. It wasn't Richard. But by Lottie's tone of voice I could tell it was one of her sons. I crossed my fingers and hoped it wasn't Karl.

"Okay," Lottie said with a weary sigh. "I'll be there later."

"The next phone call will be from Richard," I promised Grace, then headed back to the workroom to find out what was going on. "Who called?" I asked, trying to be casual about it.

"Karl. He said he'd promised Trudee he'd weed her garden this afternoon. You think he'd ever weed our garden? Fat chance."

Wonderful. After I'd just told Don I'd keep him away. "Did he call for a ride home?"

"What else? Just my luck his brothers are working till seven tonight, and Herman has gone to the Kankakee River to fish. I'll have to run out to the DeWitts' after work."

After work? That would leave almost two hours for Karl to ogle Trudee. "Say, Lottie, here's an idea. I need to deliver these roses, so why don't I swing by Trudee's house and pick up Karl for you? I'll be in the vicinity anyway."

"Don't bother yourself, sweetie. A few more hours of weeding won't kill him."

But Don might. "Honestly, Lottie. I don't mind. In fact, I'm almost looking forward to it." I picked up the wrapped flowers and my purse and took off, hoping I reached Karl before Don did.

CHAPTER ELEVEN

Don's truck wasn't parked on the DeWitts' long brick driveway, and I didn't see it in any of the open bays of their four-car garage. I heaved a sigh of relief. There was still time to rescue Karl. I hurried around the house to Trudee's backyard, where I searched her flower garden at the bottom of the sloping lawn. No Karl. So much for weeding the garden.

I turned to scan the deck that ran across the back of Trudee's house. On the deck was a long rectangular glass table with an umbrella in the center, six matching chairs, and a pair of chaise longues covered by cushions in a bright, tropical print. One of the lounge chairs was also covered by Karl, who was stretched out like a young prince, his eyes closed, shirt off, chest glistening with perspiration, arms behind his head, and blissful smile on his face. On a table beside him was a glass of ice water. I was surprised there wasn't a bowl of grapes and two fan-waving slaves nearby.

Through the sliding glass doors I could see Trudee in the kitchen, removing a tray from the oven. I tiptoed across the deck and nudged Karl's arm to rouse him from his daydream.

"M-m-m. Those pizza bites sure smell good," he said.

I crouched down beside the lounge chair and whispered, "Karl."

He opened his eyes, saw me, and sat up in surprise. "Abby! What are you doing here?"

"The question should be, what are *you* doing here?"

His face turned beet red. "I'm cooling off. I just finished weeding Trudee's garden."

"When did you become a gardener?"

"Hey, I did her a favor, and she paid me. Any crime in that?" He pulled two twenty dollar bills from his pants pocket and showed them to me. "Not bad for a few hours' labor."

"Fine. Let's go now."

He looked at his watch. "But it's only two thirty."

"Karl, Mr. DeWitt is a very large, very strong guy who has been known to lift grown men over his head when angered. And your hanging around here is making him angry. Are you getting the message yet?"

"Over his head?" I could see Karl's throat muscles work as he gulped.

I grabbed the T-shirt he'd draped over the back of his chair and thrust it at him. "Put this on and let's go before he gets home."

At that moment the sliding door opened and Trudee emerged, wearing a yellow halter-top sundress and orange and yellow polka-dot, high-heeled slides. She didn't see me at first—a pink chewing-gum bubble hid my face—but then she popped it and saw me. "Hi, Abby!" she said brightly. "I didn't hear you come up the steps. Want some pizza bites?"

I took one, thanked her, and slipped it in my mouth. I couldn't resist pizza—or even a product that claimed to taste like pizza. "I came to get Karl," I told her. "I need his help with a delivery. Let's go, Karl." I practically propelled him across the deck in front of me.

"Gee, I wish you could stay longer," Trudee called. "I just made all these hors d'oeuvres."

Calling pizza bites hors d'oeuvres was a real stretch but that was typically Trudee. "I wish I could, Trudee, but I'm in a time crunch."

"Maybe Heather will eat them." Trudee glanced at the white face of her pink leather watch. "I'm surprised she isn't home yet. Thanks for your help, Karl. You did a great job on the garden."

"No problem. If you need anything else—"

I pushed him around the corner before he could say more.

"Stop shoving," he said, twisting out of my reach. "You're worse than my mom."

"Your mom would have grounded you for being a nuisance. I'm merely taking you to a retirement home. And let's make that older sister, instead of mom, okay?"

"You're taking me *where*?"

The way he choked out that word, you would have thought I'd told him I was taking him to a manicurist to have his toenails painted puce. I opened the car door, got in, and started the engine. "Are you coming, or do you want to wait for Mrs. DeWitt's husband?"

He got in and slammed the door. "Why do I have to go with you to a retirement home?"

"Because it's on the way to your house. I promise it won't take long. It's not like you have anything better to do. Besides, you get to ride in a cool Vette."

"It would be cooler if I could drive."

"In your dreams." On further consideration, however, I decided his dream had potential. "You really want to drive my Vette?"

He sat up, his face brightening. "Dude!"

"Okay, then here's what you do. Stay away from the DeWitt house for a whole month and I'll let you take it out for a spin."

He slumped back down with a pout, looking more like seven than seventeen.

I made my delivery on Freeburg Road, then turned into the parking lot of the Lakeside Retirement Village. The so-called village was actually a cluster of brick buildings that housed both assisted-living facilities and private apartments. Each structure backed up to a large retainment pond, or "scenic lake" as it was advertised in the brochures, with a walking path around it, and benches located at regular intervals.

As I shut off the engine I explained to Karl why I was really there. His response was, "Cool. A murder investigation." But then he took one look at the elderly people walking the paths and sitting on the benches and sank farther into his seat. "I'll wait here."

I shaded my eyes to glance at the sky, where the sun loomed large and scorching. "Suit yourself. But don't blame me if you become one with the black leather upholstery."

Grumbling, he got out and followed me into the larger, center building, which housed the administration offices. At the information desk I got directions to Matilda Osborne's unit, then headed out the door to find building B, where her apartment was located. As we crossed the landscaped lawn that separated the buildings, I spotted

Pryce's father coming out of building B. Since neither us felt at ease around the other, I made a quick decision to spare us both the discomfort of an awkward encounter: I ducked behind a stone bench, where two elderly men were talking.

"What are you doing?" Karl asked, staring down at me, causing the two men to get up from the bench and walk around to see what was happening

"Sh-h! Get down here," I whispered.

He crouched down. "Why are we hiding?"

"Did you sprain your ankle?" one of the men asked, peering at me through thick glasses.

The other one said in alarm, "You sprained your ankle? Stay right there, honey. I'll go for help."

"Wait! Don't do that!" I cried as he started off.

The commotion caused Mr. Osborne to glance our way. To my surprise, he didn't scuttle off to his car. Instead, he lifted a hand to acknowledge me, then came toward us, which he would never have done unless he felt it was of vital importance. Even then it was doubtful.

"How's your mother?" I asked, walking out to meet him.

"She isn't coping well with the"—he cupped a hand around his mouth to finish in a whisper—"murder. The police questioned her for a long while this morning, and it left her so discombobulated that I insisted she take something for her nerves. Now she's claiming I tried to poison her and she won't take any of her pills. She *has* to have her heart medication."

"I'm sorry to hear that." Perfect lead-in. Now I could offer to visit—which I was sure was his goal anyway—and make myself look like a heroine. "Would you like me to stop by to say hi to her? Perhaps I'll be able to persuade her to take her medicine."

He looked extremely relieved, so I didn't feel bad letting him believe I was doing him a favor. "Thank you, Abigail. That's very kind of you to offer."

Kind, *and* smart.

"How long will this take?" Karl asked as we walked up a long hallway, checking the numbers on the doors.

"Twenty minutes, tops."

"That long?"

I could hear him grumbling under his breath as I knocked on the door of 214B. There was more grumbling on the other side of the door, then it swung open and Grandma Osborne stood there in a pair of bright blue slacks and matching knit top. She had a perturbed look on her face, but it changed to a smile the instant she saw me.

"Well, look who came to visit! And you brought your new boyfriend."

"That's it," Karl said. "I'm outta here."

I grabbed his arm before he could escape. "Grandma, I'd like you to meet Karl. He's my assistant Lottie's son." I gave Karl a little nudge. "Say hi to Mrs. Osborne."

She clucked her tongue at us. "None of that missus stuff now. Call me Grandma like everyone else does." She turned and shuffled up the hallway, calling back, "Would you like some milk and cookies, Karl?"

"No, thanks." Karl shot me a scowl as I motioned for him to follow me. "Twenty minutes," he whispered.

She led us to her living room, an airy space jammed with furniture and knickknacks collected over a lifetime. She sat down in a spindle-back rocking chair, her bony hands resting on the wooden arms, and looked at us, the chair creaking as it moved in a steady rhythm.

"We won't keep you long," I told her as Karl and I took

seats on an old-fashioned, high-backed, flowered sofa. "I just wanted to see how you were doing."

"That's very kind of you, Abby, but to tell the truth I'm not doing too well. I'm having a hard time sleeping, and just look at this." She held out her hands to show how they trembled. She stopped rocking suddenly and put a hand against her chest, as though she felt faint.

"Are you all right?" I asked.

"Palpitations. It's from that medicine my son made me take this morning. He said it would calm my nerves, but all it did was make me cotton-headed and give me palpitations. The only reason I took it was so he'd quit griping at me." She thrust out her lower lip. "So I told him, no more pills."

"I'm sure he's concerned about you. After all, you had quite a shock yesterday."

She let out a sad sigh. "Yes. It's painful to see a young man's life end so tragically."

Karl leaned toward me to whisper, "Is she talking about the dead guy?"

I gave him a discreet poke with my elbow.

"Say, would you two like some cookies?" she asked, as if for the first time. "I have butterscotch."

"No, thanks. Grandma. Would it be too upsetting if I asked you a few questions about what happened?"

She tilted her head, like Simon did when he didn't understand. "What happened when?"

"Monday evening."

"Sakes alive, young woman, didn't you hear? Claymore got married! And to such a beautiful young woman, too. Jillian is her name . . . Jillian Osborne."

I ignored Karl's nudge. "I was referring to the murder, Grandma. I'm doing a little private investigating and I was hoping we could go over what happened one more time—just in case you remember something new—but only if you're up to it. Do you remember the body we found in the gazebo?"

"Of course I do. It was awful. But I've already told the police about it."

"The problem is, the police don't like to share information."

"Phooey on them. Bunch of Neanderthals if you ask me. I'll tell you exactly what I told them. I went to the garden to get away from all that racket in the ballroom. The gazebo looked so peaceful with that soft light falling on it that I decided to go sit up there for a spell. It reminded me of the pretty little gazebo my mother had in her garden. I always loved to sit there and watch the birds." She heaved a melancholy sigh and stared into the distance.

Karl nudged me again, whispering, "Is twenty minutes up yet?"

"Butterscotch cookies!" the elderly woman exclaimed, turning her gaze on Karl. "That's what you'd like, isn't it?"

Karl shot me a pleading look.

"Tell me what happened once you were in the gazebo," I said.

"Let me think . . . You know the bench that circles the inside? I sat down there and looked around, and that's when I spotted that glass of water shimmering in the moonlight. I got up and took it, and that's when I saw that poor young man stretched out on the floor."

"Do you remember seeing anyone in or around the garden when you first walked out there?"

"Not a soul. But as I told the police officer, I did see someone sneaking around the back corner of the building."

"You were able to see someone all the way back there?" I asked in disbelief. "At night?"

"There's a light up on the roof that shines down on those stinky garbage bins in the back. Thank goodness we were upwind or the ceremony would have been completely ruined."

"Can you give me a description of the person you saw?"

"No. All I could make out was a white jacket."

"Did the jacket have tails, like a waiter's uniform?"

"It was white; that's all I could tell. Now, I have an idea! Why don't you two sit right there and I'll go get you some butterscotch cookies!"

"Let's leave now," Karl whispered, but I was busy thinking about the white jacket. Who else besides the waiters had worn one? I searched my memory but could recall only one person—Richard Davis. I hoped to heaven there were more. It was something I'd have to discuss with Marco when I talked to him that evening.

We stayed long enough to down a cookie apiece, convince Grandma to take her heart medicine, and get her to promise to call me if she remembered anything else.

At five o'clock, Lottie, Grace, and I closed up shop and headed to Café Solé, a cozy Italian eatery on the other side of the square. Lottie and I stuffed ourselves with crusty Italian bread, pasta, red wine, espressos, and tiramisu, but Grace only picked at her garden salad and fish dinner. She tried to keep up a cheerful front, but I could tell her heart wasn't in it. I hated seeing her unhappy. I had to get to the bottom of that murder.

That was what Lottie and I discussed afterward, as we headed for the Garden of Eden to pick up our floral paraphernalia. So after we'd carted everything from the storage room to Lottie's station wagon, parked at the back entrance, we went back inside to see what we could learn from the staff. We stopped at the ballroom first, but the waiters were serving salads to somber-faced men and women seated at long tables, listening to a speaker at a podium. We tried the kitchen next, where we saw a flurry of mincing, mashing, pounding, and sautéing.

"I don't think we should bother them," Lottie whispered. "They look stressed-out."

"They always look like that. Wait. I see someone I know." I held up a hand and caught Sheila's eye. She signaled back, wiped her hands on a towel, said something to her boss, and came toward us.

"Hey there, Abby. Did you come for your vases?"

"Vases, risers, kitchen gossip . . . Do you have a few minutes to talk?"

"I'm not due for a break for ten minutes, but, what the heck, the desserts are finished and that meeting in the ballroom is supposed to go on for a while. Let me grab a soda and I'll meet you out back."

Moments later Sheila came strolling out the back exit, popping the tab on her soft drink and tilting her head back for a long, lusty drink. Her brown hair was tied at the nape of her neck in a low ponytail and her kitchen coat was gone, revealing black jeans and a gray T-shirt emblazoned with the words DON'T ASK ME! I ONLY WORK HERE.

I introduced Lottie, then explained that I was looking for any bits of information she might have heard about what had happened last night. "I'm sure there's been some talk about it in the kitchen," I said.

She finished a swallow of soda. "Are you kidding me? That's all we're talking about. I mean, shoot, a horrible thing happened, practically under our noses. Now everyone's real jumpy, wondering if one of us is gonna be next."

"Did you know that the victim, Jack Snyder, was wearing a waiter's outfit?" I asked.

"We figured that from the questions the cops were asking. That's why you asked me about those uniforms last night, isn't it? Well, guess what? Anthony found one of them missing when he took inventory for the cops this morning." She took another swig from the can. "The waiters have all accounted for theirs, so it must have been stolen yesterday."

"How difficult would it be to take one?" Lottie asked.

"Hell, it'd be a snap," Sheila said, tucking a stray lock of hair into her ponytail holder. "They're hanging in a big supply closet off the main hallway. All you'd have to do is open the door, slip one inside a sack, and walk away like you belonged there."

"Has anyone in the kitchen mentioned seeing an unfamiliar waiter last night?" I asked.

"Not that I know about."

I couldn't think of anything else to ask, so I thanked Sheila for her time and gave her my business card. "If you hear anything else, would you let me know?"

"Sure, hon," she said, tucking it into her cleavage. "So, why the interest?"

"We're helping a friend get some information," I said.

Lottie put her hand to the side of her mouth and said in a confidential whisper, "Abby's a private-investigator-in-training." She patted my back, beaming like a proud mother.

"Well, good for you. Everyone could use friends like that. So do you get to work with the police?" Sheila asked, as if it were a big deal.

"Not so much *with* them," I said, "as behind their backs."

"I get it," she said with a broad wink. "In other words,

this conversation never happened. So, as long as we're keeping things quiet, let me ask you something." Sheila folded her arms and leaned a hip against Lottie's car. "I got my eye on that big handsome cop that was here Monday night, the one acting like he was in charge. You don't have a thing for him, do you?"

"Reilly?" I made a scoffing sound. "I've worked with him a few times, but that's as far as it goes." Then I couldn't resist asking, "What makes you think I have a thing for him?"

"I saw you and him with your heads together, so I figured I should ask. I don't like to muscle in on someone else's meat, if you catch my drift."

Lottie was practically vibrating with suppressed laughter.

"I'd tell you to go for it, Sheila," I said, "but Reilly might be married."

She let out a bark of laughter. "Hon, that's never stopped me before."

I didn't know what to say to that.

Sheila finished off the last of her soda and crushed the can. "I'd better get back to work before Anthony starts bellowing. Why don't I send out one of the waiters for you to talk to? He might be able to give you some answers. And if you think of it, find out what hair color Reilly is partial to in his women." She tugged on her ponytail. "I could always use a change."

The waiter Sheila sent out was Kevin Jarrett. He had a medium build and a pleasant face and looked to be about thirty-five years old. He'd worked at the banquet center since it had opened a year ago and had been a waiter for ten years before that. He reported that Jack Snyder had never been an employee there, and he was certain that the uniform had been taken from the closet after the wedding ceremony, not before, when the waitstaff would have gotten dressed.

"How many extra uniforms are there?" Lottie asked.

"Three each of the jackets and vests, and there's always a box of new berets. We keep them on hand just in case someone has a tray dumped on them or a beret falls in the food."

There was an appetizing thought. "Did you notice any new faces among waiters on the night of the murder?"

"You've never worked a banquet, have you?" he asked dryly. "Try to imagine two hundred half-crocked people demanding second helpings of food, refills of wine, and *you-call-this-coffee-hot*? Trust me, an elephant could lumber through the room and we wouldn't notice."

One more mouth-watering image to erase from my mind. "Okay, Kevin, can you think of anything even slightly out of the ordinary that happened yesterday?"

He rubbed his chin. "No. Nothing leaps to mind . . . except maybe Gunther taking off early. That was unusual. He's always here. I mean, the guy hangs out here on his day off, like he doesn't have anything better to do."

"Gunther is the dishwasher, right?" I asked.

"Yeah, dishwasher, kitchen helper, gopher . . ." Kevin shrugged.

I said to Lottie, "He's the guy who almost knocked you over when he ran out of the kitchen to take a phone call."

"I remember him," Lottie said.

"Is Gunther here now?" I asked Kevin.

"I haven't seen him today. It could be his day off, but even so, like I said before, he's usually here."

There could be any number of legitimate reasons for Gunther leaving work early and not showing up the next day, but for some reason my inner alarm was buzzing. "Have the police interviewed all the employees, Kevin?"

"Oh, yeah. All morning."

"Were they told about Gunther taking off early?"

He shrugged. "I guess so."

"What time did Gunther leave?"

"I couldn't tell you. He was here during the wedding because I saw him watching the ceremony. I don't remember seeing him after that, but that's when things got really hectic, and when that happens—"

"Right. The elephant thing. Do you know anything about Gunther?"

"Not much. The guy keeps to himself. We're pretty busy, though, moving food in and out of the kitchen. Your best bet would be to ask Sheila or one of the others inside."

I didn't think Anthony would appreciate me bothering Sheila again, so I made a mental note to get back to her, then I thanked Kevin for the information and gave him my card.

As we drove away, Lottie said, "I can almost hear those little gears grinding in your brain. What are you thinking?"

"I'm not sure what to think, but I'm going to tuck that information away, just in case Gunther's name comes up again. To quote my favorite police sergeant, Gunther is a person of interest."

Since it was not yet seven o'clock when we got back to town, I decided to take a drive over to the New Chapel Meat Market, where Vince Vogel worked, to see what I could learn from him. The market was a popular place, selling fresh beef, pork, chicken, and lamb, deli meats, cheese of all types, bakery breads, and local produce. The store had a loyal following and was always busy, especially during the predinner hours, which was why it stayed open until seven.

When I stepped inside the store, a dozen people were lined up at the glass counter waiting to place their orders, and another dozen were in the checkout line by the door. I took a numbered ticket and joined the throng, hoping the clerks worked fast.

Luckily, my number was called a short five minutes later. I asked whether Vince was there and gave my name. The clerk disappeared through a doorway in the back, and a moment later Vince stepped out, searching the faces on the other side of the counter.

Vince was an ordinary-looking man—sandy brown hair, light brown eyes, crooked nose, clean-shaven face, average height—with the upper arms of a weight lifter. He had on a white butcher's coat covered by a black bib apron that looked like it was made out of thin rubber. His hands were covered by surgical gloves. I made a mental note to check whether any fingerprints had been found at the murder scene. Surgical gloves might be an easy thing to slip in one's pocket.

"Hi," I said, giving him a little wave. "Remember me from the wedding?"

"Sure," he said with a grin. "You were the short bridesmaid."

I forced myself to smile back. "Yep. That was me—the short one. Do you have a few minutes? I'm trying to track down some information on Jack Snyder."

His grin dissolved into a look that verged on hostility, and for a moment I was sure he would refuse, but after a brief hesitation he pointed toward a door at the other end of the counter. "Go through that doorway. I'll meet you in back."

I squeezed around customers and made my way into what appeared to be a cutting room. It had two big butcher-block tables in the center—one of which had huge slabs of red meat on it—white cardboard boxes stacked on white wire shelves, a big, stainless steel door that I assumed led to a meat locker, and an array of different types of knives close at hand. I couldn't stop myself from shivering. The room was icy cold.

"Slip this on," Vince said, handing me an oversized white jacket. I put it on and had to push back the sleeves to find my hands. He took a slab of beef ribs from one table, laid it out on the other table, and picked up a cleaver.

"So," he said, "you're looking for information about Jack?" He brought the cleaver down hard into the meat, splitting it in two and making me jump.

"I'm helping a friend work on this murder case, and Claymore said you've known Jack since you were a boy, so I was hoping you might be able to shed some light on why someone would want to see him dead."

"A friend?" He hit the ribs again, splitting them neatly down the middle. He folded the two halves together, then hit them crosswise. "Is this friend a cop, by any chance?"

"Nothing like that," I said, waving away his concern. "She's simply a good friend." I didn't elaborate, hoping I wouldn't have to.

He eyed me for a moment, then pulled a new slab from the pile. "So you want to know about my history with Jack."

"It would be helpful."

He spoke in brief sentences punctuated by swift blows to the meat. "We were neighbors at one time. My family lived next door to his. They were decent people. I haven't seen Norma since Bill died. I hear she's very ill now."

He continued to work but didn't continue to talk. I glanced at my watch and saw that it was seven o'clock. I'd have to be direct. "Listen, Vince, I know Jack was responsible for some trouble you had down at IU—a false arrest, I think Claymore told me. What was that about?"

Vince took another hard whack at the meat. "Jack stole a car and told the cops I did it." *Whack.* "He was ticked off because he thought I blackballed him to keep him out of the fraternity." *Whack.* "Bastard ruined my career plans."

"Why did you leave right after Claymore's wedding Monday night?"

Whack. "I don't see that it's any of your business why I left." He raised the cleaver again, then lowered it with a sigh of impatience. "Look, if you came here to ask me if I killed Jack, just say so. I don't have anything to hide."

"Okay," I said slowly, "did you kill Jack?"

"As much as I disliked the bastard, no. Jack was scum, but he didn't deserve to die for it. And the reason I left right after the wedding was to check on my wife." He split another slab of ribs. "She suffers from terrible migraines."

I made myself a note to verify that with his wife. "What color suit did you wear?"

"Beige."

Hmm. A beige suit could look white under a spotlight in the dark.

Vince tore off a big sheet of butcher paper and wrapped a section of ribs. "Anything else I can help you with?"

I assumed that was his way of telling me he was done answering questions. I took off the jacket and hung it on a hook by the door. "No, thanks. I'll let you get back to work."

"Wait." He picked up a marker and wrote a big *NC* on the package he'd just wrapped. "Here," he said, handing it to me. "No charge. Just show it to the girl at the register as you go out."

I thanked Vince but left the gift. I felt kind of weird about accepting it, like I was taking a bribe. But why would he want to bribe me unless he was lying? I could usually tell when someone was hiding something, but I hadn't been able to get a good reading on Vince.

I definitely had to speak with his wife to see whether their stories matched. But it was too late to drop by that evening. I needed to talk to her when he wasn't around. I'd have to find time to pay her a visit tomorrow.

When I got back to the square I threw caution to the wind and stopped at Down the Hatch, even though Marco had tried to dissuade me earlier. Part of me wanted to discuss with him what I'd learned. The other part of me wanted to see what he was up to.

The bar was already crowded with the usual groups of single professionals, a contingent of college students who avoided the trendier sports bars near the campus, and stalwart senior citizens who'd been going there for four decades and weren't about to let the young people shove them out. I checked out the room but didn't see Marco either behind the bar or mingling with his patrons, so I threaded through the crowd and headed for his office in the back. But the office door was locked and no light showed beneath.

"Looking for someone?" Chris the bartender asked when I reappeared at the bar.

Before I could reply, three plastered males raised their hands, calling out, "I'm right here, baby," and "Hey, this *your* lucky day," and "Come and get it, hot stuff."

"Yeah, yeah," I said and ducked behind the bar to talk to Chris. "Where's Marco?"

"He had business errands to run."

"What businesses are open after seven o'clock?"

Chris poured a measure of rum into two glasses. "I didn't ask. Try calling his cell phone."

I wasn't keen on doing that—not after Marco had said he'd contact me. Dropping by the bar somehow seemed more innocent.

I squeezed past the crowd again only to have someone put out a hand to stop me. Figuring it was another guy who'd had too much beer, I was all set to tell him where to get off when the bar stool swivelled and I found myself staring into the face of the last man I ever expected to see at Down the Hatch. Pryce.

CHAPTER TWELVE

"**W**hat are you doing here?" I sputtered.

Pryce scoffed, as if his presence there were an everyday event. "I stopped by to see what was happening." He tried to look hip about it, as if he were checking out his 'hood, which was ridiculous considering that he was wearing a white silk sport shirt, a belt that had to be snakeskin, tan trousers with pressed pleats, and Gucci loafers with tassels.

If all that didn't make him stand out above the denim-clad customers around him, toss in the red silk handkerchief sticking out of his chest pocket. Someone needed to take a photo of him and hang it next to the ancient stuffed carp mounted over the row of booths, with a caption underneath that read, FISH OUT OF WATER.

He glanced over both shoulders, and then said in a low voice, "Don't look so surprised," as if I were embarrassing him.

Surprise didn't even come close to describing what I was experiencing. Shock. Astonishment. Knocked for a loop. Pryce never went to places where he'd have to rub elbows with the common folk.

I didn't want him to think I cared why he was there, but there was no controlling my natural curiosity. "No, really, Pryce, what brings you here?"

He shrugged. "I needed a change of scenery." He took a sip from the tall glass of beer in front of him. That was another surprise. For as long as I'd known Pryce I'd rarely seen him drink alcohol, and when he did, it was always an expensive wine. Was he becoming human?

"I hear you went to see my grandmother today," he commented.

"I did. Poor thing; she's really rattled about the murder." Several people squeezed past and I had to practically climb onto Pryce's lap to avoid them. "Sorry. It's packed tonight."

"Why don't we get a booth?" he suggested. "I'll buy you a drink. White wine?"

I was about to turn him down, but he'd already called Chris over to take the order. "Bud Light."

Chris filled up a tall glass; Pryce took it and his beer and headed for an empty booth near the front window.

Sitting across from him was eerie, like I'd jumped back in time. Since I didn't care to revisit that time, I decided to keep it brief and get out before ugly emotions bubbled to the surface. I sipped steadily on my beer as we made small talk about the weather and recently released movies—and I searched for a graceful exit line.

"I meant to thank you for the way you handled my grandmother yesterday." Pryce paused for a sip of beer. "But then you've always been nice to her."

"She was always nice to me, too," I told him honestly, and I could have sworn there was a flicker of nostalgia in his eyes.

Before things could get syrupy, I finished my drink, put my purse strap over my shoulder, and slid to the end of the booth. "So, listen, thanks for the beer. I've had a long day, so I'm going to take off. See you around, okay?" A long day. Was there a phonier excuse in existence?

"Hey, Marco!" I heard someone say.

I turned around and saw Marco at the far end of the bar, as if he'd come in through the back door. There was no way I wanted him to spot me with Pryce—it would look too much like we'd met for a date—so I decided to slip quickly out the front door.

Then I saw whom Marco was with.

She was slender, dark-haired, fashionably dressed, and exotic, with smooth olive skin that complimented Marco's Italian looks. She was also a good half head taller than me, and I was betting there wasn't a single freckle on her anywhere. I was also betting she was the reason he hadn't wanted to meet with me tonight. Who was she?

That green-eyed monster inside me whispered in my ear, *Flirt with Pryce. Show Marco he isn't the only game in town.* I'd battled this monster before. She almost always won.

"I'm sorry. You were saying?" I said, smiling at Pryce.

"I wasn't saying. You were."

Marco was now standing behind the bar chatting with one of the bartenders, while the woman waited quietly at the end. She wasn't talking to anyone and, by the way she kept glancing at her watch, she didn't look particularly happy to be there. I wanted to dislike her on principle— seeing Marco with another woman hurt more than I cared to admit—yet there was a sadness in her expression that wouldn't let me.

Suddenly Marco looked over and met my gaze. He

glanced at Pryce, then raised his eyebrows at me as if to say, *What gives?* so I gave him a smile that I hoped looked mysterious.

"Abigail?"

I turned back to Pryce and realized he had witnessed this little exchange of glances. "Gotta go," I said before he could get nosy. "Thanks again for the beer."

As I got up to leave I saw Marco escorting the woman toward the back of the bar, probably heading toward his office, so I quickly edged through the crowd to the front door. I didn't realize anyone was behind me until I stepped outside and heard Pryce say, "I'll walk you to your car."

I didn't want Pryce to walk me to my car. For one thing, it would be too much like old times. For another, he hated my car because it was yellow. He disliked bananas for the same reason—yellow. "Really, Pryce, there's no need to do that. My car is parked *way* over on Jackson." I drew out the words, trying to make it sound like an all-day hike.

"It's only one block away."

Yes it was, damn it anyway.

As we approached Bloomers, I snapped my fingers and said, "I just remembered; I need to stop at the shop and I might be a while. Why don't you go on?"

He knew I'd just given him the brush-off, but he pretended he didn't. "Maybe we can do lunch sometime."

He had to be kidding. Or maybe that was just *his* way of making a graceful exit. "Sure," I answered, playing along. "Let's do that." Then we said good night and went our separate ways. I stood by the shop door and pretended to dig for my keys while he unlocked his BMW and got in. As soon as he drove away I hurried around the corner and headed for my car.

I'd parked across the street from the Happy Dreams Funeral Home, where Jack Snyder's viewing was being held, and it looked like there was quite a crowd. As I unlocked the car, I noticed Jack's brother, Rick, standing outside, so I shut the door and walked over to express my condolences—and to see what I could learn from him.

I hadn't known Jack's parents but, despite what Jillian believed, I had known Rick. We'd worked on the high school newspaper together—he wrote articles and I did page layouts. Rick had been a congenial, conscientious student who had always seemed embarrassed by Jack's capers. Still, he'd lost his only brother. He had to be grieving.

"Hey, Rick," I said, "I'm so sorry about your brother. It must have been a terrible shock."

"Thanks, Abby." He paused to greet people coming up the sidewalk. "To be honest, I'd always feared something bad would happen to Jack. It's been really tough on my mother. You may have heard she has terminal cancer. She was hoping he'd straighten out before she . . . you know . . . passed. My hope is that the police will solve the case soon, so she can have some peace of mind."

"Do they have any leads?"

"No. Not that they've told us, anyway."

"Just so you know, Rick, I'm working on the case, too."

He seemed surprised, so I explained my connection and my concern for Grace. More people came by and shook Rick's hand, so I waited until they were gone, then I said, "I know this is lousy timing, Rick, but could I ask you two quick questions?"

"Sure."

"You probably know about the fight your brother had with Josiah Turner during the wedding, and that Jack returned dressed as a waiter sometime during the reception. Can you think of any reason why he would do that?"

"Jack was always trying to avoid Josiah Turner, so why he went back—I don't have a clue."

"Would your mother know?"

"I doubt it. We've only had brief contact with Jack since he got out of prison. I had to track him down to tell him about Mom's health."

I handed him my card. "Would you pass this along to your mother with my condolences and let her know that I'm trying to help?" I gave him a hug and left.

It was after nine o'clock when I trudged upstairs to my apartment, a modest two-bedroom with a decent bathroom, a galley kitchen, and a narrow living/dining room that sometimes got a little cramped. Fortunately, Nikki worked the three-to-midnight shift at the county hospital—she was an X-ray technician—so we were usually able to stay out of each other's way.

I unlocked the door to find Simon waiting for me, a rubber band dangling from his mouth. Simon loved to play fetch with rubber bands and plastic straws, and would happily scamper after one for hours, unless it landed on a throw rug. Then, rather than admit he was a coward, he would pretend he couldn't find the toy and send us off in pursuit of another one. No dummy, that cat.

"Sorry I'm late," I said, giving him a scratch behind the ears. I didn't bother explaining why. He'd heard it all before. I gave him a dollop of cat food, put fresh water in his bowl, and grabbed a spoon and the container of ice cream and took it to the living room. Then, sitting on the sofa with the carton in my lap and an old episode of *Friends* on TV, I dug into the creamy dessert, trying to erase the image of Marco and the exotic beauty that kept replaying in my mind.

Suddenly, Simon came galloping across the room and leaped onto the sofa right next to the container of ice cream.

"Don't even think about it," I said, turning my back on him, as if I actually expected that to deter him. He climbed across my lap and tried to poke his head inside the carton, so I held it out of his reach. But that, as any cat person would know, only made him more determined to get it. As he balanced on my knees, trying to swipe at it with a paw, the phone rang.

I set the carton on a high bookshelf and went to grab the cordless phone on the end table, only to find the handset missing. Since Nikki had a habit of carrying the phone between her shoulder and her ear as she walked around, it was anyone's guess where she'd left it. She also managed to lose the TV remote on a regular basis. I kept telling her it was a good thing we were best friends because otherwise I'd have to kill her.

I ran to the kitchen and picked up the phone there just as our answering machine kicked on. "I'm here," I cried over the sound of Nikki and me saying in unison, "Leave a number. If you're lucky we'll get back to you."

As soon as the beep sounded I heard Marco's sexy voice say, "Hey, is everything okay?"

"Are you kidding?" I tried to give him a carefree laugh, but it came out as more of a sneer. "Everything is great. Why?"

"You left the bar without saying good-bye."

He'd actually noticed? "I had things to do, and you seemed"—I had to inhale in order to finish the sentence—"busy."

I'd thought that would make him come clean about the mystery woman but I was wrong.

"Yeah, I've got this thing I've got to deal with. But I found something interesting on Richard Davis," he said. "Are you free to talk?"

Was that his way of asking if Pryce was there? Or was I reading too much into his words, hoping for a little counterjealousy? I decided not to give him a direct answer—just in case—and sat down on the kitchen floor with my legs folded yoga-style and my back against the cabinets. "Tell me about Richard."

"For starters, he's not the model citizen you think he is."

I got an uncomfortable flutter in my stomach that always foretold bad news. "He's not?"

"I'm holding a copy of his arrest record."

"He has an arrest record?" The flutter grew stronger. "Please tell me it was a traffic violation."

"Not exactly. Try murder one."

CHAPTER THIRTEEN

My head thunked against the hard wood of the cabinet as that flutter turned into a full-blown stomach clench. Grace's beau had been arrested on a murder charge. She was dating a possible killer.

"Are you okay?" Marco asked.

"I think my brain just crashed. Was Richard acquitted? Did he jump bail? Is he on the lam?"

"Let me tell you what I have. This is a report from the NCIC—the National Crime Information Center. Basically, it's an FBI rap sheet, and it shows that Davis was arrested in Texas three years ago for killing a man. What it doesn't show is the outcome of the case."

"So we don't know if he was found innocent or not?"

"No, we don't. I'll have to try to reach the detective who was in charge. Keep your fingers crossed he's still around."

"What should I tell Grace?"

"Nothing. Listen to me, sunshine; you can't say a word about this to anyone. It would put my source in jeopardy. Besides, you don't want to alarm Grace before we have all the facts, and you certainly don't want to let Davis know you know. That could put *you* at risk."

I scoffed at the notion of Richard doing me harm. "He and I talked at some length, Marco, and I didn't get a bad feeling about him."

"Yeah, well, remember this. Whatever he did or didn't do, he *was* arrested for murder."

"Then how do I *not* say anything to Grace?"

"By pressing your lips together."

"I'm going to need a staple gun."

"Do what you have to do."

"On the other hand," I said, tucking my feet under me, "maybe Grace knows. I mean, think about it. Richard is aware that he's a suspect. He has to figure the police will dig into his past. He might have wanted to prepare her ahead of time."

"You're not off the hook. You still can't say anything. Anyway, I'm not so sure he would tell Grace. It would depend upon how close they are. I doubt the police will do anything about the information until they know more anyway, but at least now you know why they've zeroed in on him."

"You know what this murder charge could mean, Marco? That the cops will ignore their other suspects and focus solely on Richard. And that would be a huge mistake." I got to my feet because my toes were cramping. "Remember Vince Vogel? Okay, listen to this and tell me if it doesn't set off any alarms in your head. First, we have Claymore's grandmother, who saw a person in a white coat near the back of the building minutes before she found the body. Second, we have Vince Vogel, a butcher who wore a beige suit to the wedding, who left just after the ceremony, and who, by the way, swings a mean hatchet. FYI, beige can look almost white at night under the right light."

"A valid point. Go ahead."

"Third, Vince still harbors quite a grudge against Jack. And last, he gave me a package of beef ribs—free of charge."

I waited, but there was only silence on the other end. "So what do you think, Marco? Any alarms going off?"

"Sorry, sunshine; what you have is circumstantial, and before you argue that point, think about the number of guests who were dressed in light-colored jackets that night, including Richard Davis. Add to that the fact that it was dark outside, and Claymore's grandmother is ninety years old. Do you really trust her night vision?"

"So you don't hear any alarms?"

"No. I'd have to classify this as mildly interesting."

"I don't know, Marco. My alarm has never been wrong before . . . Actually, it's more of a buzz—but no matter, don't you think you could at least run this information past the police on the off chance it will help Richard?"

"I'm sure they've checked Vince's story out, but if it will make you happy, I'll mention it to Reilly."

"It would make me ecstatic . . . Wait. Did you say Reilly? I thought Detective Williams had taken over the case."

"Nah. Reilly is still the go-to man."

I fumed. The go-to man had lied to me. "Were you able to find out anything on Josiah Turner?"

"He's clean. One traffic ticket years ago. That reminds me. When are you going out to see him?"

"Tomorrow, if I can."

"If you want company, just ask. I'll be glad to go along."

Did your other company desert you? that jealous little wag in my head wanted me to say. But I didn't, so we hung up on a good note.

When I returned to the living room, Simon was sitting on the sofa, calmly cleaning his face—and my container of ice cream was missing from the shelf. I looked around and found it and the spoon beneath the coffee table.

"Bad, bad boy," I called, shaking my index finger at him. He paused to give me a look that said, *Who? Me?*

Luckily, the frozen dessert hadn't had time to melt onto the carpet. I got a clean spoon and started to dig in, then peered into the carton for a closer look. Were those tongue marks? Was that fur stuck to the sides?

"You little thief," I yelled. "You ate my ice cream." In response, Simon took off down the hallway, probably to seek asylum with the dust bunny brigade under Nikki's bed.

"You are *so* banned from this room!" I took the container into the kitchen and turned it upside down in the sink, letting the ice cream melt into the drain. I didn't see Simon the rest of the evening. I'm sure he and the troops were under the bed plotting a hostile takeover.

Nikki surprised me by coming home at eleven o'clock instead of after midnight. I had put on my pj's and washed my face and was ready to call it a night when I heard her come in.

"What are you doing home so early?" I asked. She had dropped her shoes at the door and her purse on the counter and was searching the freezer for something to eat.

"I worked a double shift today, so they let me leave an hour early. Where's the ice cream?"

"Talk to Simon."

Nikki raised an eyebrow. "How did he get the freezer door open?"

"Okay, so I left the carton sitting on a shelf—a *high* shelf. If someone hadn't misplaced the living room phone, I wouldn't have had to take the call in the kitchen. Have one of my chocolate bars instead and I'll give you the latest news on the murder investigation."

Nikki crouched in front of a kitchen cabinet and began to rummage through the contents. "They're dark chocolate. You know I hate dark chocolate. Don't we have an old box of Girl Scout cookies around here somewhere? Oh, wait. Here they are."

"I wouldn't eat those. They're old."

"They're not *that* old." She opened the box, stuffed a cookie in her mouth, and smiled, smashed cookie all over her teeth. Suddenly, she made a horrible face and raced for the sink to spit it out, only to see the empty ice cream container there.

I grabbed a paper towel off the rack and pushed it into her hand. "Didn't I tell you?"

"What I want to know ith," she said, wiping soggy traces of cookie off her tongue, "who called and ruined my chanthes of having ithe cream tonight?"

"Marco called, and you're not going to believe what he—" I was all set to tell her about Richard's arrest record when I remembered Marco's warning.

"Not going to believe what?" Nikki asked, putting mugs of water in the microwave to heat.

"Not going to believe . . . who showed up at Down the Hatch this evening."

We made decaf lattes and took them to the living room, where I caught her up on all the events of the day, including seeing Pryce at the bar and Marco with the mystery woman.

"Seriously, Abby, you should have taken my advice and gone after Marco big-time so this wouldn't have happened."

"It's not that easy, Nik, especially when he's helping

me with an investigation. We have to be professional about it, otherwise we wouldn't get anything done."

"Then it's a good thing you've got Greg Morgan waiting in the wings."

"Morgan? Not in *my* wings."

She sighed impatiently. "One of these days you'll have to get over that high school snub."

"It's not the snub, Nikki; it's his personality. Morgan is so conceited, he's jealous of his own reflection. You remember that disastrous dinner date we went on, where he talked about himself for four solid hours? I don't ever want to do that again. I wouldn't be having lunch with him tomorrow if I didn't need information."

"You're right. Scratch Morgan. Next subject—Pryce. What's behind his sudden mixing with the lower classes? Is there a cute waitress at the bar who's caught his eye?"

I nearly spit out my drink. "Nikki, would Pryce date a waitress? What would his mommy say?"

She smacked herself on the forehead. "What was I thinking?"

"Pryce is up to something, I'm sure of it. Marco thinks he's had a change of heart because I have my own business now and his parents have decided I'm acceptable, but I'm not buying it."

"I'm with you. You've owned Bloomers for three months. Why would he all of a sudden be interested in you again?"

"Like I said, he's up to something."

"There's one way to find out." Nikki finished her latte and stood up. "Take him up on his lunch offer."

By ten o'clock Wednesday morning, the temperature outside had already reached ninety degrees and the air was so humid that there were water droplets on

Bloomers' bay windows. That kept a lot of shoppers off the square and in the air-conditioned malls, which was not good for most downtown businesses. But it hadn't hurt mine—thanks to the coffee parlor. It hummed with clerks and secretaries from the courthouse and surrounding offices who had stopped in for iced teas and iced coffees. Not only did they fill up the cash register; they also kept Grace occupied, and that was a very good thing.

Grace had come to work that morning with the worrisome news that the police had grilled Richard again, this time for more than five hours. She couldn't make sense of it. Richard was above reproach. How dare they question his integrity! I knew then that Richard hadn't told her about his arrest, and it took all my willpower—not to mention a few glances at that vicious stapler on my desk—to keep from spilling Marco's information.

"You look nice, sweetie," Lottie commented as we worked on arrangements. "You'll bowl over Mr. Gorgeous Deputy Prosecutor at lunch today."

"Whatever gets me the information I need." I tried to sound blasé about it, but secretly I was pleased that she liked my choice. I had put on a flared skirt and pale yellow blouse that I hoped minimized my ample bust. I wanted to bowl the man over, not knock him out.

The bell jingled in the shop, so I jumped up to get it, knowing Grace had her hands full in the parlor. I walked through the curtain and saw Sheila Sackowitz admiring one of my silk flower arrangements. She was wearing purple cotton pants with a white T-shirt that sported the phrase IT'S MS. BITCH TO YOU. Her face was bare of any makeup and her brown hair stuck up at odd angles in front, as though she'd tried to spike her bangs. She had a plastic bag from the Dollar Store in her hand and a denim purse hanging from her shoulder.

"Hey there," she said with a big smile when she saw me. "Isn't this one helluva heat wave? If I hadn't needed a birthday gift I wouldn't have stepped a foot outside until it was time to go to work. Look, I even remembered my coupon. Hey there, Lottie. That's the way to stay cool."

Lottie had just come from the back with an armload of fresh carnations and was arranging them in the display cooler. She waved from behind the glass door.

Sheila picked up a hand-painted ceramic vase, checked the price on the bottom, and set it down. She did the same with a porcelain dove. "I'd forgotten what a nice shop this is," she said in a way that meant, *Wow—too expensive for me.* Then she spotted a pair of tall, vanilla, tapered candles set in a shallow basket of dried flowers. She turned over the tag to see the price, then said happily, "I'll take this."

I rang up the total, which came to under ten dollars with the coupon. As Sheila pulled crumpled bills from her purse, she said, "I'll have to bring my friend Deb around. She loves this kind of stuff."

Never one to turn down an opportunity to do a little sleuthing, I said, "Do you have time for a cup of coffee?"

"Are you kidding me? I love coffee. I don't drink as much as I used to—I'm too busy working my butt off in that kitchen—but when I was at the bank I'd suck up a gallon every day."

"Then wait until you try our coffee. It's the best in town."

"You don't have to sell me, kiddo," she said, following me into the parlor. "Would you look at this fancy wallpaper? And these cute little white tables and chairs. Don't they call this style Victorian? Hey, are those scones?"

I took her up to the counter to meet Grace, then, armed

with cups of coffee and a plate of Grace's scones, we headed for a table in the corner. I was hoping to learn more about Gunther, the absentee dishwasher, but after fifteen minutes of listening to Sheila complain about her rotten ex-husbands—all four of them—her crummy job, and her drunken father, I was beginning to wonder whether that was going to happen anytime soon.

"Sheila," I said, when she stopped to munch on her second scone, "I have a question for you. What do you know about Gunther?"

She gazed at me as if my ears had sprouted feathers. "Tell me you're not interested in that loser. Oh, wait. This is for your investigation, isn't it? Well, I don't know much . . . Let's see, his last name is Bundle. Gunther Bundle—ain't that a kicker of a name? He lives in the trailer park over by the university. He's about thirty years old, he has a short fuse, and he isn't too swift"—she pointed to her head—"upstairs."

"That name isn't familiar. Is he from this area?"

"Not that I know of," she said, stuffing her mouth with buttery scone. "He's a strange one. Always hanging around. Except, now that I think about it, he didn't show up for work yesterday." Her forehead wrinkled as she slurped her coffee. "He might have called in sick, though. Grace, these scones are dee-lish," she yelled across the room.

Two women talking quietly at a nearby table stopped to turn and glare. I gave them an apologetic smile.

Sheila glanced at her watch and gasped. "Oh, lordy. I gotta get home and change for work. I'm sorry to cut you short, Abby. You want me to have Gunther call you from the center?"

"Thanks, but if I need to talk to him I'd rather do it in person. It always helps to see someone's reactions to my questions rather than just hear them."

"Yeah, well, good luck with that," she said, rolling her eyes. "He's not what you'd call sociable." She drained her coffee cup, gathered her packages, and rose. "Good to meet you, Grace," she called. "I love your scones."

"Thank you, dear," Grace whispered. If she was hoping to send a message, it didn't work.

"Any time, Grace," Sheila called back, then headed for the door. "Well, this was a real treat, Abby. Maybe I'll see you out at the center soon, huh?" Halfway out, she paused to add, "Say, you wouldn't have another coupon handy, would you?"

I pulled one from beneath the front counter. "Here you go. Thanks for answering my questions."

"No problem. Mention me to your friend Reilly." With a wave, she was gone.

"What a chatterbox," Lottie remarked. "I didn't think you'd get a word in edgewise. So are you going out to the Garden of Eden to talk to Gunther?"

"I don't think so. Other than Gunther leaving work early, there's nothing to tie him to the murder."

"I'm sorry to interrupt," Grace said, "but shouldn't you be getting ready for your lunch date with Mr. Morgan, dear?"

My lunch date! Yikes. I had ten minutes.

CHAPTER FOURTEEN

The clock in the nearby church tower had just tolled one o'clock as I cut across the courthouse lawn to reach the restaurant on the opposite side of the square. Because of the humidity I couldn't move too fast or my hair would frizz up like a big red Brillo pad, but I also hated to keep anyone waiting, so I held down the ends of my hair and plowed forth.

Rosie's Diner liked to advertise itself as being "'fifties inspired," but the truth was that it had actually been built in the nineteen fifties and never redecorated. It had avocado green vinyl booths, a jukebox in the back, and graffiti carved into the wooden stall doors in the bathroom that said, among other things, *Class of '59 rocks and rolls!* Not to mention the infamous *Janey Sadenberger loves Tommy Thurman*, the couple who later became *The Magic Act of Jane Berger and Tom Thurm* and was now *J. Sadenberger, plaintiff, vs. T. Thurman, defendant,* in a custody battle over a white rabbit named Merlin.

Rosie's offered standard diner fare: hot and cold sandwiches, breakfast anytime, and a daily special of either meatloaf and mashed potatoes or fried chicken and mashed potatoes. It was Greg Morgan's favorite place, partly because it was handy but mostly because the waitresses rolled out the red carpet when he walked in. The only surprise was that they didn't lift him on their shoulders and carry him to a booth. He was already there when I walked in, holding court with three waitresses at a highly visible front booth while other diners grumbled about the poor service. I slipped onto the bench opposite him and had to clear my throat several times before he noticed I was there.

"Abby! Good to see you," he said. Two of the waitresses shot me dirty looks, huffed in annoyance, then sashayed away. The third pulled out her ticket pad and scowled, obviously not thrilled to see me, either.

"Know what you want?" she said to me, scratching a hip.

I reached for a menu stuck behind the napkin dispenser and opened it, skimming the list I knew by heart anyway. "Why don't you start, Greg?" I said.

"Hon, I already *know* what he wants," the waitress said with a laugh that came out as a deep, hoarse rumble. Quite an attractive come-on. All she needed was a lipstick-smudged cigarette dangling from her lips.

"Ladies first," Morgan said to me.

"I'll have a grilled ham and cheese on rye."

"Swiss, American, cheddar, or mozzarella?" the waitress asked in a bored voice.

"Swiss."

"All we got today is American."

I rubbed my left eyebrow, gazing at her thoughtfully. "I can't help wondering why you asked, then."

"They tell me I have to ask, so I ask. What'll you have, doll?" she said to Morgan.

"Burger and fries—hold the onions—and a Diet Coke."

She wrote it down, winked at Morgan, and sauntered off, hips swaying, shoulders slouched forward.

"Excuse me," I called. "I'd like some iced tea with that." She didn't acknowledge my request, so I gave Morgan a sad shake of the head. "She's something else."

He leaned forward, chin planted on one hand, and gazed at me with vivid blue eyes that put the sky to shame. If I hadn't known what he was like underneath that gorgeous face I'd have fallen for him just because of those eyes. "Funny," he said wistfully, "I was thinking the same thing."

"Greg, honestly, does that line work on *anyone*?"

"You'd be amazed." He paused to bestow a smile on a flirtatious fortysomething female who had to be on the lam from the fashion police, then he said, "Fill me in on what I missed Monday night."

"The main thing you missed was walking up the aisle with me. I can't think of anything else really interesting except, of course, the murder. Other than that, it was your average wedding."

Morgan snickered. "Have you heard what the police have dubbed the case? The Jack-in-the-Pulpit murder."

"I figured someone would get around to that. Have you heard who their top suspect is?"

"No, who?" he asked, as if I were telling *him* a joke.

"There is no punch line here, Greg. I'm asking you who their top suspect is."

Morgan wasn't quick on the uptake, but he was pretty fast on the recovery. "Right. I knew that. They're looking at several people."

I leaned in to say in a whisper, "Josiah Turner, Vince Vogel, and Richard Davis?"

"And one more."

"Who is it?"

He shrugged. "I haven't actually studied the file."

"Yeah, right."

"Come on, Abby. You know I can't divulge information."

I paused as the waitress plunked down our drinks. I was impressed that she'd actually remembered my glass of tea. "I'm not asking you to divulge the whole name. Just give me the person's initials. Are they M.T.—as in Melanie Turner?"

"Why are you so curious?" he asked, unwrapping his straw.

"I can't tell you. You'll blab to the police."

He scoffed. "I wouldn't do that to you."

"You did it to me two months ago!"

"That was an accident. And it wasn't to the police; it was to my boss." He saw me trying to hold back a laugh, and since he knew my mouth was full of iced tea, he said, "Fine. I'll read the file and see what I can do for you. Now would you swallow, please? This is a new suit."

I swallowed. "I knew I could count on you, Greg. Now I have one more, itty-bitty favor to ask."

He glowered. "You're pushing it."

I paused as the waitress delivered our sandwiches, then I leaned toward him and said quietly, "All I need for you to do is take a peek at the autopsy report when it comes in and let me know the results."

Morgan was about to chow down on a limp french fry, but at that he stopped. "Do I look like a complete idiot to you?"

I couldn't bring myself to answer that, so I sat back and reached for my glass instead.

"It's unethical," he said. "You're asking me to put my

career on the line, and for what? So you can satisfy your curiosity?"

"For heaven's sake, all I'm asking for is the cause of death. Even if your boss found out, you wouldn't lose your job. Everyone in the courthouse adores you, and you know it."

He couldn't argue that.

"Besides, it's more than idle curiosity."

"So what is it, then?"

I took the top slice of bread off my sandwich and squirted mustard on the ham. "Are you sure you want to know? It has to be off the record. You can't breathe a word to anyone."

He had another fry and thought it over. "Fine. Off the record."

"Okay, here it is. My assistant Grace is dating Richard Davis."

Morgan made a circling motion with his hand. "And . . ."

"And . . . that's why I'm trying to find out who killed Jack."

"That's it?" he said with a laugh. "You want me to stick my neck out because your assistant is seeing one of the suspects?"

"Would you feel better if I were spying for a foreign government? Yes, that's it, Greg. I'd like to know Grace isn't in any danger, but I don't want the whole town to know I'm investigating. Is that a good enough reason? *Now* will you get me that information?"

He toyed with his fork for a moment, looking perturbed. But then his gaze met mine and his mouth curved into a wily grin. "I might be persuaded to help you."

There it was—the dreaded dinner invitation. I sat back and folded my arms. "All right. When do you want to go?"

His grin faded. "Go where?"

I felt my face begin to burn. "To dinner."

He rubbed an earlobe, looking sheepish. "Actually, I was thinking along the lines of a dozen roses for my secretary's birthday. But if you want to go to dinner—"

"Roses it is. When do you want them?"

"Tomorrow."

"You'll have that information for me then?"

He grinned slyly. "Like I said, I need the roses tomorrow."

"Deal." I tucked into my sandwich, smiling inside. That had worked out a lot better than I'd thought.

After leaving the diner, I cut across the street to Down the Hatch to see whether Marco had dug up anything new. As usual, the bar was filled with its regular lunchtime clientele: lawyers, judges, bankers, secretaries, and other local businesspeople. I stopped to say hello to my former employer, Dave Hammond, and several secretaries who frequented my coffee parlor, then made my way to the back.

"Looking for the boss?" a waitress named Kim asked as she cleared a table.

"Yes. Is he in his office?"

"He had to go out. He should be back any minute. You want to sit and have something cold until he gets back?"

"No, thanks." I saw an opportunity to do some fishing, so I grabbed it. "So what's up with Marco lately? He's never here."

She started to reply, then shut her mouth.

"I'm here," Marco said, walking up behind me. "Come on back."

I glanced at Kim and she gave me a shrug.

I followed Marco to his office, where he pulled out one

of the black leather chairs for me, then took a seat behind his desk. I could tell immediately that he wasn't in the best of moods.

"Find out anything new from Morgan?" he asked, opening a desk drawer and removing his notes.

"Not much, other than the police are looking at four suspects—Josiah Turner, Richard Davis, Vince Vogel, and a fourth whose name he claims not to know. It took some doing, but I managed to convince Morgan to check into that and the autopsy report for me." I wiggled my eyebrows. "Want to know how?"

He pinned me with a look that answered my question. Okay, so he didn't want to know.

"What else do you have?" he asked.

"Nothing. Zip. Zero. Nada. I hope you've got something, because I'm starting to get nervous."

Marco sat back, tapping his pen on the desk as he looked over his notes. "I tracked down the name of the detective who handled Davis's case in Texas and put in a call to him, but I got a machine, so I left a message. I'll follow up on that again tomorrow." He took a folder from a drawer and slid it across the desk. "Here. Have a look."

Inside was the report he'd read to me on the phone. It was exactly as he'd described it, with just enough information to worry me and not enough to know whether I had good reason to be worried. "Why doesn't it tell how the case was settled?"

Marco shrugged. "The Feds work in mysterious ways."

"I'll ask Morgan about it when I see him tomorrow." I paused, hoping Marco would want to know why I was seeing Morgan tomorrow. Then I took a long look at Marco's tense features and said, "Are you okay? You seem kind of distracted."

"I'm fine," he said instantly.

He wasn't fine, but since he wasn't in a mood to discuss it, I let it go.

"When are you going out to the Turner farm?" he asked.

"Soon." I was procrastinating and we both knew it. I wasn't sure why I had such a fear of Josiah. It wasn't like he'd ever been cruel to me; it was just that he always seemed so angry—on the verge of exploding—and I wasn't in any hurry to be there when that happened.

"You'd better move that up to soon-*er*. The prosecutor is pushing hard for the cops to name their man." He checked his watch. "What do you have planned for the next hour?"

"I can spare an hour. What do you have in mind?"

"A little drive to the country to talk to Josiah."

Distracted or not, he was still my hero.

I made a quick stop at Bloomers to let Lottie and Grace know my plans, then hopped into Marco's dark green Chevy Caprice, and we headed out of town to the rural farmland that surrounded New Chapel. I directed Marco to the narrow road that branched off Route 2, then ran about five miles, the last mile sloping down to a creek. There were only three homesteads on the road. The Turner farm was the last.

We wound through cornfields almost as tall as me before I spotted the old two-story white frame house. Marco pulled up the gravel driveway on the left side of the house and stopped the car. "Ready?" he asked, unbuckling the seat belt.

I gave him a nod, gathered my purse and my courage, and got out while Marco walked to the front of his car and did a visual sweep of the area, probably a habit he'd developed in the army. There was an old wood-frame one-car garage at the back of the driveway, and beyond that, a large red barn, a chicken coop, a tall silo, and several smaller outbuildings. A wooden porch ran across the front of the house, on which were arranged pots of red geraniums and two cane-back rocking chairs. The storm door was standing open, but the screen door was shut.

On the right side of the house was a flower garden, where I could see tall spires of red salvia, white phlox, purple globe thistle, blue and pink delphinium, and stalks of lavender. Next to the garden was a big square of lawn partially shaded by a row of maple trees that ran along the outside edge, probably planted as a windbreak for the house. A playpen had been set up in the shade, and I could see a tiny figure inside. On the far side of the lawn I spotted the ankles of a woman who was apparently hanging wet bedding on a clothesline. I was betting it was Melanie. I didn't see Josiah and breathed a sigh of relief.

"People still hang clothes out to dry?" Marco asked.

"Josiah has plenty of money. You'd think he could spring for a dryer."

As we drew near the flower garden, I took a closer look at Melanie's delphiniums. The spikes had to be more than eighteen inches high, the individual blossoms were gargantuan, and the intensity of the colors—the richest violet, the iciest blue, the hottest pink I'd ever seen—was incredible. I came to an immediate halt, gasping in amazement.

Before I knew what was happening, I found myself yanked into a crouch position beside Marco.

"Who is it?" he hissed in my ear, his body beside me radiating tension. "Turner?"

"Flowers," I wheezed, trying to catch my breath.

There was a pregnant pause, then Marco muttered

something under his breath, stood up, and hauled me to my feet. "Don't gasp unless you mean it." Apparently, my gasp had startled him, kicking in his police and Army Ranger training.

I straightened my clothing with a huff, resisting the urge to defend my gasp, and made myself a note to ask Melanie what she fed her blossoms. At that moment she peered out from between sheets—no doubt to see what the commotion was—saw us, and nearly tripped over her feet in her rush to get to the playpen, as though she were afraid we'd harm the baby.

"Hi, Melanie," I called, trying to be extra cheerful and therefore harmless. "How's it going?"

She held the baby tightly against her chest and watched us with frightened eyes. "What are you doing here? Who's he?"

"This is my friend Marco—maybe you remember him from the wedding. He was one of Claymore's groomsmen. I couldn't help admiring your beautiful flowers. What kind of fertilizer do you use?"

"Cow manure," she said, eyeing Marco with suspicion.

Cow manure—good product, but not something that would go over well in the flower shop. I smiled at the little girl, who had chubby cheeks and wide eyes and wore a pink sunsuit with bunnies on it. "She's beautiful," I said. "What's her name?"

"Josie," Melanie said tersely.

Josie sounded awfully close to *Josiah*. I wondered whether that had been Melanie's attempt to ingratiate the baby with her father. Speaking of whom, I noticed that Melanie kept glancing at the fields around us, probably keeping an eye out for him.

"How old is Josie?" Marco asked, letting the baby wrap her fingers around his thumb. He looked so domestic that I wanted to throw my arms around him and give him a big sloppy smooch.

"She's nine months."

Since Melanie didn't seem inclined to chattiness, I tried the sympathetic approach. "Actually, Melanie, we stopped by to express our condolences."

She said nothing. She wasn't making this easy.

"It must be rough losing the father of your baby," I said. "I'm sure you had some feelings for him."

She hunched a shoulder as if she didn't really care, but I caught the flash of agony in her gaze before she looked away. She did care. The problem was how to get her to admit it. I was about to try flattery when Marco pulled out his private investigator's license.

"We're investigating Jack's murder. I need to ask you a few questions about Monday night."

The blunt approach. How typically male. Marco just didn't understand the subtle touch needed with an introvert like Melanie.

She put the baby in the playpen and straightened, giving a little sigh of resignation. "What do you need to know?"

I pulled out my notebook and pen and wrote, "Blunt approach can be highly effective with introverts," then readied myself to take notes.

"Why did you and your father leave the reception early?" Marco asked.

Her gaze did a quick sweep of the fields. "Josie was sick. I didn't want to leave her too long."

"Who was watching her?" Marco asked.

"Mrs. Walsh, our neighbor up the road."

"What time did you get to Mrs. Walsh's house?"

"Around ten fifteen."

As I jotted it down, Marco said, "Did your father stay home after he brought you back, or did he leave again?"

"He stayed home."

"Did you see Jack after the fight?"

She shook her head hard. "No."

"Do you know of any reason why he might have wanted to come back to the reception?"

"No."

Marco's eyes narrowed as he studied her, and I could tell it made her nervous. She began to scratch her forearm, leaving long red streaks on her skin.

"Was he coming back to the reception to see you?" Marco asked bluntly.

"No!" she said instantly.

"Had you had any contact with Jack since he got out of prison?"

She hesitated.

The screen door shut with a bang, causing Melanie to gasp and Marco to turn quickly and reach for a gun that wasn't there. Josiah came rushing down the front porch steps, his big work boots thudding, a look of rage on his face, and a shotgun in his arms.

"Let's get out of here," I whispered to Marco, slipping my notebook and pen in my purse in preparation for flight.

"We're not going anywhere," he replied in a steely voice. Then he calmly turned to face the charging bull.

CHAPTER FIFTEEN

"What the hell is going on?" Josiah demanded, striding toward us. His face was dark red with fury and his chest was puffed out like a pigeon's. Fortunately, he wasn't aiming the gun at us—yet.

"We're talking to Melanie," Marco replied calmly. "Not that it's any of your business."

"Melanie *is* my business." Josiah marched past us, reached into the playpen, scooped up the baby, and thrust her at Melanie. "Get yourself into the house. You're done talking to them."

He turned defiantly, legs planted firmly on the ground, and glared first at Marco, then at me, giving me a harsh once-over. "You've always been a little snoop, haven't you?"

"Papa, don't," Melanie said in a pleading tone.

"Did you hear what I told you?" he snapped back.

"She's an adult, Turner," Marco said as Melanie hurried away. "She can make her own decisions."

"Here's *my* decision," Josiah said. "I'm giving you to

the count of ten to walk yourselves over to that car and get in."

I had no problem with that. In fact, I would have gladly sprinted to the car, but Marco put a restraining hand on my arm, saying nothing.

"One," Josiah said, drawing the shotgun up to take aim.

Before he could count to two, Marco reacted as only an Army Ranger could, and suddenly Josiah's arm was twisted behind his back, Marco's arm was around his neck, and the gun was on the ground. He had moved so swiftly that I had to blink to be sure it had really happened.

The look on Josiah's face was one of utter disbelief, complete mortification, and a surprising note of fear. He attempted to break free, but Marco's grip was iron-strong. I rocked back on my heels and watched Josiah squirm. It was so satisfying to see the tables turned.

"Do you have something to hide, Turner?" Marco asked in a voice so icy it made me shiver.

Josiah was so outraged he could barely talk for all the spittle flying. Marco released him and gave him a push forward, then bent to pick up the shotgun. He opened it to eject the shells then turned it around so I could see that both barrels were empty. Josiah had been bluffing.

"Start talking," Marco commanded.

Josiah thrust his chin forward in an attempt at bravery even as he rubbed his sore shoulder. "I don't have anything to hide. Why would you ask me that?"

"Because you're behaving like a guilty man. What do you know about Jack Snyder's death that you haven't told the police?"

"Melanie, call the sheriff," Josiah shouted.

"Yes, do that, Turner," Marco said evenly. "Get the sheriff out here so I can tell him about your warm reception."

"I told the police everything I know," Josiah yelled.

"Then you shouldn't mind telling me." Marco glanced at me and lifted an eyebrow in Melanie's direction, which I took to mean, *Go talk to her.*

I moved away from the men, then hurried across the lawn toward the front steps. Melanie was standing inside the screen door, the baby in her arms, watching the proceedings. When she saw me approaching, she backed away. By the time I got to the door she was out of sight.

"Melanie?" I said through the screen. I could see straight up the hallway to a room at the back that had to be the kitchen, judging by the old-fashioned black stove against the wall.

"Please go away," I heard her say from somewhere close by.

"What were you going to tell us?"

"I can't talk to you."

"Don't worry about your father. Marco has him under control."

I didn't hear anything, so I cupped my hands around my eyes and looked through the screen. On my right was a doorway that probably led to a parlor. I was guessing Melanie was just inside the doorway.

"I'm going to put my card inside the door," I told her. "Take it, please, and when you get a chance, call me, okay? I just want to find out who killed Jack."

I opened the screen door and tossed my business card inside. "I'm leaving now, Melanie. You might want to pick that up before your father returns."

I walked down the steps and turned to look back in time to see her dash to the door, snatch the card, tuck it in the pocket of her dress, then dart away.

"Let's go," Marco called.

I looked around to see him striding toward his car, so I

hurried after him. Josiah was standing where Marco had left him, glaring at us as if he'd love nothing better than to shoot us both. As soon as I was buckled in, Marco backed the car onto the road and took off, wheels digging into the gravel, kicking up a cloud of dust.

"Did Josiah tell you anything more?" I asked.

"Not much. He swears he didn't see Jack after the fight. He took his daughter home because the baby was sick. What did you find out?"

"Melanie wouldn't talk to me. I finally slipped my business card in the door. She knows more, Marco. She was on the verge of telling us when her father showed up."

"What do you say we pay a visit to the babysitter?"

"Do you have time?"

He glanced at his watch. "I have until four o'clock."

"Let's do it."

We had to drive uphill to reach Mrs. Walsh's house. Her home was similar to that of the Turners—a narrow two-story with a wide front porch, a patch of lawn on one side, and several outbuildings in back. As we walked up the porch steps, a middle-aged woman came to the door. She had on a pair of jeans and a blue denim blouse, with an old-fashioned apron tied at her waist. She appeared to be older than Lottie but younger than Grace.

"May I help you?" she asked with a curious smile.

"Mrs. Walsh, I'm Abby Knight, and this is Marco Salvare. I'm related to your neighbors, the Turners. Well, actually, it's my cousin Jillian who's related"—I glanced over at Marco to see him giving me a *get on with it* look, so I finished with—"but that's not why we're here."

"Is there a problem with Josie? Is she sick?"

"No problem with the baby." Marco held up his PI license for her to read. "I'd like to ask you some questions. You babysit for Josie sometimes, don't you?"

Mrs. Walsh stepped out onto the porch, obviously deciding we weren't dangerous. "Yes, I do."

"Did you babysit Monday night?"

"Yes, why? Is this about the murder?"

Marco fixed those sexy eyes on her, a hard thing for any female to resist. "We're trying to verify a few facts. Would you mind helping?"

"Not at all."

I pulled out my notebook as Marco asked, "What time did they bring the baby here?"

"It was just about seven o'clock."

"What time did they return?"

"Let me think." She looked down at the wooden boards of her porch, one hand on her chin. "I had the TV on. There was a show on PBS I wanted to see at ten o'clock, but the baby was fussing, so I played with her instead. They came shortly after that."

"Was the baby fussing because she was sick?" I asked.

"No. Just the normal fussing of a sleepy baby."

"She wasn't ill?" I asked, glancing at Marco to see if he'd caught it.

"Not that I could see. I'm sure Melanie would have told me if Josie wasn't feeling well."

"Did you know Jack Snyder?" Marco asked.

"I knew him through his mother. We were in Women's Club together for years, until she got cancer." Mrs. Walsh clucked her tongue in disgust. "Poor Melanie was heartbroken when Jack took off. Personally, I was glad he left. He would have dragged her right down into that cesspool of his life."

"Had you seen Jack in the area recently?" Marco asked.

"He came by here a few weeks ago, but Josiah chased him away. He stands guard over that poor girl like she's his prisoner. I'm not saying I'd want to see Melanie with Jack, but it's not right of her father to keep her and the baby locked up like he does. I told Melanie she needed to get a job and get out of that house. I even volunteered to watch the baby until she could get on her feet, but she won't even entertain the idea."

"Do you think she's afraid to leave?" I asked.

"It wouldn't surprise me, although she says it's because she can't abandon her father. Sometimes, when I see Josiah drive away, I'll hurry over to the house to give her a little female companionship. That's the advantage of living up on this hill. I can see him come and go."

Marco glanced at me to make sure I was getting it all down. "How did Melanie appear to you on Monday when she came back for the baby?" he asked.

"Nervous. Kind of flushed in the face, too. While I was packing up the baby's things in the diaper bag, she kept glancing at the screen door like she expected her father to come barging in after her."

"When they left," Marco asked, "did they turn toward their house or go back the other way?"

"They went home." Mrs. Walsh pointed down the road. "See that rooftop? That's their house. I can see their lights come on at night, so I always know when they're home. That cheapskate won't leave a light burning otherwise. It might cost him a few nickels."

"That's all I have," Marco said. "Thanks for your help."

I pulled out my business card and handed it to her. "If you think of anything else, please give me a call."

"You own Bloomers?" she asked, reading my card. "I bought this wreath at Bloomers years ago." She pointed to a very faded grapevine wreath hanging on her front door. "Didn't Lottie Dombowski own the store at one time?"

"Lottie's still there," I told her, pulling out a coupon,

"as feisty as ever. Here you go. Twenty percent off a new wreath."

"My goodness. Thank you so much."

"What do you know?" I said as I climbed into Marco's car. "The baby wasn't sick after all. Maybe Josiah saw Jack at the banquet center, killed him in a fit of rage, then rushed Melanie home. And she's too frightened to say anything."

"It's a possibility," Marco said as we headed back to town. "But that doesn't answer the question of why Jack returned. Another thing to consider is that maybe Melanie killed Jack and her father is protecting *her*."

"It couldn't have been Melanie. She's too meek. And her father wouldn't have allowed her a moment alone with Jack anyway. If one of them is the killer, it has to be Josiah." I wiped a smudge off the side window with my fingertip, thinking it through. "Mrs. Walsh said Jack came around here a few weeks ago but Josiah chased him away. Maybe Jack disguised himself as a waiter so he could talk to Melanie during the reception without her father seeing him."

"For what reason? He dumped her."

"So you're saying it's not possible for a man to have a change of heart about a woman?" I was thinking specifically about Pryce's renewed interest in me.

"Do you honestly believe Jack would take up with her even though he was doing his best to avoid paying child support?"

I slumped against the seat. "Then you come up with a reason."

"Don't get your hackles up," Marco said. "I think Josiah is a strong suspect, and I'm going to have a little talk with Reilly to tell him why. But what we need is a more realistic scenario."

"Well, we still have Vince Vogel," I reminded him. "And don't forget there's always the dishwasher, Gunther, to consider. Did you ever run either of them past Reilly?"

"I've been a little busy," he said vaguely. "I'll get to it tomorrow. Where do you stand with Vince?"

"I still need to talk to his wife to verify his alibi. You wouldn't happen to be available around six o'clock this evening, would you?"

"No."

I blinked in astonishment. No? Just like that? Had I called him my hero?

The look on my face must have tipped him off that I was feeling a tad bit wounded, so he gave me an apologetic glance. "Sorry, sunshine. I can't say any more than that. It's a private matter."

A *private* matter. I turned to stare out the window, imagining steamy meetings between Marco and the mystery woman. So he'd been a little busy, huh?

"Let's see if the White Sox won today." Marco punched a button and the radio came on.

The insensitive oaf. There I was, stewing in an emotional turmoil that Marco had caused, and he was thinking about baseball. Mars and Venus at their worst.

As soon as he pulled up in front of Bloomers to let me off, I got out and said in a not-so-friendly voice, "Thanks for going with me. I'll see you around."

"Hey," he said before I could walk away, "I know you're stressed about this, but take it easy, okay? We'll figure it out."

I wished I could figure him out.

Back at Bloomers, Grace and Lottie were waiting eagerly to hear what had happened at the Turner farm.

Since there were customers having beverages in the parlor, we huddled on the other side of the curtain, where I gave them a quick account and assured Grace that once Marco had discussed the situation with Reilly, Josiah was almost certain to be the focus of the police investigation.

Grace put her arms around me and gave me a hug. "Thank you, dear. I can't tell you how relieved I am."

Lottie waited until Grace left, then she said quietly, "Do you really believe the police will go after Josiah and leave Richard alone, or are you just trying to make Grace feel better?"

"A little of both."

Lottie was putting together a swag made from grapevine, deep and pale pink miniroses, and ivy, a perfect accent to hang above a door. "I'm worried about Grace. All this fretting is taking its toll on her nerves. She couldn't even eat her lunch today. She said her stomach wouldn't hold it."

I didn't like hearing that. Grace had been a good friend and mentor during the year I worked at Dave Hammond's law office. When I got the word that I'd been booted out of law school, Grace had been there for me, always ready to lend a shoulder—or a quote—to help me get on with my life. I owed her the same opportunity.

The phone rang and we heard Grace answer it from the front. A moment later she brought in an order on which she'd written *Rush*. "I'll take this one," I told Lottie.

The flowers were for a hospital patient, so I chose vibrant colors for their cheery effect: hot pink carnations, purple asters, orange gerbera daisies, yellow sunflowers, and white mums, then I arranged them in a white wicker basket with a handle, perched a little bluebird on the edge, tied on a bright orange bow, and stuck in a get-well card.

"It's lovely, dear," Grace said, coming in with another piece of paper. "This lady would like her order by five. She said to call if it would be a problem."

And have her go elsewhere? I checked the clock on the wall. "It's only four. I've got time."

The bell jingled, so Grace went up front. She was back almost immediately, or at least her head was. She poked it through the curtain to say in a low voice, "Pryce is here to see you."

I glanced at Lottie and she lifted her eyebrows. I slid off the stool—being short, I never could make a smooth transition—and stepped through the curtain, with Lottie on my heels. Pryce was walking around the shop, hands clasped behind his back as he studied the various flower arrangements on display.

"Hi," I said, heading toward him. "What's up?"

He didn't smile—not that I expected it—but he did seem relieved to see me. I hadn't expected that, either. "Do you know where my grandmother is?"

"*Should* I know where she is?"

He held out a slip of paper on which had been written in a spidery hand, *Went to Abby's place for ice cream. I'll be home when I feel like it.*

CHAPTER SIXTEEN

I showed the note to Lottie, who was trying her best to maneuver herself around so she could read it over my shoulder.

"Your granny hasn't been here," Lottie told Pryce. "We don't even serve ice cream."

"Wait a minute," I said. "I know where she went—Luigi's Italian Ices. It's near the Dunes. I took her there once and told her it was my favorite place for ice cream. She loved it. She probably took the trolley. It runs right past there."

Pryce glanced at his prized granite-faced Swiss watch—most people chose pets that looked like themselves; Pryce chose watches. "I really don't have time for this. I've already canceled two of my afternoon appointments."

"Then don't worry about your grandmother," I told him. "She got there by herself. She'll get home by herself."

"I can't do that. She's supposed to be at her doctor's office at five o'clock for her pneumonia vaccine—I volunteered to take her since my parents are packing for their trip to Spain."

"Did she forget about the appointment?"

"It's more likely that she's hiding from me. She has an irrational fear of needles." Pryce heaved an Oscar-worthy sigh. "I don't know what to do. A bout of pneumonia at her age could do her in. Somehow she has to be convinced to go—but you're probably the only one who could coax her into it."

I blinked at him as he tightened the knot of his hand-painted silk tie, smoothed the lapels of his suit coat, and adjusted his French cuffs. He'd pleaded his case and was waiting for my decision. Would I volunteer to save his grandmother from a fate worse than a prick in the arm or condemn her to live out the remainder of her life lurking in ice cream parlors?

"I really don't have time for this, either," I wanted to tell him, but since I felt partly responsible for Grandma being at "my place," I couldn't very well tell Pryce to take a hike. "Fine. I'll try to coax her into it."

His breath came out in a relieved huff. "Okay, then. My car's out front. We'll just take a quick ride out there."

Not a quick ride, not a quick hop, not even quicksand would make me get into the car with Pryce. I noticed Lottie standing by a display table, shifting arrangements around, no doubt stalling so she could hear my answer. There was silence in the coffee parlor, too, probably for the same reason. Grace was a practiced eavesdropper.

"I need to make a flower delivery at the hospital," I said. "I'll take my car and meet you at Luigi's."

With Pryce following a safe distance behind—he'd never trusted my driving—I got off the highway at the Dunes State Park exit and took the road that snaked around the lake, parking in front of a row of tourist shops, one of which was Luigi's Italian Ices. Through Luigi's window we could see beachgoers looking for cool relief from the summer sun, standing three-deep at the glass-fronted cases and filling the tables along the side. Sitting near the back was Grandma Osborne, licking chocolate ice cream off the sides of a waffle cone and chatting with a teenaged couple with matching tattoos and nose rings.

Pryce took my arm and led me past the shop. "Okay, here's the plan. I'll stay out here—I don't dare let her see me or she'll bolt. You go inside, circle around her, and herd her toward the door."

I stared at him. "What are you, a cowboy? Your grandmother isn't a runaway horse, Pryce. I think you can come inside."

Two girls in swimsuits and see-through cover-ups strolled past, pausing to glance at Pryce's dark suit.

"You know what?" I said. "You're right. It would be better if I went in alone. But it's hot here on the sidewalk, and this might take a while. Of course, if you get tired of waiting, you could always throw a lasso around Grandma's neck and haul her out."

I ignored his scowl, walked into the shop, and got into the line nearest to her table. Then I looked around and feigned surprise. "Grandma, what are you doing here?"

"Having ice cream." She displayed her empty containers. "So far I've had two cones, a banana split, and three shakes."

"Are you here alone?" I asked, sitting down in a wrought iron chair at her table.

"I certainly am. I took the trolley. Wasn't that smart?"

"You have no idea. I'm going to pick up a dish of Italian ice, then head back to town. Do you want to ride with me?"

She squinted at the wall clock behind the counter, and I could tell she was doing some calculating. "Not yet."

She turned away from me and resumed her conversation with the teenagers.

That called for plan B. I bought strawberry-flavored Italian ice, then meandered back to Grandma's table. "Mind if I join you?"

"It's a free country."

"How are you feeling today?"

"I woke up. That's good enough for me." She eyed the spoonful of red ice as I slid it into my mouth. "That looks yummy."

"It is yummy." I pushed the clear plastic dish toward the middle of the table so we could share. "Have some."

As she dug in, the teenagers at the next table got up and left. However, their trash didn't, and moments later a white-coated busboy came over with a garbage bag to haul it away. Grandma paused, watching him, her spoon almost to her mouth; then she said, "The fellow in the white coat was carrying a black plastic bag."

I glanced at the busboy, who was now wiping off another table. "Yes, he was picking up the garbage."

"I'm not talking about *that* person," she said, stabbing a gnarled index finger at the unsuspecting employee. "I'm talking about that fellow in the white coat I saw sneaking around the back corner of the banquet center. He was carrying a black plastic bag, too. Seeing that young man over there made me remember."

"You're sure it was a garbage bag?"

"I'm sure. The fellow had it in his arms, like he was taking out the trash. I probably wouldn't have noticed him if it hadn't been for the noise."

"The noise coming from the ballroom?"

"No, *that* was a racket. This noise was more like a brick hitting the sidewalk. I turned around to see what had caused it and that's when I saw the fellow in the white jacket."

"Did he cause the noise?"

"How should I know? I *heard* it; I didn't *see* it. Are you going to finish that ice?"

"You can have the rest." I pushed it toward her, then sat back to think about what she'd said. A white coat and a black plastic garbage bag. Had Grandma seen a possible witness to the murder? Had she seen the murderer himself? Or, as my logical mind reminded me, had Grandma merely seen someone taking out the garbage?

I'd have to inquire at the banquet center as to who took out the trash on Monday night. In the meantime, I tucked that information away to tell Marco later.

I caught Grandma glancing at the clock, and remembered Pryce waiting outside. "Don't you have a doctor's appointment this afternoon?"

"Doctors," she grumbled. "Always wanting to pump me with chemicals and poke me with sharp needles. In my day a doctor would stick a few leeches on your arm, give you a good dose of laudanum, and send you on your way. We were tough people back then. We didn't need a pill for every little pain."

"You can't avoid your doctor forever, Grandma."

She scraped the last smear of pink ice out of the bowl, then leaned back with a contented sigh. "Well, it was fun while it lasted. Okay, let's go face the music. My grandson is about to melt out there anyway."

I blinked at her in surprise. "You knew Pryce was here?"

"Pshaw! He's had his face pressed against the glass for the last five minutes and he's the only one wearing a three-piece suit. I may be old and forgetful, but I'm not blind."

We threaded our way through the crowd with Grandma in the lead. As soon as we exited the shop, Pryce walked up from behind and, with what was supposed to pass as a shocked look, exclaimed, "Grandmother! What a surprise."

"Put a sock in it, suitboy," she said. "I knew you were here. Now give me your arm and help me to the car. I'm feeling a little queasy from all that ice cream."

Pryce paled. "You're not going to throw up on my leather seats, are you?"

"I haven't decided yet." She glanced back at me. "Are you coming, Abby?"

I gave her a hug. "I can't. I have a delivery to make. My car's parked down the street. Good luck at the doctor's."

"Abigail," Pryce called as I walked toward the Vette. "Thanks for the assistance."

"No problem, Tex," I called back. "I always enjoy a good roundup."

He didn't find that as amusing as I did.

It was nearly five o'clock when I got back to Bloomers. I filled the ladies in on Grandma Osborne's escapade as I pulled flowers for the bouquet I planned to take to Vince Vogel's wife. I wanted to drop by the Vogels' house around five thirty, figuring that if she worked outside the home, she'd be getting in about that time. The flowers were my foot in the door.

As I wrapped the red zinnias, yellow daisies, and white bachelor buttons in floral paper, Grace came back to tell me that my aunt Corrine was there to see me.

"Woo-hoo!" I cried, jumping up. "It's payday."

I followed Grace to the front, imagining the happy chime of the cash register when I stuck that fat check for the wedding flowers inside. Thanks to Trudee's pay-ment—after months of barely being able to cover the ex-penses of running the shop, not to mention the mortgage, Lottie's and Grace's salaries, and a new pair of flip-flops every now and then—I'd finally reached the breakeven point. With this wedding fee I'd be dollars ahead—even with the discount I'd given my aunt and uncle. They were family, after all.

Lottie hadn't been too keen on my waiving the cus-tomary one-third down, but, as I'd reminded her, I knew where they lived. Besides, my aunt had assured me that I'd get the entire amount as soon as the wedding was over. Because of the murder, that hadn't happened Mon-day night. But it was about to happen now.

Aunt Corrine greeted me with a perfumed hug, then leaned back to study me. "My, aren't we looking cheery."

Anticipating a big bundle of dough tended to do that to me. I was practically salivating. "Things are looking bright today," I told her.

"Marvelous. Guess what? I brought something else to brighten your day"—I rubbed my hands together. *Lay that baby on me.*—"a message from Jillian."

A message? I didn't want a message. I wanted my check.

"She said to tell you—you're going to love this—that you were absolutely right about Claymore. He isn't a total jerk after all." My aunt laughed liked it was the most hilarious thing she'd ever heard. "Isn't that just like Jil-lian? He isn't a *total* jerk."

I forced a laugh. "Yes . . . just like her."

"Okay. That's all I have," she said as two customers walked in the door. "I'll let you get back to work."

Did my aunt truly not remember her promise? "About the wedding," I said as Lottie came through the curtain.

My aunt paused, one hand on the brass handle. "Yes?"

"I was wondering . . ."

She smiled at me. "Wondering what?"

Wondering why the customers looking at the wreaths had suddenly become quiet. I moved closer to my aunt and said in a low voice, "I was wondering when . . ."

I couldn't do it. I tried to open my mouth to finish the sentence, but my jaws seemed to be locked.

"Abigail, you keep losing your train of thought. Are you all right?"

"Am I all right? Of course I'm all right," I said with a light laugh. "I was just wondering when Jillian and Claymore would be home."

"Not until next Wednesday."

"Wednesday. Okay. Got it." *Fraidy-cat,* that little voice inside taunted. I shot Lottie a sheepish look, but she was helping the customers.

"I'm off to the photography studio to pick up the proofs," my aunt said. "I do hope the police will be done with their evidence gathering soon. They confiscated the wedding video, you know, and I can't have it put on a DVD until they give it back. Heavens, I just thought of something. I hope the videographer didn't film anything gory. Wouldn't that be embarrassing?"

It was evident who Jillian took after in the tact department. At least my aunt had jogged my memory. I'd have to ask Morgan whether the police had learned anything from the video.

I turned to go back to the workroom, then stopped. There had been two video cameras at that wedding. "Aunt Corrine," I said before she could get out the door, "what happened to the film the other cameraman shot?"

"What other cameraman?" she asked, trying to look innocent.

"I know Jillian spirited him out of the reception, Aunt Corrine."

She nibbled her lower lip. "You won't tell the police, will you? I wouldn't want to get my daughter in trouble."

"I won't tell them, but someone else might, and then we'd all be in trouble."

She looked like she might faint. "We can't let that happen, Abigail. I'd never be able to show my face at the country club again. How about if I give it to you and you turn it in?"

"Me?" I sputtered.

"The video is being processed right now. I'll pick it up tomorrow morning and drop it off here." She gave me another hug. "Thank you so much, darling. And by the way, if I haven't mentioned it, the wedding flowers were lovely. You did a magnificent job. Bravo."

Behind me, I heard Lottie clear her throat in a way that meant, *There's your opening.*

My aunt departed and I turned with my head bowed, knowing I was in for a Business 101 lecture. "Okay, I admit it. I'm a coward. Why is it I can face down a bully but I can't ask my aunt for my fee?"

"Don't beat yourself up over it," Lottie said. "Send the bill to your uncle."

"He won't even look at the wedding bills. When Uncle Doug saw the estimate for Jillian's reception dinner, he washed his hands of the whole thing. It was either the chocolate fountain or the six hundred calf brain canapés that pushed him over the edge."

"Perhaps your aunt hasn't yet recovered from the ordeal of putting on a wedding," Grace offered. She always tried to see the positive side of the situation. "Perhaps she'll bring the check when she returns tomorrow."

"If she doesn't," Lottie said, "she gets a bill."

"That would look so tacky," I said.

Lottie snorted. "Tacky is not paying your bills. We'll give her a few more days, and if she still hasn't coughed it up, I will personally send her a statement."

"Fine, but I'm warning you, there'll be hell to pay. My aunt will be totally humiliated, Jillian will never forgive me for embarrassing the family, and my mother will have a field day with it. She and my aunt have always had this little competition going." I sighed forlornly. "I'll probably have to dye my hair black and move into the witness protection program."

"Sweetie, business is business," Lottie said. "Your aunt will just have to suck it up. Am I right, Grace?"

We both looked at Grace. Under normal circumstances this would have been her cue to step in with a quote.

"I'm sorry," she said with a sad sigh. "I've got nothing."

She really was in a bad way.

At five o'clock I pulled my bouquet for Vince's wife out of the cooler and closed up shop for the day. As I locked the door I glanced up the sidewalk and saw Marco coming from Down the Hatch. I raised my arm to catch his attention but jerked it down again when I saw the dark-haired woman follow him out. I watched with a mixture of envy and curiosity as he escorted her to his car and opened the passenger-side door for her.

As she slid inside the car, Marco's head suddenly turned my way. He gave a brief wave, then got into the car, and they drove away.

Well, *that* confirmed why he'd declined to accompany me to the Vogels' house.

I stomped off with an annoyed huff. What was he doing, sneaking around town with a stranger?

He wasn't sneaking. It's broad daylight. And she

obviously isn't a stranger to him, my better self chided. *Besides, it's not like the two of you have agreed not to see anyone else.*

There were times when my better self annoyed the hell out of me.

I was so preoccupied with thoughts of Marco and the mystery woman that I missed two turns and almost blew through a stoplight before I found the Vogels' address. I got out of the car and marched up the front walk of the green aluminum-sided ranch home, determined to put those thoughts aside and concentrate on finding the murderer, which was a lot more important than Marco's private life. I rang the doorbell and silently rehearsed my opening line: *"Hi, you don't know me but . . ."*

I waited a moment and rang again, and when no one came to the door I opened the screen and knocked on the heavy storm door. I was just about to head back to my car when I noticed an elderly lady watching me from the house next door. She was sitting on her front porch in a wicker rocking chair, a book in her hand. And I had a bouquet in mine.

"Hello," I called, walking across the lawn toward her. "Do you know when Mrs. Vogel will be home?"

"Suzanne? She should be home soon. Are you a friend of hers? I don't remember seeing that cute little sports car around here before."

I had a hunch that this woman knew everything that went on in the neighborhood. "Suzanne didn't make it to my cousin's wedding Monday and I was worried about her. I stopped by to see how she was doing."

The woman was all too willing to share the gossip. "You must not have heard what happened to her. Her migraine got so bad Monday she ended up in the hospital that night. Vincent felt terrible for leaving her, even though he was only gone for an hour. They've got her on medication now, but I have to say she gave us quite a scare."

I thanked her for the helpful information, gave her the flowers, and crossed Vince's name off my list of suspects.

CHAPTER SEVENTEEN

"**Y**ou're still up?" Nikki asked me late that night. "Do you know it's after midnight?" She flopped down on the sofa, startling Simon, who had curled up next to me and gone to sleep. Nikki had her hospital duds on, and there was a brand-new carton of ice cream in her hands.

"When did you get home?" I asked her.

"Just now. Didn't you hear me come in? Why are you watching C-Span?"

I blinked at the television screen. "I'm not sure."

She took the remote and clicked the TV off. "What's up with you, Ab?"

I picked up the sofa pillow and hugged it to my chest. "There's way too much on my mind. It's really getting crowded in there."

"So what's got you in a twist?"

"For one thing, I've got to clear Richard soon because Grace is suffering. Then there's my aunt, who still hasn't paid for the wedding flowers—and I saw Marco with the mystery woman again."

"Aha! Now we're getting to the real problem." She

dug into the ice cream and said through a mouthful, "Did you try to call Marco?"

"No way. What if *she* answers?"

"Put on your sexiest voice and ask to speak to Lover Boy. That'll get her."

I let out a frustrated sigh. "I really believed we had some potent chemistry, but I guess the sizzle was all on my side."

"Wait a minute. It's not like you haven't experienced some heavy lip-lock with him. Remember that cozy little picnic in his office?"

"I kissed *him*, Nikki—and I practically wrestled him to the blanket to do it. There's a difference."

"No, no. I'm talking about that time when you were standing by the kitchen sink and he was ready to leave but first he kissed you and you said you'd never figure out the male species. Then there was the time you had just escaped from that crazy Tom Harding in Bloomers' basement and Marco came charging in to rescue you, found you on the floor, knelt down, and laid one on you. Oh, and what about when that Crown Victoria was following you, and Marco told you he didn't want anything bad to happen, and then he pulled you in his arms and . . . *bosh!*"

Nikki had an amazing recall for kiss stories. I hunched a shoulder. "Yeah, but were those I-find-you-irresistible kisses or gee-you're-still-alive kisses?"

"You know what you need? Ice cream." Nikki put down the carton and trotted to the kitchen. "I'll get you a spoon."

"Sure. I need to pack on a few more pounds. That'll really make me attractive."

She came back and handed me a spoon. "This is Skinny Cow. Very low calorie. Try a bite."

I slid some in my mouth. "Not bad," I muttered through the melting sweetness on my tongue.

"See? You don't even miss the sugar, do you?"

"Just don't tell me what chemicals they're using as a replacement." I started to dig out another bite, then stopped. "Great. I'm beginning to sound like Grandma Osborne. And that reminds me. You won't believe what she did today."

I pushed all thoughts of Marco out of my head and told Nikki about Grandma and Cowboy Pryce. From there we turned to the perplexing puzzle of Jack Snyder's killer, and then suddenly we were back to discussing Marco again. By the time we had worn out the subject of the mystery woman I could barely keep my eyes open, so I took myself off to bed, resolving to stop trying to figure out anyone carrying the Y chromosome and instead concentrate on a more important matter—helping Grace.

I woke up Thursday morning feeling recharged and ready to track down the killer—with or without Marco's help. Naturally, that would be the day when a bundle of orders would come in—twelve of them to be exact, all funeral arrangements that had to be delivered to the Happy Dreams Funeral Home by two o'clock that afternoon. On any other day those orders would have had me jumping for joy. Today they felt like an annoyance.

"Let's rent a van," Lottie said.

"Good idea," I said. "Once I get paid for Jillian's wedding I'm going to see about buying one. I can write it off as a business expense."

"I'll call the rental company we used for the wedding," Grace said.

Seeing her drawn face only added to my frustration. I wanted the old Grace back. I missed her ready quotes and the pleasant tunes she hummed throughout the day. Their absence was like a black hole, sucking up all the light. Even Lottie kept shooting her worried glances as we shared our first cups of coffee in the parlor. But Grace wasn't one to vent. She bore it all with her classically British stiff upper lip.

Lottie and I took fresh cups of coffee and headed back to the workroom, where, for a few hours, I concentrated on nothing but my flowers. Midway through the morning, though, Grace came back to tell us that Sheila Sackowitz had returned, and she'd brought a friend.

"Great. The chatterbox is back," Lottie said with a roll of her eyes. "I think I'll go pick up the van."

"Coward," I said. "That's okay. I don't mind Sheila coming in, as long as I can get her to chatter about Monday night."

"Hey there, kiddo," Sheila called when I stepped through the curtain. She threw a skinny arm around my shoulders and dragged me against her, practically into her armpit—it was one of the drawbacks of being short.

"Didn't I tell you I'd be back? This is Deb Bartoli. She fills in at the banquet center when they need an extra waitress. Deb, this is Abby Knight, owner of this cute little shop."

I extracted my head and reached out to give Deb's hand a shake. She was a stout woman, taller than me but a head shorter than Sheila. Both had on baggy knit pants and a T-shirt, but Deb's was pink with a teddy bear on it, whereas today Sheila's had a logo that read, HANDS OFF, ASSWIPE.

"Deb needs to pick up some flowers to take to her mother in a nursing home." Sheila tapped her head and whispered, "The old lady·lost her marbles, you know?"

Deb was standing at the display cooler with her hands

cupped around her eyes, peering through the glass, which was steaming up from her breath. I suggested we open the door and she could take a look, but the array of colors and textures seemed to make it even harder for her to select, so I ended up suggesting an arrangement for her. When the door finally closed, the flowers shuddered in relief.

"Hey, come on in the parlor, Deb," Sheila called from the doorway. "I ordered us coffee and some of Grace's delicious scones. Do you have time to join us, Abby?"

"I'll make time," I told her. I finished wrapping Deb's bouquet and took it to the parlor, where Deb was munching on one of Grace's pride-and-joy scones and Sheila was telling Grace how to make cranberry muffins—her specialty, as it turned out.

Grace, with her usual good manners, was standing at the table, coffeepot in hand, listening politely. "I'll have to try my hand at it," she said when Sheila had finally finished.

"I'll bring some by for you to sample," Sheila offered. "You'll love 'em. Hey, here's an idea, Abby. You might want to think about selling them here. I could make a couple dozen every morning and drop them by on my way to work. I'll give you a real deal on 'em—cost plus twenty percent."

"I'll give it serious thought," I told her, adding a few drops of cream to my coffee. I immediately glanced at Grace and gave her a discreet shake of my head. Grace would run me through the coffee grinder before she let someone else do her baking.

The bell over the door jingled and I heard my aunt Corrine's voice. I tried to focus on what Sheila was saying, but my mind was too busy sending my aunt a telepathic message: *Pay Abby for the flowers.* So I sipped my coffee and nodded at whatever Sheila was saying.

A few minutes later, the bell jingled again, then Grace came back to the parlor, picked up a carafe, and walked over to refill our cups. At my quizzical glance, she leaned over to say quietly, "Your aunt said to tell you the wedding video will be ready tomorrow." Then she gave me a little shrug that meant *No check.*

Great. Now Lottie would send a bill, my aunt would be humiliated, my mother would be delighted, and I'd be banished from the family. I grabbed the pitcher of cream, laced my coffee with it, and took a gulp, hoping the butterfat would numb my brain.

"Wedding video?" Sheila exclaimed. "Damn, I'm glad no one taped any of my weddings. There's no way I'd want to watch those disasters happen again." Both women guffawed. Then Sheila said, "I wish you could have seen little Abby here in her bridesmaid dress, Deb. She was something, let me tell you, especially when she fell on her ass and took another bridesmaid down with her."

The women chortled and slapped their knees. I dumped the rest of the cream in my cup and looked around for another pitcher.

"Sorry," Sheila said, wiping her eyes. "I just had to tease you about it." To Deb she said, "That was the night I had to work late 'cause that blockhead Gunther took off work early."

At the mention of Gunther, my brain snapped to attention. "I have a question for you, Sheila. Has it always been Gunther's job to take out the garbage?"

"Since I've been there it has. It's one of the few things he can't screw up." She snickered.

"Is the garbage packaged in black plastic bags?"

"Sure is, why?"

"Because someone wearing a white jacket was seen carrying a black garbage bag near the back of the banquet center around the time of the murder, but it was too dark to make out a face."

"Yep, that would be Gunther," Sheila said. "Anthony always sends him out with the garbage around nine thirty."

"Are you're sure it was Gunther who took it out Monday night? Did you actually see him leave the kitchen with the bag?"

"Hell, no, but that doesn't mean anything. You've been in that kitchen. You know how crazy it gets back there."

"Does the banquet center have security cameras outside the building?"

Sheila and Deb looked at each other and laughed. "Are you kidding?" Sheila said with a snort. "They pay us minimum wage. You think they're gonna spring for security cameras?"

"So do you really believe Gunther might be a killer?" Deb asked me, her chin propped in her hand, which still contained part of a scone. "I've always thought he looked like the type."

"I wouldn't make that leap," I said. "That's not fair to Gunther. But if he was outside at the time the murder happened, he could have *seen* the murderer. Of course, security cameras would have helped."

"I wouldn't be surprised if Gunther did it," Sheila said, sipping her coffee. "You know what they say—once a jailbird, always a jailbird."

"Wait a minute," I said. "I didn't know Gunther had been in prison."

"I just found out myself, as a matter of fact," Sheila said. "You know, ever since Monday, people in the kitchen have been talking about him. I guess Gunther's only been out a few weeks."

Jack had been out a month. It might have been a coincidence, but that little alarm in my head didn't think so. I needed to interview Gunther, but I wanted to run it by Marco first.

"Well, this has been great, but I've got to get home," Sheila said. "Thanks for the coffee and goodies. We should do this again—hey, maybe when I bring those muffins around."

I darted a quick glance at Grace and caught her pained look. As soon as Sheila and Deb were gone I said, "Don't worry. Sheila's muffins could never compare to your scones." I left her smiling for the first time in days and went to the workroom to call Marco.

Chris the bartender answered on the second ring. "Sorry, Abby. Marco's on an important call. He asked not to be disturbed."

Important call. Right. He was probably talking to that exotic, dark-haired beauty.

"Did you say something, Abby? Hello? I think we have a bad connection."

It wasn't a bad connection. It was my brain sizzling. Who needed Marco's help anyway?

CHAPTER EIGHTEEN

L ottie and I finished the funeral orders at twelve thirty in the afternoon, with no breaks for anything but coffee and handfuls of microwave popcorn to quiet the growls in our stomachs. Once we had everything loaded in the van, I volunteered to make the deliveries so I could dash out to the Garden of Eden afterward for a little chat with Gunther.

"Whatever it takes to help our Gracie," Lottie said, shutting the back gate. "I'll hold down the fort here."

At the banquet center, I passed the ballroom, where employees were inflating balloons, setting out plates and flatware, and hanging a banner that said, HAPPY 35TH ANNIVERSARY, CLAUDE AND JUDY. I continued past and was about to go into the kitchen when Kevin the waiter came out carrying a round tray filled with glass tumblers.

"Hi," I said cheerily. "Remember me? Well . . . here I am again."

"Sure, I remember you, Abby," he said, giving me a coy once-over, which couldn't have been easy to do with that huge tray in his hands. "Still working on that murder?"

"You bet. Is Gunther around?"

"He's in the kitchen. Hold on and I'll get him for you."

Other waiters were scurrying between the kitchen and ballroom, so I walked up the hallway to get out of the traffic. In a moment Gunther pushed through one of the kitchen's swinging doors and looked around.

"Hi there," I called, holding up my hand.

He looked bewildered, but maybe that was normal for him. "You want to talk to me?"

"Yes, just for a few minutes."

His bulk nearly blotted out the light as he lumbered toward me. "Who are you?"

"I'm Abby Knight, the florist who did the arrangements for the wedding this past Monday."

His heavy eyebrows drew together. It wasn't ringing any bells.

"Maybe if you picture me holding a stack of white boxes in front of my face?" I positioned my arms and pretended to be balancing a wobbling pile of cardboard. Then I peered around my imaginary tower and smiled, hoping a little humor would jog his memory.

"Yeah, I think I remember that. So, what do you want?"

"I've got a friend who's in serious hot water and I was hoping I could get some information from you that would help clear his name."

"From me?"

"Yes. You know, like did you see anyone hanging around the garden when you took out the garbage Monday night, the exact time you left work . . . that kind of thing."

"I already told the cops everything I know."

"Is there any reason why you can't tell me, too?" I asked with a smile. "I have just a few questions. It won't take much time."

I could see his jaw muscles working, as if he were growing impatient with me. "Look, I can't help you. I didn't take out the garbage Monday night, so I couldn't have seen anyone hanging around."

"Then who did take it out?"

He gave me a *duh* look. "I don't know. I wasn't there."

"So that means you left work before nine thirty?"

His jaw worked again and I could sense he was about at the end of his patience. "I don't know. I didn't look at the clock. That's enough questions now. I'm gonna get in trouble if I don't get back to work."

"Wait, Gunther. Please. I'm almost finished. Why did you leave work early that night?"

"I got sick," he answered just a little too defensively.

"Did you know the man who was killed—Jack Snyder?"

He hesitated, a wary look in his eyes. "No."

"Weren't you in prison with him?"

At once Gunther's jaw tightened and his fists clenched. He took a threatening step toward me, and I backed up against the wall. Why was the hallway always empty when you didn't want it to be? All I could think of was Marco's admonition to make sure I never interviewed a suspect without witnesses around.

"You listen carefully, stubby," he sneered, putting his big face inches from mine. "It's no secret I did my time, but I don't need you or the cops persecuting me for it. Yeah, I left work early. Yeah, I knew Snyder from prison, but I didn't kill him; got it?"

I nodded, swallowing hard, trying not to shift my gaze away. It was never good to show fear. Besides, I was still trying to absorb the fact that he knew the word *persecuting*. It didn't seem the kind of word a blockhead would use.

"Finished with your nosy questions now?"

"I'm finished," I whispered, deciding not to press my luck.

Gunther's hands relaxed and he straightened, allowing me to draw the first good breath I'd had in minutes. "Don't bug me again," he said.

"Okay," I squeaked.

I glanced at him just before he turned away, and that's when I caught a sly glint in his eye. Suddenly I had a sneaking suspicion that he wasn't such a blockhead after all.

Gunther walked away, and I hurried in the opposite direction. I knew two things for sure: Gunther was a brute, and my questions had upset him. Obviously he was touchy about his prison record. But was there anything to tie him to Jack's murder? So what if Jack had come to the Garden of Eden. There must have been other parolees who'd been guests at an event there. And who was to say Gunther hadn't been sick that night? Certainly not this stubby person.

I got into the van and drove back without even switching on the radio. I was frustrated. My investigation kept hitting blank walls, and I had a strong feeling I was missing something important. The only thing I could think to do was to turn my focus back to the most obvious suspect—Josiah.

At two thirty I whipped together the bouquet of roses I owed Morgan and was out the door in ten minutes, heading for his office at the courthouse to exchange flowers for facts. I took the wide center staircase—the ancient elevator's groaning cables spooked me—and marched up to the Formica-topped desk of the prosecutors' one and only secretary, a fashionably dressed woman in her mid-thirties whose habit of wearing narrow, blue-tinted glasses low on her long, thin nose gave her voice a distinct nasal tone.

I held the wrapped bouquet behind my back, since it was purportedly for her, and waited for her to stop typing and look up at me. But since she didn't seem so inclined, I said, "Excuse me. I have a delivery for Greg Morgan." And just so she wouldn't ask, I added, "I'm the florist from across the street."

She reached for the phone, informed Greg I was there, and continued typing, without once glancing at me. My grip tightened on the flowers. I was tempted to smack her on the head with them.

"Abby, come on in," Morgan called from his doorway just in time, sparing the woman the embarrassment of having to wear her bouquet.

I walked into his cramped office and took a seat on an ancient wooden chair as he shut the door and went to sit behind an equally ancient oak desk. There were files everywhere—on filing cabinets, in boxes, even stacked on the floor. Prosecutors were notoriously overworked and underpaid, although you'd never know by the way Morgan dressed. Of course, it helped that he lived rent-free with his mother.

I handed him the wrapped bundle. "Here you are; one dozen of my finest."

Morgan took a peek inside the green paper and gave me a smile. "Super. Kirby will be thrilled."

The only Kirby I'd ever heard of was a brand of vacuum cleaner my aunt used—yet somehow it seemed fitting. Kirby looked like she'd had all the air sucked out of her head.

"So," I said, "what did you find out about the murder investigation?"

Morgan sat back, resting his hands on the arms of his

chair. "Let me state once again that I'm bound by ethics not to divulge case information."

"And let me state once again that you promised we would trade favors."

He held up his hand, palm out. "Answer the question, please. You do realize I'm bound by those ethics, don't you?"

I faked a yawn. "Yes, Greg, I realize that."

"Okay then." He shuffled through papers, found the one he wanted, and put it on the edge of his desk. "How's the flower business?" he asked, nudging the paper with his elbow. It slipped over the side and landed on the wooden floor under my chair. He wasn't actually divulging anything. I was accidentally getting a peek at it.

I folded my hands together in my lap, resisting the urge to reach under the chair until he'd given a signal. "The flower business is fine."

"Good. Would you excuse me for moment? I have to deliver this file next door. I'll be right back."

He left the room and shut the door while I grabbed the paper and flipped it over to read it. Across the top was the title: *Office of the County Coroner: Autopsy Report.*

Bless Morgan's ethical little heart.

Most of the report was technical information, but finally I found the details I needed. I pulled my notebook and pen from my purse and began to write. The time of death was estimated to be approximately nine thirty p.m. Cause of death was blunt trauma to the right temporal area. Toxicology showed no amphetamines or alcohol.

I heard footsteps approaching and, fearing it might be someone other than Morgan, I tossed the paper onto his desk and tucked away my notebook just as the door opened. Morgan walked in, shut the door, and glanced at me as he walked around his desk and sat down. "Are we square now?"

"Almost. There's this business about a fourth suspect."

He folded his hands on the desk and leaned toward me to say quietly, "I can tell you this much. The fourth suspect doesn't matter anymore."

"Why not?"

"Take a guess."

"The cops have picked one of the other suspects?"

Morgan shrugged as if he didn't know, but his grin was saying yes.

"Is it Josiah Turner?"

This time he didn't bat an eye or twitch a lip, making it impossible to know whether I'd hit it right, so I told him why I felt there was a strong possibility that Josiah was the killer, just in case the police had come to a different conclusion. But after I'd finished, Morgan didn't look impressed, and that concerned me.

"Don't tell me the police have cleared Josiah, because there's no way they could have," I said.

"They don't need to clear him."

My stomach tightened. Had the cops verified the murder charge on Richard's rap sheet? I had to bite my tongue to keep from asking, because I couldn't let Morgan know Marco had a source. It wouldn't take a mental giant to figure out that source was a cop.

"Be straight with me, Greg. Is there enough to make a case against Richard Davis?"

Morgan gazed straight at me with those baby blues and said, "He's being booked as we speak."

CHAPTER NINETEEN

❧

I dashed across the courthouse lawn and headed straight for Down the Hatch to tell Marco the bad news. I was breathing hard and my stomach was in a knot, not only from what Morgan had told me but also from worrying about how it would affect Grace. And I was annoyed with Marco, who was supposed to have checked out Richard's murder charge but had been so preoccupied with a certain exotic beauty that I just knew he'd forgotten to call the detective back. If I didn't get an ulcer from everything that was happening, I'd be amazed.

I burst into Marco's office and found him sitting behind his desk, calmly eating nachos smothered in meat, cheese, and salsa. The room smelled of spicy chili and cilantro, which normally would have had me drooling but now only made my stomach feel worse.

"Hey!" he said in surprise, swallowing a mouthful of food. "I've been trying to track you down. Don't you return messages anymore?"

I sank into one of his leather sling-back chairs and

leaned my head into my hands, afraid I was going to be sick. "They're arresting Richard—right now."

There was silence for a moment before he said, "Where did you hear that?"

"From Morgan. I was just over at his office. What am I going to tell Grace?"

"That you did your best."

My head came up with a snap. "Obviously I *didn't* do my best, and neither did you."

"Wait a minute," he said, but I was on a roll.

"I've been running around like a headless chicken trying to juggle all these"—I waved my hand in the air, searching for the right word—"these *crises* around me while you're off with"—I did the hand motion again, like a coach signaling a play, unable to bring myself to utter the words *another woman*.

"Did you ever get back to that detective in Texas?" I demanded. "Oh, I forgot. You've been busy. Heaven forbid that a murder investigation that *you* volunteered to help me with should interfere with your personal life. And by the way, I *always* return my messages." With a final huff I lifted my chin to show I was finished.

Marco had stopped eating and was now leaning back in his chair, his gaze level, his only reaction to my tirade being a raised eyebrow, as if to say, *Is that so?*

Then he very calmly stood up and came around the desk, reminding me of a large cat who appears to be lazily trolling the high grass when actually he's planning a surprise attack. He stopped in front of my chair, leaned his backside against the edge of the desk, and folded his arms across his chest. "You'd better check your voice mail and your answering machine to see if they're working, because I left a message on each. I also tried to reach you at Bloomers. Grace took the call."

I'd missed two calls and a message? No way. To prove it, I dug in my purse, flipped open my phone—and saw that I'd forgotten to recharge it. Now that I thought about it, I couldn't remember even glancing at the machine when I got home from work the evening before. And clearly Grace wasn't at her best or she would have remembered to give me the message.

"Well?" he said.

I shut the phone, dropped it into my purse, and gave him a sheepish shrug. "Sorry. My fault."

He pinned me with his cool gaze as he crouched down in front of me. "No, sunshine," he said at last. "My fault. I *have* been busy and I should have explained why."

My heart gave a lurch. I remembered Grace saying many times, *"Be careful what you wish for."* I tried to brace myself for his explanation, suddenly not wanting to know anything about the woman. I should have kept my big mouth shut.

"Gina"—he began, and I let out a groan. Even the woman's name sounded exotic—"is going through a rough time."

A rough time? That wasn't exotic. That was lame.

"Her husband can't decide if he wants to stay married, and it's tearing her up inside."

Oh, brother! That was probably the second-oldest excuse in the book, trailing only the my-husband-doesn't-understand-me lament.

"Let me guess," I said. "She turned to you for comfort."

Marco gave me a quizzical look. "Why wouldn't she? I'm her brother."

I almost swallowed my tongue. "Gina is your sister?"

"I told you about her."

"Is she the one with the little boy?"

"No, that's my other sister. This is the one who married the used-car salesman."

"No, Marco, you've never mentioned her. I would have remembered."

He looked puzzled for a moment, then his face cleared. "You thought I was dating her, didn't you?"

My thumbnail suddenly needed my undivided attention. "Yes—not that it matters." I could say that now only because I knew who the woman was.

"You were jealous of my little sister." His eyes crinkled with laughter.

"I wasn't jealous. It was more like a slight twinge of envy."

"*Envy?*"

"Whatever. Like you've never felt that way."

"I didn't say that." He suddenly looked uncomfortable.

I blinked, trying to understand. "What are you saying? You *have* been jealous? Over me?"

"I didn't say that either. On a completely different topic, I happened to see you leaving with your ex-fiancé yesterday—not that it mattered."

A different topic? Right. "Grandma Osborne was on the lam and Pryce asked me to help find her."

"But why did he ask for *your* help?"

Was that a glimmer of jealousy in Marco's eyes? I decided to play naive and see. "I guess Pryce thinks I'm a good detective." I shrugged. "Go figure."

"So . . . how did that work out?"

"I found her."

"And Pryce was grateful?"

"Highly grateful."

Exactly how high would that be? his gaze asked, and that's when I knew I had him. Strangely, now that I'd proved I could make Marco jealous, I didn't feel good about letting him suffer. "You know what?" I said with a smile. "I couldn't care less about his gratitude. I mean, come on. We're talking about *Pryce,* for God's sake."

Marco cupped his palm against the side of my face, his eyes searching mine. For a moment we simply gazed at each other. His face was absolutely still, preventing me from reading his thoughts, but that didn't stop me from drinking in those dark eyes, that firm mouth, that strong, straight jaw that just begged to be nuzzled . . .

I held my breath and waited.

Suddenly, his mouth curved into that sexy grin, and just like that we were copacetic. Even the knot in my stomach had eased. More important, something had strengthened between us, a bond that would have to be explored when the time was right. But not yet.

"We've got work to do," he said as he got to his feet, all business once again. "And just so you know, I negotiated a temporary cease-fire between my sister and her husband." He went to his desk and pulled out a fresh sheet of paper. "Now, tell me what Morgan said."

I gave him the scoop on Richard's arrest, then flipped open my pad and read him my notes on the autopsy report. After Marco had finished making his own notations, I said, "It seems like the police are so focused on Richard that they're missing the obvious. Look at this. The time of death is listed as approximately nine thirty p.m. We know Josiah and Melanie didn't get to Mrs. Walsh's house until a little after ten. That would leave plenty of time for Josiah to do Jack in. So put that together with the fistfight and the lies Josiah told, and there you have it— the perfect suspect. Why are the cops ignoring that?"

"Probably because they have more on Richard. His arrest down in Texas must have tipped the scales against him. Trust me, cops don't take murder charges lightly."

I sat back in frustration. "So how do we get them to take a closer look at Josiah?" My stomach growled, reminding me it hadn't been fed recently. "Are you going to eat the rest of those nachos?"

Marco pushed the plate toward me. "Help yourself."

As I scarfed down the food, he said, "Here's what I think you should do. Start with the weakest link—Melanie. If you can make her believe you have proof that she had a hand in Jack's death, she might be frightened enough to tell you what really happened."

"You keep using the word *you*—as in me. Aren't you going with me?"

"If you want me to. This is your case, sunshine. I'm just backup."

It sounded like a plan to me. I phoned Mrs. Walsh and discovered that Josiah was out in the field on his tractor. It was his usual custom to work until five o'clock, she told me. I glanced at my watch. Three o'clock. We had less than two hours.

We left Marco's car in Mrs. Walsh's driveway, then hiked to the Turners' house, keeping a sharp eye out for Josiah's tractor. Marco stood guard outside the house while I went to the door and knocked, hoping I could convince Melanie to let me into the house.

"I can't talk to you," I heard her call.

I peered through the screen door and saw her standing a few feet back. "Please, Melanie; I promise this won't take long. I just need to ask you a few questions about Jack. I know he came here to see you a few weeks ago."

The baby crawled up behind her and tried to pull herself up using the hem of Melanie's long cotton skirt. She picked the child up and moved closer to the door. "How did you know that?"

"A lot of things come out during an investigation, such as the fact that you lied about Josie being sick Monday night."

I saw her face turn white, so I moved in for the kill. "I don't personally think you killed Jack, but there's some strong evidence that says you had a hand in it, and I'd hate to see you arrested for something you didn't do. Think of Josie, Melanie. Who'd raise her if you went to prison?" It was pure bluff, but Marco had promised me it was an effective tactic.

Melanie bit her lower lip, and I could see she was wavering.

"I'll be gone before your father gets back," I said. "Just answer a few questions to clear up any doubt about your involvement."

She shifted the baby to her other hip, then glanced over my shoulder to the fields beyond the house. "Okay," she said, pushing the door open to admit me, "but you'll have to be quick."

I followed her into the big farm kitchen, an old-fashioned affair with a black-and-white linoleum floor, a coal black stove, laminated counter tops that were curling back at the outside edges, and a small, round-topped refrigerator that looked like it had been purchased in the nineteen sixties. Luckily, the windows were open, so Marco could position himself to listen in.

Melanie pulled out a chair at the pine table in the middle of the room and sat down with the baby on her lap. I followed her example and sat adjacent to her, leaving my notebook in my purse on the floor beside my chair. I didn't want to pull it out just yet. I needed time to let her feel safe with me.

She ran her fingers through the baby's fine brown hair, not looking at me. "What do you want to know?" Her voice was a mixture of wariness and defiance.

"Why Jack came back to the reception after the fight with your father." I waited for her to answer, and when she only continued to stroke the child's hair I decided to try a long shot. "He came back to see you, didn't he?"

Her chin started to quiver and her eyes filled with tears. She pulled a tissue from her skirt pocket, wiped her eyes, and was on the verge of speaking when Josie started banging on the table with her plump baby hands, clamoring, "Ma-ma-ma-ma."

"I'm sorry," Melanie said, sniffling, and set Josie on the floor between our chairs. She gave her a stack of plastic measuring cups to play with, then sat down again and folded her hands on the table. "I hadn't heard from Jack in months, then one day he showed up here begging me and Josie to go with him to see his mother. He told me she was dying of lung cancer and he'd get his inheritance only if his mother believed he'd be a responsible father to Josie. Otherwise she'd leave everything to his brother. But I knew that even if she left Jack the money, we'd never see a penny of it, and I wasn't about to lie to a dying woman, so I told him I wouldn't do it. What kind of person would ask me to lie to his own mother on her deathbed?"

Now I understood why Jack had come back. It wasn't that he cared for Melanie or wanted to start supporting his child; it was all for money. Not wanting to break Melanie's concentration, I eased my notebook and pen out of my purse and made quick notes as she wiped bitter tears off her cheeks.

"When Jack finally got it through his head that I wasn't going to change my mind, he tried to convince me he had a big deal in the works and that he was about to come into some money that he'd split with me right away—but I'd still have to go with him to visit his mother. I asked him what this big deal was, but all he'd say was that he had a contact at a bank, some woman he'd started seeing.

"It was one scam after another with Jack." Melanie stopped to wipe her eyes and blow her nose. "The next time I saw him was at Jillian's wedding."

I glanced down by my chair and saw Josie happily rooting through my purse. She looked up and smiled at me, a tube of lipstick in one hand, a tampon in the other. I gently dislodged both items and decided to keep my purse in my lap. "Did Jack know you were going to be there?"

"I'm sure he figured it out. It was no secret that Jillian was having a big wedding."

I read over the questions Marco and I had crafted. "Did you see Jack dressed in a waiter's uniform?"

"I was aware of a waiter clearing away the empty plates at our table, but I didn't really notice him in that costume. Then I heard his voice in my ear and I panicked. The last thing I wanted was for my father to recognize him and cause another scene. So I excused myself from the table to go to the ladies' room, knowing Jack would follow me. That's when he told me he had great news about his so-called big deal. I told him I didn't want to hear about it and that I had to go back to the table before my father caught us, but he grabbed my hand and wouldn't let go until I'd promised to meet him at the gazebo. 'Be there in fifteen minutes, Mel,' he said."

Her voice broke on the last sentence. She held the tissue to her eyes for a long time, then took a shaky breath. "I'm sorry."

"That's okay. I know it's upsetting to you. What time did that conversation take place?"

"I'm not sure. Around nine fifteen, I think."

"Did you keep that meeting with Jack?"

"No," she said at once. "I couldn't have even if I'd wanted to. We left almost immediately after that."

"I know Josie wasn't sick, Melanie. So what was your hurry?"

She looked away, her face a mask of anguish.

"Did you tell your father that Jack asked you to meet him in the gazebo?"

"I had to," she cried. "When I went back to our table I tried to pretend nothing had happened, but my father can read me like a book. He kept at me until I confessed everything." She covered her face, weeping softly.

"Melanie?" I waited until she lifted her head to look at me, then I said, "Did your father meet Jack in the gazebo?"

Her chin quivered and tears spilled onto her cheeks. "I don't know," she said, then broke into heavy sobs. Upon hearing her mother's distress, Josie joined in, holding out her chubby arms for her mother to pick her up.

Melanie wiped the tears from her own face, then plucked her baby from the floor and bounced her on her lap, murmuring soothing words against the top of her head until she quieted. Josie hiccuped noisily a few times, then spotted my green pen with BLOOMERS printed on it. She stretched out a hand, making grunting noises until I rolled it across the table and got another one from my purse. Josie grabbed the pen and banged it against the wood, her tears forgotten.

"Tell me exactly what happened after you told your father what Jack said."

Melanie sniffled a few times. "He was furious. He told me to stay put, that he'd see to everything. I begged him not to make a scene but he said he only had to use the restroom. When he came back he was in a terrible temper and he wouldn't talk to me, except to say we had to get home."

"How long was he gone?"

"Ten minutes . . . I don't know. It seemed like forever." She gazed at me through red-rimmed eyes and whispered raggedly, "I think he killed Jack."

I was stunned that she'd admitted it. "Did you tell this to the police?"

She grasped my hand, squeezing it in her cold one. "I can't tell them. My father—"

With a frightened gasp she turned toward the window. In the distance I could hear a tractor engine chugging. We both glanced at the clock on the wall. It was only three forty-five.

Melanie jumped to her feet. "He must be coming in for more fuel. You have to leave right now."

I had no problem with that.

CHAPTER TWENTY

Clutching the baby in one arm, Melanie ran up the hall to the screen door and pushed it open, and I dashed out. My heart raced as I rounded the corner and nearly ran into Marco. He grabbed my shoulders to steady me.

"Josiah is coming," I said, breathing hard. "We need to leave—now."

"Let's go." He strode off toward the car with me right behind. We slid in, he started the motor, and we took off.

I swivelled to watch out the rear window, and once we were well away from the farm I turned excitedly. "Did you hear what Melanie said? She thinks her father killed Jack. Isn't that great news?" I pounded the dashboard excitedly.

"You did a good job, sunshine. Congratulations."

I opened my purse and dug through the contents. "I have to call Reilly and let him know he's arrested the wrong man."

"Whoa. You're getting ahead of yourself. Melanie's confession doesn't clear Richard. It only throws doubt on her father's story. If you call Reilly and tell him he made a mistake, he'll get defensive, and you'll never get his co-operation. What you need to do is *share* this with him and hope he'll decide to give Josiah a closer look. That was the original plan, wasn't it?" Marco handed me his cell phone. "He's in my phone book. Give him a call and ask him sweetly if he'll meet with us."

I could do sweetly. I held the phone to my ear and waited while it rang. After the eighth ring I was all prepared to leave a message when he answered. I stammered in surprise, "Reilly! You're there."

"Brilliant deduction, Sherlock," he growled.

I pressed my lips into a thin line, a good retort on the tip of my tongue.

"Sweetly," Marco reminded me.

Right. This was going to be harder than I thought. "Sherlock. Haha. That's funny, Reilly," I said, forcing a laugh.

"All right, what gives?" he demanded.

"Marco and I were just sitting here chatting about how you—being the top-notch cop you are—might be interested in some new information that's come to light about Jack Snyder's murder."

I glanced at Marco and he gave me a thumbs-up.

"I thought I told you to bug Detective Williams about the case," Reilly snapped.

"Right. Like I'd fall for that line again," I said, then got a poke in the arm from Marco.

"Sweetly," he warned.

"What I meant, Reilly, was that Marco told me *you* were the go-to man."

"The goat what?"

My sweetness subscription was about to expire. "Not *goat*. Go-to. Go. To."

Marco held out his hand and I gave him the phone.

"Hey, man, it's me. Gotta talk. Okay." He glanced at me as he dropped the phone in his pocket. "It's all set. We're meeting him at the bar at five o'clock."

"You got all that in two seconds?"

"You'd have to be male to understand."

Thank goodness that would never happen.

With an hour to go before our meeting with Reilly, I hurried back to Bloomers, praying Grace hadn't heard the news about Richard's arrest, but I was too late.

"I sent Grace home," Lottie told me. "She got a phone call that upset her so much she was shaking. She tried to pretend nothing was wrong—you know how she is—but she couldn't even pour coffee without spilling it. I told her to take off early."

"Damn. I wanted to tell her myself and soften the blow."

"What blow? What did she hear?"

I let out my breath. "That Richard was arrested for Jack's murder."

Lottie gasped. "Oh, dear Lord. No wonder she was shaking. Poor Gracie. After all these years she finally meets someone she cares for—and this has to happen." She paused. "You don't think Richard is guilty, do you?"

"No, I don't. Not after what Melanie told me. Josiah Turner is the one who should be in jail, and now I've got to meet with Reilly and convince him of that."

"Is there anything I can do?"

"Call Grace and tell her that justice will prevail."

Lottie gave me a high five and went to the phone. I crossed my fingers and hoped my message would make Grace feel better, because it wasn't working on me.

*   *   *

At six minutes after five o'clock, Marco slid into the booth beside me. Just my luck, I was too keyed up to appreciate that the man with the sexiest swagger in town was sitting inches away. All I could think of was how Grace must be suffering.

Marco put a hand on the back of my neck and kneaded the muscles. "Relax, will you?"

Relax? When Richard's life was at stake? I stopped drumming my fingers on the table so I could look at my watch. "Where's Reilly? He said he'd meet us at five."

"He'll be here. Do you want a drink?" He motioned to Kim, one of the waitresses, who came right over.

"I'll have an iced tea," I told her. "I need to keep a clear head so I can present my case . . . I can see you rolling your eyes, Marco. Don't make fun. I'm serious about this."

"I'm not making fun, and you're not presenting a case. We're trying to get him on our side so we can gently steer him toward Josiah. We have to be smooth about this, sunshine, so we don't ruffle his feathers. Remember, Reilly's meeting with us as a favor to me. He doesn't have to do this. Now, how are you going to talk to him?"

"Sweetly," I grumbled.

As Kim was delivering my iced tea and two tall glasses of Beck's, Reilly strolled in, spotted us, and came over. He'd changed out of his uniform and into a tan knit shirt and a pair of blue jeans that fit him rather nicely.

He took a seat opposite us, and Marco pushed one of the beers toward him. "My treat. I thought I remembered it was your favorite."

I gave Marco a grateful glance. He knew how to do smooth.

Reilly nodded his thanks, took a long pull from the glass, then sat back with a sigh. "Long day."

"I'll bet it was," Marco said, "and I want to thank you for seeing us. I wouldn't have bothered you unless it was important."

"I appreciate that." Reilly eyed me as he took another sip, then said to Marco, "You want to tell me what this is about before she wiggles onto the floor?"

Marco gave me the nod, so I pulled out my notes and gave Reilly the whole accounting of my conversation with Melanie. Then I sat back to let the information sink in. "So there you have it. What do you think of Josiah now?"

Reilly looked skeptical. "Did Melanie see her father with Jack?"

"No," I replied.

"Did she say what he used as a weapon?"

I shook my head.

"Did her father confess anything to her?"

I toyed with my straw. I could see where he was going with this, and I didn't know how to stop him. "No, he didn't confess anything to her, but—"

"So what do you have? Her suspicion that he killed Jack? I can't go after Josiah for that."

"But he lied about the baby being sick," I said.

"So? What does that prove?"

"That he's a liar," I said, starting to bristle.

Marco laid a hand on my shoulder, his way of telling me to calm down. "You have to understand, Sean, Abby's assistant has been dating Richard Davis, so naturally Abby is concerned, and that can make her a little touchy at times. Do you guys really have a strong case against Davis? Is there anything you can tell us to help us out?"

Marco was so smooth, I could have ice-skated across his lap.

Reilly hesitated, his gaze moving from Marco to me.

"All right. I suppose I can tell you—it's going to be a matter of public record anyway. First of all, Davis has a strong motive. Jack stole a lot of money from him. Second, Davis has an alibi that can't be verified. Third, he was involved in a murder back in Texas a few years ago."

"How involved?" I asked.

"We're still trying to determine that. The detective who worked on the case is apparently away on a fishing trip."

You didn't even wait to find out if Richard was guilty before you arrested him? I wanted to say. But that wouldn't have been smooth, so I pressed my fingers against the icy glass, forced a smile, and tried a different tactic. "So did you ever recover a weapon?"

Reilly's response was on the flinty side. "No."

I felt Marco press his knee against mine in warning, but I forged ahead, knowing I might not get another opportunity. "What about the wedding video? Did Richard turn up on that?"

"No." Now his gaze was flinty, too.

"Have some sugar for your tea," Marco said, tossing a packet my way. He knew I never used sugar in iced tea.

"Okay, so here's a thought," I said, pushing the packet aside. "While you're waiting to hear from the detective in Texas, why can't you take another look at Josiah?"

Reilly finished his beer and set the glass down with a thunk. "You want me to take another look at him? Then give me something worth seeing." Abruptly, he stood up.

As we watched Reilly stride out of the bar, Marco said, "That wasn't smooth."

"I know and I hate myself for it."

"Yeah, right. Well, you can scratch Reilly from your resource list. We won't get any more cooperation from him."

"No, I mean it. I didn't want to alienate Reilly. I just got so frustrated with him that I couldn't help myself. Do you really think I blew it?"

"Yep."

"Maybe I should send him a big bouquet of daisies. No, make that roses. Nothing says *I'm sorry* like a dozen roses." At Marco's scowl I sighed and plopped my chin on my hand. "Okay, forget the roses. Would it help if I talked to Melanie again?"

"Would she talk to you after that close call you had?"

"Probably not. Do you want to have a sandwich with me? I don't think well when the gurgles from my stomach are louder than my thoughts."

Marco called Kim over to give her our orders, then we went back to brainstorming, although what my brain was doing would hardly be classified as a storm. A sprinkle maybe.

"Let's take another look at the suspects," Marco said. "You've crossed off Vince Vogel. What about Melanie?"

"I've crossed off Melanie, too."

"That leaves Richard and Josiah." He saw me about to object to Richard and held up a hand. "You have to leave him in until we hear from Texas."

"Fine. So we've got Richard and Josiah—and there's always the dishwasher, Gunther. We've never really checked out his story."

"Remind me about Gunther."

I counted off what I knew on my fingers. "Gunther knew Jack from prison. He left work after the wedding ceremony without telling his boss. He wears a white coat. And he takes out the garbage—although he denied that he'd taken it out Monday night. I told you Grandma saw someone with a garbage bag, right?"

"It's thin," Marco said. "Besides, I'm sure Gunther has

been cleared by the police. They would have interviewed all the banquet center employees."

I held up my hands. "Then I'm stumped. I don't know what else to do."

Marco sat back, thinking, and finally shook his head. "We need a fresh lead, sunshine, otherwise this investigation is dead in the water."

Which meant Richard was in trouble big-time.

CHAPTER TWENTY-ONE

Since I'd taken so much time off work, I left Marco's bar and went back to Bloomers to do a little catching up—opening mail, paying bills, and taking care of orders that had come in after the shop had closed. When I finally locked up and headed for home, the sun had set, so I flicked on the headlamps, buckled my seat belt, and eased out of the parking space. I drove with the top down and the radio on, but I was too preoccupied with the murder case to enjoy the ride.

It wasn't until I was almost home that I noticed that the same pair of headlights had been behind me for a long time. I noticed them because the left one was dimmer than the right. I turned on the next street to take a different route, just to be on the safe side, then I glanced in the mirror and the headlights were gone. With a sigh of relief, I pulled into the parking lot, got out of the car, and started for the building.

Suddenly, the slam of a car door made me jerk to the left, where I saw a figure in black move quickly toward me. There was no question that the person was coming at me.

"Back off!" I shouted, threading my keys through my fingers to use as a weapon.

"Abigail, it's me," came a whispered female voice.

I let my breath out in a rush. "Aunt Corrine? What are you doing here?"

She got closer and I could see the lower half of her face beneath a wide-brimmed black hat. "I brought you this," she whispered. She pulled something out of her black raincoat and slipped it to me. "It's the video."

"It's not raining. Why are you dressed like that?"

She glanced over her shoulder. "I don't want anyone to see us."

"Did you follow me home?"

She nodded. "I didn't frighten you, did I? I'm sorry, darling. It's just that—you know—my community standing is at stake." She patted my cheek. "I'm so glad you're taking care of this for us. Your mother would be proud of you—but you mustn't tell her. She'd love nothing more than . . . well, that's not important now. What's important is that we're no longer hiding evidence."

I glanced at the plastic case in my hand, on which she'd written in black marker *Jillian's Wedding*. That gave me an idea. I wasn't going to be turning it in until morning, so in the meantime, would it hurt to preview it?

But first there was the little matter of my fee. I had to ask for it before Lottie sent out that statement. "Aunt Corrine," I said, as she started away.

She stopped and glanced back with a smile. "Yes?"

I opened my mouth, but the words wouldn't come out. What was wrong with me? "Get your headlights checked. One of them looks weak."

Simon was waiting for me in the kitchen doorway. I bent to scratch under his chin, but he was already moving toward the refrigerator door, where he put one paw on the door and looked up at me with an innocent expression.

"Don't feed him," I heard Nikki call. "He ate an hour ago."

I set the DVD on the counter and walked into the living room, where Nikki was lounging on the sofa in shorts and a tank top, watching a show on TV that appeared to be about a bunch of really filthy, half-naked men and women holding a powwow. "What are you doing home so early?" I asked her.

"I traded today for my Saturday off. One of the other techs needed to take her son to the doctor . . . Is that a worry line between your eyes? Did something happen?"

I felt the area between my eyebrows. Yep, there it was—a worry line. "Something happened all right. Richard Davis was arrested."

"Oh, no. That's awful."

"No kidding. And I'm completely out of ideas on how to help him. Even Marco is stumped." I sank down on the sofa and leaned my head against the back. "I feel terrible, Nikki. I let Grace down."

"I'm so sorry." She patted my shoulder just as Simon jumped up, plopped on my lap, and started to clean his paw.

"Look there," Nikki said, getting up. "Simon is sorry, too. Do you want a beer or wine or something?"

"I'll take anything, as long as it's cold."

"What's this?" she called from the kitchen. "Did you rent a movie?"

"That's the wedding video Jillian managed to sneak out from under the cops' noses. My aunt dropped it off. I have the privilege of turning it in to the police so my cousin doesn't get into trouble."

"I don't know how you put up with Jillian."

"At least now that the wedding is over I won't have to see her often."

"You're going to watch the video before you turn it in, right?"

"You read my mind. I probably shouldn't—I'm pretty certain it would still be considered evidence—but I've reached the point of desperation. Do you want to watch it now?"

Nikki came back with two cold cans of Miller Lite and the DVD. "And miss another fascinating episode of *Survivor*? Puh-leez." She snorted. "Let's do it."

I powered on the DVD player, inserted the disk, punched the Play button, and sat down beside Nikki on the sofa.

"Okay, what are we searching for?" she asked.

"I don't know. Just keep your eye out for anything that seems out of place or unusual."

The video began with Jillian mugging for the camera as she sat in a chair at the beauty salon, having her hair and manicure done. "She shouldn't use so much conditioner," Nikki commented. "It makes her hair look oily."

I fast-forwarded through images of Jillian applying mascara, being zipped into her gown, getting in and out of the rented white stretch limo, waiting inside the glass doors with all the bridesmaids lined up in front of her, and sticking her tongue out at the camera as the music started.

"Oh, look. There you are," Nikki said. "That dress doesn't look any better on film, does it?"

The next scene showed Jillian and her father walking up the aisle, with all of us evenly spaced in front of her. "You really are short next to those girls," Nikki remarked. "Omigod, there's Marco. Could he be any yummier in that tux? And what's up with Pryce? He looks like a stone statue. Claymore isn't much better. If he stood any straighter he'd fall over. Remind me what Jillian sees in him again? Oh, right. Money."

The camera panned the crowd and I pointed out my brothers and their wives, Melanie and Josiah, and various Knight relatives and friends.

"So, what are we looking for again?" Nikki asked.

"Anything unusual. And keep your eye out for Jack in his waiter's disguise."

"I'm not sure I remember what he looks like."

I jumped up to get the newspaper photo out of my purse. As I returned with it she pointed to the screen and said, "There's something unusual."

I hit Pause. "What? I don't see anything."

"You don't see that Afghan hound sitting in the third row next to that man with the rug on his head?"

"That's not an Afghan hound; that's Claymore's cousin Arielle, and the man with the rug is Claymore's uncle Oscar."

"Someone needs to get Arielle on *Extreme Makeover, Wedding Edition*."

"Are you going to provide commentary throughout the entire video?"

"Yeah. It'd be pretty boring otherwise."

The ceremony began and we watched silently until Nikki suddenly cried, "Stop!"

I hit the Pause button again. "What?"

"You didn't tell me about your fall. Rewind that last part. I want to see it again." She reached for the remote and I held it away.

"We're looking for evidence, Nikki, not for laughs. Get ready. Here comes the fight."

As the minister talked to the bride and groom, a bellow could be heard in the background. The cameraman turned the lens toward the back of the garden, where Josiah was clearly visible pounding the heck out of Jack. Then the view was blocked when everyone around them jumped to their feet. I hit the Rewind button, then we watched it again.

"Who are those people standing in front of the banquet center?" Nikki asked.

I paused the tape and Nikki pointed to three white-coated figures. I got down on my knees in front of the TV for a better look. "That one is Sheila Sackowitz." I tapped the first little figure on the screen. "She works in the kitchen. She mentioned she'd snuck out to watch the ceremony. I've seen the woman beside her, too. She's one of the cooks."

"Ew. Bad hair day for her. Who's the ape-man?"

I squinted at the blurred face. "It looks like Gunther."

"The dishwasher, right?"

"Right."

"So he saw the fight with Jack Snyder, whom he knew from prison."

I turned to look at her. "That's right. Interesting connection, isn't it?"

I hit the Play button and we watched as Jack was escorted out of the garden and Josiah was taken to the banquet center. The three white-coated figures had disappeared. Then the ceremony resumed, followed shortly by the fireworks display. The cameraman had apparently been unable to decide which to film, so he filmed a little of both, moving back and forth until we were dizzy from watching it.

"Jillian's going to love that," Nikki remarked.

"They can edit it out. There was another cameraman filming the ceremony. Jillian made sure she was covered from all angles."

The next scene showed the bridal party forming a receiving line just inside the banquet center doors. The first guest to come through was Vince Vogel, who offered his congratulations then turned and headed out again, dodging guests streaming in from the garden. Through the glass doors I caught a glimpse of Richard and Grace standing on the sidewalk outside, a cell phone pressed to Richard's ear.

At that moment one of the guests blocked the camera lens, but in the next frame I could see Richard put away his phone, give Grace a kiss on the cheek, then head off to the left, toward the parking lot.

I stopped the tape. "There. Did you see that?"

"I saw Richard walk away. What does that prove?"

"That he didn't lie about getting a phone message. See the time stamp in the corner? It says eight forty-eight p.m., which verifies what he told me." I grabbed a piece of paper and pen and wrote it down.

Melanie Turner came into view next, offering Jillian and Claymore her best wishes. Her father was right behind, his frown lifting for a second as he congratulated the newlyweds.

"Want me to make popcorn?" Nikki asked.

"Not right now."

"How about decaf lattes?"

"Later."

She sighed and settled back against the sofa as a procession of guests paraded across the screen. After a few more minutes, she rose. "I'm taking a break. I need something to eat."

While she was gone I watched the bridal party troop back to the gazebo for posed photographs. While the photographers set up their shots, the cameraman panned the area, doing a circular sweep of the garden and surrounding area, then along the side of the building all the way to the rear, then continuing on around, catching the bridal party again as we went through various poses.

He kept turning until finally the parking lot came into view, panning past my yellow Vette and various Knight and Osborne family autos. I paused the image so I could take a closer look. There was no sign of Richard's red Cadillac. The time stamp read 9:02 p.m.

Then the video cut to the reception and Pryce's toast; the camera kept switching from him, to the guests falling asleep at the tables, to the waiters bringing in trays of food. I watched closely, hoping for a glimpse of Jack in his waiter's disguise.

Nikki returned with a big bowl of popcorn, which we nibbled as we watched Jillian and Claymore make their way among the tables to greet the guests. I spotted the waiter Kevin and was about to point him out to Nikki when suddenly the camera panned to the back of the room, and there was Melanie talking to Jack.

"There they are!" I cried, hitting Pause. "Just like Melanie described. Look at the time stamp. It's nine twenty."

The video played for a few more minutes, then suddenly we saw Josiah barreling toward the exit. "And there he goes!" I shouted, jumping to my feet. Simon's back arched in alarm, then he jumped from the sofa and took off down the hallway. The time stamp on the video, I noted, read 9:29 p.m.

We hunched closer to the set, keeping our eyes sharply focused, but there were no further views of Josiah, Melanie, or Jack. We watched as guests began to leave the ballroom, then the videographer filmed Jillian running out to the gazebo. But unlike the first cameraman, who followed her and had his memory cards confiscated, this one hung way back to pan the crowd behind the police lines. I didn't see either Melanie or Josiah, but I did spot Richard standing with Grace. "There, Nikki. That verifies that Richard was back by nine fifty."

"Does it help him?" Nikki asked, stuffing popcorn in her mouth.

"It shows that his car was gone before the murder and there after, which backs up the times he gave, and it also proves Melanie was telling the truth about talking to Jack and about her father leaving the ballroom afterward." I flopped against the back of the sofa. "But it's not enough to clear Richard. I've got to find something else." I hit Rewind.

"What are you doing?"

"I'm going to watch it again. Maybe I missed something."

Nikki stuck it out with me, polishing off most of the popcorn followed by two glasses of water and her decaf latte, which prompted a trip to the washroom. She settled onto the sofa again just as the cameraman was panning the garden area. As the video rolled along the side of the building, Nikki said, "Pause it." Then she got right up to the television and tapped her finger against the screen. "Who are these people?"

I crouched beside her for a better look. At the back corner of the building was a figure in a white coat and part of a big green metal garbage bin. Then another white-coated image became visible, carrying a shiny black plastic bag, which he hefted into the air as if it weighed nothing and tossed into the receptacle. Then he turned and the two seemed to be talking. In fact, by their arm gestures, it looked more like an argument was under way.

"I can't make out their faces," Nikki said, squinting, "but doesn't it look like that white coat has tails?"

"Damn. It's so grainy . . . but I think you're right." I checked the time on the video: 9:27 p.m.—just minutes before the murder. "Nikki, that might be Jack!"

"Is there some way to get an enlargement of their faces?" Nikki asked.

"I'm sure there is. I'd have to call around town and see, but I'm supposed to turn the video in to the police in the morning."

"They don't know you have it, right? So would it hurt to keep it a little longer, and see if you can find someone who can enlarge that frame for you?"

"If Reilly finds out, I'll be in major trouble."

"Then you'll just have to make sure he doesn't. Now, what about this other guy?" She tapped the second face on the screen. "Could that be Gunther?"

"Gunther said he didn't take the garbage out that night because he'd already left, but you know what? He lied to me about knowing Jack. Why should I believe him about the garbage?"

I paused as a chilling thought popped into my brain. What if Gunther hadn't lied? What if that *was* Jack wearing the tailed coat and it was someone other than Gunther with him? I had to find out, because *that* person could have been the last one to see Jack alive . . . or the first one to see him dead.

I glanced at the clock on the bookcase. It was ten minutes after nine. Perfect.

"Where are you going?" Nikki called as I dashed to the kitchen for my purse and keys.

"To the banquet center. I've got to get to the bottom of this. Want to come?"

"Is there danger involved?"

"Possibly."

"Cool. I'm right behind you."

We took Nikki's car and pulled into the Garden of Eden at nine twenty. I had gambled that there would be an event taking place that night, so I was relieved to see that the parking lot was full. Armed with what I had seen on the video, I knew I had to confront Gunther, but first I wanted to stand where the cameraman had stood and watch Gunther's movements as he carried the garbage bag to the bins.

We crouched behind the shrubs in the garden area and waited.

"I hope they spray for mosquitoes out here," Nikki whispered, swatting at something.

"Keep your head down," I whispered back. "Gunther should be coming out any minute."

"We're not going to be able to see his face from here," she warned.

"Doesn't matter. Just watch how he moves."

I'd barely finished my sentence when Nikki grabbed my arm and shook it, whispering, "There he is."

I held my finger to my lips and watched as someone in a white coat came out with a garbage bag and hefted it into a bin.

"Is it him?" Nikki whispered.

"It's him."

I heard a gasp and looked around just as Nikki fell back onto the lawn, shaking her leg and slapping her right thigh, then her rear. I turned to shush her, but she was in a panic. "Spider," she said in a barely audible shriek. "I think it crawled into my shorts."

Fearing Gunther had heard her racket, I raised my head to peer above the shrubs.

Oh, yeah. He'd heard. "Get ready," I said. "Here he comes."

CHAPTER TWENTY-TWO

Because I believe that the best defense is a good offense, I jumped up, helped Nikki to her feet, and whispered, "Act fearless." Then, with her behind me, I strode out of the garden area and met Gunther halfway. "I was hoping to find you," I told him.

"Were you spying on me?"

"How dare you make such crazy insinuations!" Nikki said—staying safely behind me.

"It's okay, Nikki. Gunther knows I'm collecting information on the murder case."

His nostrils flared and his beady eyes narrowed. "I thought I told you to leave me alone."

"You did, and I have, but something just came to light and I thought you should know about it."

"You have a really short memory, don't you? The cops *cleared* me. You got that now?"

At least he hadn't called me stubby. I knew he was about to turn away, so I blurted, "The thing is, Gunther, I have a video of Monday night's wedding that shows you taking out the garbage."

That took him by surprise. He took a step closer and shook a huge fist in my face. I felt Nikki shrink back, but I held my ground.

"I didn't *take* out the garbage Monday night!" he shouted in my face, his onion-laced breath nearly making me gag.

"So you say," I muttered.

He looked like he was ready to pop me in the jaw. "Go ask around the kitchen!"

"I already did."

"Someone told you I took it out? Who? Was it that gossipy bitch Sheila?"

I gave him a little shrug. "I can't reveal my sources."

His jaw muscles were working overtime and his hands twitched as though he were ready to plant a few black-and-blue marks on my face. Then suddenly his whole body relaxed and a sly look came over his face. "You think I don't know what you're doing? Well, guess what? I do. You're trying to trap me into saying something. The thing about that is, I didn't do anything, so pull up your trap and *go home*." This time he did walk away, smugly.

Frustrated, I called, "Oh, yeah? Well, the police might have second thoughts once they see the video."

It didn't faze him. He lumbered around the corner and was gone. My plan had failed.

"I don't think you should have told him about the video, Abby," Nikki said.

"I know. It was an amateurish thing to do. It just slipped out." In fact, as soon as those words had come out of my mouth I knew I'd goofed. I had a sudden image of Marco saying, *You have to be smooth, sunshine.* I was so far from smooth I could have sanded the bark off a tree.

"Nikki," I said, as we headed toward her car, "let's just keep that little slip between us, okay?"

When I walked into Bloomers the next morning, no one called out, "Good morning, dear. How are we today?" No coffee machine gurgled. No one hummed in the parlor. "Grace didn't make it into work?" I asked Lottie as she came through the curtain.

"You just missed her call. She isn't feeling well, so I told her to stay home and rest. Did you see the morning paper?"

"I did, but I wish I hadn't." Richard's arrest had made the front page.

"I'm sure seeing that didn't make Grace feel any better," Lottie said. "I made instant coffee, if you want some."

We sat down together as we usually did, and discussed the orders for the day, but it didn't feel right without Grace there. "I think I'll go see her at lunch," I said. "Maybe I can cheer her up."

I took my messages from the spindle and looked them over as I headed toward the workroom. Two were from my mother, reminding me of our family dinner at the country club that evening, a ritual that I forced myself to endure because it made her happy. Life with an unhappy mother was not a pleasant experience. The other message was from Pryce. It said only that he would call back. I crumpled it up and tossed it in the wastebasket.

I glanced at my watch. I really wanted to discuss the video with Marco, but it was too early to call. I had learned never to phone him before nine o'clock because of the late hours he worked. I picked up the handset at my desk and called my mother instead.

"So you haven't left the country after all," she said, breathing hard, probably walking on her treadmill.

"It's not that I haven't thought about you," I hastily assured her.

"You had time to talk to Aunt Corrine."

The blade of guilt sliced through my rib section. "She stopped by, Mom. I didn't call her. Anyway, I'll have a chance to chat with you this evening."

"Oh, you're going to squeeze us in, then."

No one could heap on the guilt like my mother.

"By the way, have you been paid for the wedding flowers?"

She had to be psychic. "What made you think of that?" I asked.

"Well, you said your aunt stopped by, so I assumed it was to pay you. She did pay you, didn't she? Abigail? Why are you hesitating?"

"Okay, let's just suppose someone in your family owed you money and didn't seem to remember that she owed it. Would you, A, wait for her to remember or, B—"

"Aha!" she cried triumphantly. "I thought so. Do you want me to call her? I'll pick up the phone right now. Just say the word."

Across from me, Lottie was shaking her head, as if she couldn't believe what I'd just done.

"No, Mom . . . thanks just the same. Think about how it would look for me to send my mother to collect my fees. Not so good."

"I suppose you're right. But you know how I worry and you said money was tight. You're not behind on the mortgage, are you?" She held the phone away to say loudly, "Jeff, your daughter is in financial trouble."

"Mom! No! That's not it. The bank isn't foreclosing. I'm holding my own. I just didn't know if I should send a bill, or call Aunt Corrine to remind her, or write it off."

My mother held the phone away again and called in a

cheery voice, "Never mind, Jeff." Then to me she said firmly, "Send her a bill."

"Thanks for the advice," I said. "I'll see you at seven o'clock tonight."

"Wear something nice, Abigail."

Damn! I had been planning to wrap myself in a bath rug. I glanced at Lottie, who was looking rather pleased with herself. "Your mom said to send your aunt a bill, didn't she?"

"You know she did."

"And?"

"I'll send it."

"Good girl."

But I hadn't said when. I decided it might be a better idea to mention it to Jillian first to save face all the way around.

With Grace gone, Lottie and I had to take turns manning the parlor. Lottie took the first shift at nine o'clock so I could call Marco. As it turned out, I could have called much earlier.

"You've been up since seven?" I asked in amazement.

"Remember that cease-fire I negotiated?" he said in a quiet voice, as though he didn't want to be overheard. "It fell through." In the background I could hear a woman weeping. "So what's up?" he asked.

"Go take care of your sister. This can wait until later."

"Sunshine, will you just spit it out?"

I was hoping he'd say that. First, I gave him a rundown on what I'd learned about Richard's coming and going from the video. As I suspected, Marco didn't think it would be enough to convince the cops to change their minds. So I went on to describe the little figures in the white coats, and then I told him about my confrontation with Gunther at the banquet center.

"You confronted him alone?" Marco sputtered in disbelief. "What were you thinking?"

"I had to find out who those two figures on the video were. I suspected one was Jack and the one with the garbage bag was Gunther, but I couldn't see the faces clearly enough to recognize them. Then I thought, what if Gunther was telling the truth? Maybe he wasn't the one who took the garbage out Monday night. But that raised the question of who did. Which led me to the conclusion that whoever is on that video might be the killer. Anyway, I didn't go alone. Nikki was with me."

"Thank God for that. You didn't tell Gunther about the video, did you?"

I twirled a strand of my hair. "Well, it kind of came up in conversation."

I thought I heard Marco's teeth grinding. "I can't believe you did that."

"He made me angry."

"So you just *blurted* it out about the video?"

"I think we've already established that."

There was a long pause, then Marco said in a very controlled tone, "Let me clue you in on something, sunshine. One of the first things you learn in the police academy is to keep your cool and make your suspect blurt things out, not the other way around."

"I know. You're absolutely right. I have to learn better control."

"There you go."

"It's just that I get furious when someone tries to push me around."

"I know you do. That's okay. You're learning. Just try not to do it again, okay?"

"Okay."

"Now, you have to turn that video over to the police. You can't hold on to evidence."

"I'd really like to identify those two faces before I do that."

"Listen to me carefully. You've done enough. Turn it in and let the police draw their own conclusions." The weeping in the background turned to wails. "I've got to go."

I heard the call-waiting tone and said, "Me, too. I just got a beep. Have fun." Then I hit the Flash button and said, "Hello?"

"Abby, hey, it's Joey. Is my mom there?"

"Hold on." I went up to the front, got Lottie on the phone, and took over for her in the parlor. A moment later the phone slammed and I saw her storm back to the workroom, so I followed to see what had happened.

"I'm going to wring Karl's neck," Lottie ranted, grabbing her purse. "He snuck off to the DeWitts' this morning instead of going to work. Just wait till I get my hands on that kid. I'll be back as soon as I pick him up."

"Whoa, Lottie. Calm down. You can't drive over there in that temper. I wouldn't want to be in the car in front of you. Let me go. I have to make a delivery anyway."

I wrapped up the arrangement I'd just finished, hopped in the Vette, and took off. Damn Karl's teenage hormones. I didn't have time to deal with his lust. I had a killer to find.

I ran through the video in my mind, picturing quick flashes of Josiah and Jack fighting, Gunther watching the fight from a distance, Jack being assisted to his car, then reappearing later as a waiter. Then I pictured the scene in the ballroom—guests eating, waiters serving, Melanie talking to Jack, her father rushing out soon after. What about the dance scene? What about the reception line?

What about when the photographer had run out after Jillian to see the dead body? Had I missed anything?

I pulled up in front of the big DeWitt manse just in time to see Don park his pickup truck at the back of the brick driveway. I jogged after him, into the backyard, and looked around in a panic, but there was no Don in sight. There was no Karl in sight either. I hurried up the wooden steps onto the big deck, where I came to a complete, horrified stop.

Lying on the chaise longue was a discarded white T-shirt imprinted with a rock band logo. Underneath the chaise were a pair of white socks and a scruffy pair of Nikes with no laces. I knew exactly whom they belonged to. But that wasn't the worst part. On the other chair was the top half of a pink bikini.

At least she still had on the bottoms. I hoped.

"Trudee?" I heard Don call in a voice heavy with suspicion. He must have seen the clothing, too.

I knocked on the screen door, but he didn't hear me, so I slid it open and stepped inside. "Don? It's me, Abby."

"Trudee?" I heard again, from the front of the house.

With my heart in my throat, I raced up a hallway and came out in the foyer. Don stood at the bottom of the stairs, hands on his hips and a murderous look on his face. He glanced at me in surprise. "Abby?"

"Listen, Don, I know this looks bad, but—"

From above there was a heavy thump, then feet running.

"Trudee!" he bellowed, starting up.

Suddenly a door opened in the upstairs hall and seconds later a familiar female head appeared—not a blond, Barbie doll head, but a spiky pink head with raccoon eyes that were wide with alarm. "Dad?" Heather asked. "What's wrong?"

"Where's your mother?"

"I don't know. Shopping maybe?"

At that moment another head appeared, followed by a half-naked body.

"Karl!" I gasped.

"What are you doing up there, boy?" Don demanded. "And where's your shirt?"

I could see Karl's throat muscles move as he swallowed. "I was h-hot, s-sir. I left it outside."

"Dad, chill out!" Heather exclaimed. "I have a test tomorrow and Karl offered to tutor me. Summer school algebra, remember? We were studying on the deck and got all sweaty, so we came inside to cool off. Geez."

I motioned for Karl to come down. "Your mother is waiting for you. We have to go."

Karl and Heather exchanged longing looks, then she said, "Call me?"

He beamed happily and trooped down the steps. I had to press my lips together to keep from laughing. I'd thought Karl was hanging around the house because of Trudee, and he'd only been trying to see Heather.

"See there? Everything worked out," I said to Don.

He motioned me to one side. "I'm sorry for bothering you with this. I feel so foolish."

I tried to think of one of Grace's quotes about foolishness, but all I could come up with was *A fool and his money are soon parted,* and somehow I didn't think he'd find that helpful. "I understand the feeling," I said and patted him on the back. Then I had Karl collect his clothing and I took him home.

When I got back to the shop, the parlor was bustling with clerks and secretaries on their midmorning breaks. I grabbed a coffeepot and for the next half hour we ran our tails off as tables filled and emptied and filled again.

By eleven the parlor had nearly emptied out, so Lottie returned to the workroom and I manned the cash register. I was ringing up the last customer when the bell jingled and Pryce strode in. He had on one of his custom-made suits—a sharply tailored navy gabardine with a white shirt and a red and navy patterned tie. He acknowledged me with a nod, then wandered into the coffee parlor and took a seat by the bay window.

Something was up. Pryce had never stopped in for coffee before.

I glanced toward the curtain, hoping Lottie would sense a disturbance in the force and come to my rescue, but she didn't, so I had no choice but to wait on him. "Fancy meeting you here," I said, strolling over. "What can I get for you?"

"How about"—he squinted at the chalkboard above the coffee counter on the back wall—"a decaf coffee with a sprinkle of cinnamon?"

"Anything to go with that? A scone? Chocolate biscotti?"

"What are you doing for lunch?"

"Lunch?" I sputtered. *Stop staring like an imbecile and say something! Tell him you're not taking a lunch break today because you're shorthanded.* But all I ended up saying was, "Why?"

"Because I thought maybe you'd want to grab a sandwich somewhere—with me."

For some reason, the only thing that I seemed capable of uttering was, "Why?"

"Why?" he repeated, looking puzzled. "Because I'm hungry?"

That was Pryce trying to be funny. "No, really," I said.

"I was just passing by and thought of you." He tried on a smile that was a little too tight.

I didn't buy it. Pryce never "just passed by" anywhere. His routes were carefully calculated for accuracy and expediency before he ever set foot on the sidewalk. I pulled out the wrought iron chair across from him and sat on it.

"Okay, that's it. I can't stand it any longer. You haven't given me the time of day for months on end, then suddenly you just happen to pass by my shop and—bingo—decide you want to have lunch with me? What's going on, Pryce? Are you"—*Did I dare say it?*—"angling for us to be an item again?"

He seemed taken aback. Then he shifted uncomfortably, adjusted his tie, and looked around, as if to be sure he wouldn't be overheard. "I'd hoped to have this conversation over a nice glass of chilled wine, but since you brought it up, there is something I've been wanting to discuss with you. I just wasn't quite sure how to go about it."

He glanced around again, then said, "Do you think I could get that coffee first?"

CHAPTER TWENTY-THREE

I poured Pryce's coffee, put a generous sprinkle of cinnamon in it, and took it back to the table. I tried to pretend I was sitting down with a casual acquaintance to discuss a movie I'd seen, but as I put the coffee in front of him I caught a whiff of his cologne and memories came flooding back, reminding me that we had once been much more than casual acquaintants and that what we were about to discuss was a whole lot different from critiquing a movie.

Could he be serious about getting back together?

I sat down across from him, watching as he lifted the cup to his lips. This was the man I'd wanted to spend my life with, have kids with, grow old with. Could I ever feel that way about him again? My mother would certainly be elated. She'd always felt Pryce was the one for me.

Then there was Marco. Just the thought of him was enough to produce a rush of excitement. Did I want to lose him? Did I even have him? Was there a future with him?

"Good coffee," Pryce said, savoring the first sip.

I folded my hands and put them on the table, trying not

to look as edgy as I felt. "So . . . what was it you wanted to discuss?"

For a moment he stared into the swirling depths of his coffee, as if trying to find just the right words, then he put down the cup, cleared his throat, and looked at me. "Do you remember that last Christmas we were together? We were alone in your apartment, you had music on, and I'd brought over that expensive bottle of champagne?"

He had to throw in the *expensive* part. I gave him a shrug, not wanting him to know that every moment of that night was crystal clear in my mind. It just wasn't something that could be put in a machine and taped over. "Vaguely."

"You gave me that black and yellow striped T-shirt—" which he'd said made him look like a giant bumblebee, and two days later exchanged for something more to his "taste"—"and I gave you that amethyst and pearl brooch."

I could see it all in my mind's eye. It was Christmas Eve and we were due to go to my parents' house for dinner. Nikki and I had put up a live tree too early that year and the needles had started to drop. Pryce had asked for the vacuum cleaner so he could clean them up. I even remembered the CD I'd put on—*A Rockin' Sockin' Christmas*. It hadn't been Pryce's favorite.

He reached across and put his hand over mine. "I pinned the brooch on your sweater and told you I wanted you to wear it because it had been passed down from my grandmother to my mother."

My stomach fluttered at the memory. It had been a very romantic moment, a rare occasion for Pryce. "I remember," I said, and I couldn't help but gaze at him with renewed affection.

"Could I have it back?"

I gave my head a little shake, in case my ears had become plugged and I'd heard him wrong. "I'm sorry. What?"

"That amethyst brooch. Could I have it back? It's a family heirloom. My mother asked me to ask you for it."

I blinked at Pryce, trying to wrap my mind around what he'd just said. The little voice in my head whispered, *What are you waiting for? Give him a good smack on the head and tell him to get lost. While you're at it, smack yourself for being an idiot.*

Since I wasn't about to pummel either one of us, I settled for pretending his request didn't faze me in the least.

"Sure," I said lightly, sliding my hand from beneath his. "You can have the brooch. Drop by the shop tomorrow and I'll have it here for you."

He pretended to wipe sweat from his forehead. "Whew. That went better than I expected. I was afraid you'd be—what's the word I'm looking for?—prickly."

"Me?" I exclaimed, trying to smile. "Prickly?"

He folded his arms and leaned back, grinning in that arrogant way of his. "I remember very well how prickly you'd get when you believed you'd been offended."

When I *believed* I'd been offended? "Really?" I said sweetly, plotting Pryce's swift demise.

"Oh, yeah." He rolled his eyes.

We laughed. Then I rose, picked up his cup of coffee, and poured it onto his lap.

"There's another one for your memory book, Pryce."

At noon, I got into the Vette and zipped over to Grace's tidy green bungalow on Greenleaf Street. The home was located on a narrow corner lot, with a small English garden on the side and a screened porch in the front. I let myself into the porch, then knocked on her door. "Grace, it's me," I said.

I heard her call, "Come in," so I opened the door and stepped into Grace's world.

There was a museumlike quality about her house—with furniture that smelled of beeswax, graceful wing-back chairs flanking lace-curtained windows, crocheted doilies adorning curved-leg cherry tables, and oil paint-ings of apples and pears decorating walls of creamy swirled plaster—yet it also had a sense of being lived in, with fabrics worn smooth and floorboards that creaked with age.

The house was long, its rooms telescoping from front to back—living room, dining room, kitchen. The two bedrooms were on the left side, one off the living room, the other off the dining room. The bath was off the kitchen, built in a day when the tubs sat on clawed feet and bathing was a Saturday observance.

Grace used the front bedroom as her office, and that's where I found her, sitting at her desk looking through a stack of papers. She saw me in the doorway and got up at once. And although she looked pale and gaunt, her first concern was for me. "Are you all right, dear?"

"I was just in the neighborhood and thought I'd drop by." I shrugged, like it was no big deal. "How are you?"

Tears filled her eyes, something I'd never seen before, but she quickly blinked them away. "I'm okay. Thank you for asking. Would you care for tea? I have a fresh pot steeping."

"Sounds great." Nothing made Grace happier than brewing tea.

"Have you had lunch?" she called, starting for the kitchen. "I have egg salad finger sandwiches in the icebox.

That's a refrigerator, dear, if you didn't know. Make yourself at home. I'll be back with a tray."

I wandered around the living room, a virtual museum of twentieth-century English culture. I bent to look at sepia-toned photos on top of the television in the corner and picked up my favorite, a snapshot of Grace's husband in his GI uniform. I admired her hand-painted plates and an assortment of china figurines in a corner hutch. Then I came to her office door and couldn't resist stepping inside to see my favorite collection of all—Grace's Elvis Presley memorabilia, three bookcase shelves dedicated to the King of Rock and Roll.

She had mugs and pencil holders, a two foot tall plaster bust of Elvis, a radio shaped like a pink Cadillac, a small dueling saber in a fancy sheath, a pair of miniature blue suede shoes, and a ceramic model of Elvis's home, Graceland. There was even an Elvis doll in a white sequined jumpsuit.

Then I spotted a framed black-and-white photo of Elvis in army uniform, tucked back in the corner. I hadn't noticed it before, so I picked it up for a closer look and saw something handwritten across the bottom. *To Grace, from your hound dog.* Underneath was a date: 1959.

From her hound dog? No way.

I heard the rattle of cups and went back to the living room just as Grace came through the wide arched doorway of the dining room. "Here we go," she said, setting the tray on the coffee table in front of the sofa. I took a seat, sniffing the gentle fragrance of oolong tea that wafted from the delicate china teapot hand painted with pale pink cabbage roses. On the tray were a matching sugar bowl and creamer, two cups in saucers, two tiny sterling teaspoons, white linen napkins, and a plate of sandwiches cut in thin strips.

"Would you mind pouring?" she asked. "My hands seem a bit unsteady."

I filled both cups, wondering whether talking about Elvis would cheer her up and take her mind off Richard, at least for a little while. Plus, I was nosy. "Grace, that autographed photo of Elvis Presley on your shelf—I've never seen it before. Where did you get it?"

"From Elvis. Didn't I tell you about that? Would you care for sugar?"

"No, thanks. I'm sure I would have remembered your meeting Elvis. How did it happen? What was he wearing? Was he hot? Did your husband meet him, too?"

She smiled at the memory. "It was a long time ago, before I met my husband. I believe I told you I was a nurse in the English army, stationed in Germany. Elvis was stationed there, too, and we struck up a friendship of sorts. When he got out of the army he sent me the autographed picture, and I've been a loyal fan ever since."

They'd struck up a friendship of sorts? I looked at Grace, trying to imagine her as a young, sexy nurse, someone who might catch the King's eye. Yes, I could see it. She had elegant features—high cheekbones, a generous mouth, a long, graceful neck—and a slender body that was once probably very curvy. Replace her short, gray, layered cut with long black hair and of course she would catch his eye. Was it merely a coincidence that Elvis had named his home *Graceland*?

Her hand shook as she lifted the teacup to her lips. She seemed to have aged five years in the past week. It reminded me of the reason I'd come. "I'm sorry about Richard's arrest."

She put down the cup with a sad sigh. "That poor man. He's been under such a terrible strain, first with the long interrogations, now this. They even had someone follow him to my house the other night. Richard said they'd probably tapped into his telephone line, too. He called me shortly before he turned himself in—his lawyer had notified him of the warrant. He tried to sound optimistic but I can tell he's worried. I just don't understand this investigation. Wouldn't you think someone would have seen him drive away from the banquet center after the ceremony, or have noticed his return? As you know, his Cadillac does attract attention."

"I have good news in that regard, Grace. I viewed one of Jillian's wedding videos—I'll tell you how I ended up with it some other time—and it clearly shows Richard leaving the banquet center when he said he did. It also shows that his car wasn't in the parking lot at the time of the murder."

Her eyes lit up. "That's wonderful, Abby."

"There's more. On the video, just before the time of the murder, two tiny faces in white coats appear. I think one of them is Jack, and the other might be the killer, but I can't see the faces well enough to identify them. But if the police can enlarge it—"

Grace sat forward excitedly. "Do you still have the video?"

"Yes, it's in my purse."

"Abby, I have a television magnifier! It's tucked away in my closet. Stay right there and I'll find it." She jumped up and hurried into her office.

"What's a television magnifier?" I called.

"It's a piece of clear vinyl that fits over the screen and enlarges whatever is behind it. It was popular in the sixties."

That would explain why I'd never heard of it. I took the video out of the plastic case and popped it into her DVD player on top of the television.

"I know it's here somewhere," she called.

While I waited, I gobbled a few finger sandwiches. My cell phone rang, so I swallowed hurriedly, ran for my purse, and pulled out my phone. Seeing the name on the display, I flipped it open and said excitedly, "Lottie, good news! I think I found something on the video that will help Richard. Grace and I are going to watch it now and see if we can make out those blurry faces."

"You might want to hold off on that for a little while, sweetie," she said. "Melanie Turner just called and she sounded pretty frantic. She wants to talk to you right away."

"Melanie?" I was amazed. I hadn't thought I'd hear from her again. Melanie wouldn't call me unless she had more information about Jack's murder. Lottie gave me the number and I punched it in, then paced the living room, waiting for her to answer.

"Abby?" she said, at once, her voice tight and edgy. "I need to talk to you. Would you come over?"

I hesitated, remembering my last close call. "Are you alone?"

"Yes. Please. It's important."

"Okay, I'll be there in ten minutes." I shut the phone and went to the office to tell Grace why I had to leave.

"I can't find the magnifier anyway," she told me. "I'll have to pull out some of those boxes in the back of the closet, but I should have it by the time you return. What do you think that phone call means?"

I knew she was hoping Melanie would have news that would clear Richard, because I was hoping the same thing. "I'll let you know as soon as I find out. In the meantime, when you find that magnifier, feel free to watch the video."

* * *

As I sped out of town, I tried to reach Marco to tell him what was going on, but he wasn't answering his cell phone. I called the bar and Chris said he'd left in a hurry. No doubt his sister had suffered another crisis. I turned onto the country lane that led to the Turner farm and slipped my phone back into my purse. As I drove up the gravel driveway I could see Melanie waiting for me at the door, her face pinched and anxious. I hurried up the porch steps and went inside.

Suddenly, there was a blur to my right, and Josiah came at me. It happened so fast all I could do was raise my arms to cover my head, but he only pushed the heavy door shut behind me.

"Sit down," he thundered. "We have to talk."

My lungs gave a wheeze as I resumed breathing, then I smelled the pungent odor of manure coming from Josiah's dusty overalls and wondered if breathing was such a good idea after all.

"Talk about what?" I asked, casting them both nervous glances. "Melanie, what's going on?"

"What's going on is that you've been harassing my daughter," Josiah replied.

I glanced at Melanie again, but she wouldn't look at me. Had she told him about my last visit? Was she that intimidated by him? I curled my fingers into my sweaty palms and tried to look outraged. "Harassing her? I don't know what you're talking about."

He held up one of my green Bloomers pens. "I believe this belongs to you."

I shot Melanie an accusing glare and she looked like she was ready to cry. "He found it on the floor," she said, wringing her hands.

"Sit down," he commanded, indicating the worn navy checked sofa behind me.

I really didn't want to do that. "Look, I don't know what you've got in mind," I said, edging away from him, "but Marco knows I'm here. In fact, he's probably driving out here right now. So why don't you stand away from that door?"

He pointed behind me. "Sit *down*, damn it."

I sat because I didn't have much choice. Melanie sat right beside me, her eyes glued to her father. I wondered if she was there to keep me from trying to escape through the kitchen.

"You are not going to keep tormenting Melanie like this," he said, shaking a thick finger at me. "Her nerves can't take it. She's got a child to raise."

"I wasn't trying to torment her," I told him. "I was trying to find out who killed Jack Snyder."

I saw Josiah glance at Melanie, so I turned to look at her. "What? Do you know who killed him?"

She bowed her head. "It wasn't my father."

CHAPTER TWENTY-FOUR

My mouth fell open. Had Melanie killed Jack? I glanced quickly from Melanie to Josiah, but he only sank into an old wooden chair, pulled off his wire-rimmed glasses, and covered his face in his work-roughened hands.

I laid a hand on her arm and said gently, "Melanie, what are you telling me?"

"She's telling you I didn't do it," Josiah replied wearily. He put his hands on his knees and rubbed the fabric with his palms. "But I did go to meet him in the gazebo."

"So his death was an accident?" I asked, still not getting it.

"No! I don't know! I went out to the gazebo to tell him to stay away from Melanie, but Jack was already dead when I got there."

I shook my head, trying to absorb the startling news. "He was dead? You didn't fight with him?"

"As God is my witness," Josiah said, "I never laid a finger on Jack. He was lying there on the floor with blood all over his face. He wasn't breathing, he wasn't moving, and I got so scared, I ran back for Melanie and we left."

Josiah raked his fingers through his thinning brown hair and said in a broken voice, "I just wanted him to leave my daughter alone, that's all. He'd tortured her long enough."

Melanie rose and went to stand beside him, her hand stroking his shoulder in a surprisingly touching gesture. "It's okay, Papa."

"So neither one of you killed him?"

Josiah looked incredulous and Melanie gaped at me, a horrified expression on her face. "Me? How could you think such a thing? He's Josie's father. I couldn't hurt him."

"I didn't mean to offend you, but what was I supposed to think? You lied to get me out here, and then your father nearly attacked me. Look, I'm really sorry. I wish you'd been honest with me right from the start. Have you told the police what happened?"

Josiah shook his head. "I can't. I'm afraid of what they might do."

"So you lied to them, too."

"I had to, don't you see?" Josiah said, leaning forward. "Who'd provide for my family if I went to prison? I'm the one who puts the food on the table and keeps the roof over their heads. It's *my* responsibility." He thumped his chest. "Nothing's going to jeopardize my family. Nothing." He thrust out his chin and sat back. I knew he was stubborn enough to mean it.

I turned to Melanie. "Listen to me, you might have seen something that would help find Jack's killer. You have to tell the police. There's a man sitting in jail right now who could be facing the death penalty and who's probably innocent. Do you want that on your conscience?"

Tears filled her eyes. "No," she whispered, blinking

them away. She patted her father's slumped shoulders. "Abby's right, Papa. You need to tell the police. It'll be okay, I promise."

It struck me suddenly that Melanie really loved her father, and he clearly loved her. It also struck me that neither one of them was guilty. But if they hadn't killed Jack, who had?

The answer had to be on the video.

"Okay, listen," I said. "I might have a lead to the real killer, but I need you to contact the police right away and tell them what you told me. Will you do that? Please?"

Josiah rose with a sigh. "I'll do it right now."

"Thank you." I dashed out the door, jumped into the Vette, and searched for my cell phone in my purse. "It's me," I said when Grace answered. "Did you find the magnifier?"

"I'm still looking."

"Okay, I'm on my way back to Bloomers. I'll stop by your house as soon as I close up shop."

"I'll leave the door unlocked in case I don't hear you knock. I may still be digging through that closet."

I phoned Marco next and got his voice mail again, this time with a new message. "Not answering. Speak," it said. I told him about Josiah's confession, feeling pretty proud of myself. Amateurish perhaps, but I was putting that puzzle together. With a little luck, those faces on the video would be the last two pieces.

"Call me as soon as you get this," I said, "and would you please record a different message, because the one that's on there now sounds like a load of—"

A beep cut me off. It was just as well.

Late that afternoon I was snipping away at a bunch of house bamboo for a large Oriental-themed arrangement that a customer wanted first thing in the morning, when I heard Sheila's voice in the outer room. Oddly, she didn't sound like her normal, chatterbox self. A few moments later the curtain parted and she stuck her head through. She didn't *look* her normal chatterbox self either. Her hair seemed to have been hastily combed and her long face was stretched taut as though something had unnerved her.

She noticed the stems in my hand and said, "Am I bothering you?"

"No. Come on in."

She was wearing baggy jeans and a T-shirt with a slogan that said DANGER. PMS ZONE, and she had a large paper sack in her hands. "Can I sit here?" she asked, pointing to Lottie's stool.

"Of course."

"Thanks," she said, then eased onto the stool as if she were in pain and put the sack on the table, wincing as she lowered her arm. Then I noticed a discoloration on her jaw.

I stopped what I was doing and went over. "Sheila, what happened to you?"

She covered the mark on her face and gave me a reproachful glance. "You talked to Gunther last night, didn't you?"

"Why?" I asked with a sinking feeling.

She raised both sleeves over her shoulders, revealing finger-shaped bruises.

"Oh, my God. Don't tell me Gunther did that."

"You shouldn't have told him what I said, Abby. That was just between us girls. He was all over me, accusing me of gossiping and persecuting him . . . I've never seen him so mad."

I stared at the marks in horror. "I'm so sorry, but I

swear I never mentioned your name. He didn't even seem angry after I talked to him."

She let out a wavering sigh and covered her shoulders. "What's done is done. I don't hold it against you. I know you didn't mean to get me in trouble."

"I won't go 'see him again, Sheila, I promise. I hope you reported him to your boss."

"No way. Anthony would fire us both. He hates fighting among his staff. Besides, I don't know how Gunther would react if I got him in more trouble."

"He's a bully, Sheila. You can't let him threaten you. If you can't talk to Anthony, then go to the police."

"Yeah, right," she said, rolling her eyes. "That will make things better. Look, I can take care of myself. Don't worry about me."

She started to get up, then noticed the sack. "Oh, I almost forgot these," she said dejectedly. She removed a wicker bread basket and set it on the table. The basket was mounded with golden muffins, covered with plastic wrap, and topped with a big pink bow. "I made cranberry muffins yesterday—I promised I'd bring them for Grace to try—but Lottie says she stayed home today."

"She wasn't feeling up to par, but I'm sure she'll appreciate the muffins when she gets back." I could imagine how much Grace would appreciate them.

The phone rang and Lottie answered it up front. A moment later she peeked through the curtain. "Phone call, Abby."

There was an awkward silence as we waited for Sheila to make a move to leave, and when she didn't, I said, "Excuse me a moment," and got up.

"That's okay," Sheila said with a sad sigh, as if it hadn't occurred to her that she might be intruding. "You go ahead."

I glanced at Lottie and she shrugged.

As I reached for the phone, Sheila eased off the stool and began to explore the room, gazing at the silk flowers and vases on the upper shelves, touching and peering, even opening the big cooler to look inside. She picked up the pruning shears Lottie had left on the table and looked them over.

I turned my back on her and said into the telephone, "Abby Knight."

"Josiah is off the list?" I heard Marco ask. I could tell by the crackling in the background that he was on the road somewhere.

"He's off the list," I said. "Where have you been? I've left messages all over the place."

"Averting another crisis, at least for the time being. I told my sister to go see a marriage counselor for the next one. Have you turned in the video?"

"No, Grace has it, and before you start lecturing me on the rules of evidence, here's why. Grace has a device that will magnify the faces, so I'm going to stop by after work and watch the video on her television. But don't worry. I promise I'll turn it in afterward."

Behind me, I heard Lottie exclaim, "What the hell happened to your face?"

I glanced around to see Sheila holding up her sleeves as she relayed her story.

"Did something happen?" Marco asked.

I said quietly, "Sheila is here. It seems Gunther roughed her up because of my visit last night."

"She reported him, didn't she?"

"I think Lottie is trying to convince her to do that right now," I whispered.

"All right. Let me know if you identify the faces on the video. And if you want me to turn it in for you, bring it down to the bar. I'll be there the rest of the day." He lowered his voice to husky, a tone I hadn't heard in a while, which meant things really had improved on his end. "Maybe we can even sneak back to my office with a couple glasses of bubbly."

Images of the two of us getting cozy on his carpet skated through my mind. Maybe I'd hunt down a loaf of French bread and a hunk of cheese and make it a full-fledged party for two—except that I wouldn't be able to make it. Damn! If I didn't show up for dinner at the country club, my mother would worry and my father would have an APB issued within the hour. I had this horrible picture of Marco and me getting cozy inside, while a SWAT team gathered outside.

"I have to go to dinner at the country club tonight," I said with a disappointed sigh. "Family duties. You know how that goes."

"Yeah, tell me about it."

"Can I have a raincheck? Like for tomorrow night?"

"You got it, sunshine. Someone just beeped me. I'll see you later."

I hung up smiling broadly and turned to find Sheila tucking her paper sack under her arm. "Thanks for talking to me," she said with a hangdog look. "I know you're busy, and I got lots of stuff to do. It's my day off and you know how those chores pile up."

"Did you want to leave the muffins for Grace?" I asked. "We have a refrigerator in back. I'll put them inside and make sure Grace gets them."

"That's okay. I think I'll just bring them by tomorrow."

We watched her clomp out of the shop, then Lottie shook her head in frustration. "She really should report that man to the police."

"Sheila certainly seemed frightened of Gunther, didn't she?" I said, returning to my bamboo project.

Lottie snorted from inside the cooler, where she was pulling flowers for another arrangement. "Wouldn't you be?"

"I don't know. Something doesn't feel right. We've seen Sheila in action. Does she seem the type to be cowed by a dishwasher she refers to as a blockhead?"

"I hear those wheels grinding again," Lottie said, emerging from the cold. "What are you thinking?"

"I'm thinking there has to be a reason that little alarm is buzzing in my head."

"Maybe the alarm is telling you it's almost five o'clock and we still have these orders to finish."

I glanced at my watch. "You're right. I'd better stop talking if I want to have time to watch the video with Grace before I go to dinner."

Half an hour later, I set the alarm, locked the shop, and dashed across the street to my car. Just as I started the engine, my phone rang. I flipped it open and said, "Hey, Marco, I'm on my way to Grace's now."

"Abby, I—Reilly—banquet"—his voice sound like popcorn popping—"found—body—"

"What? A body? I can't hear you, Marco. You're breaking up."

"—body at the banquet center—stabbed with—"

"Whose body?" I shouted.

There was dead air on the other end, but my mind wasn't dead. Far from it. It seemed to be going seventy miles an hour. All I could think of was that Sheila had gone to report Gunther to Anthony after all, and Gunther had killed her.

Then Marco's voice came back. "Are you there? Can you hear me?"

"You're coming in clear now. Tell me what happened."

"Reilly just called from the banquet center. There's been another murder."

"Was it Sheila?"

"No, Gunther."

Gunther? I was so stunned I had to shut off the engine. "Marco, Gunther was the only one left on my list."

"Better start a new list. He was stabbed_with a kitchen knife out by the garbage bin."

"Oh, my God, Marco. Sheila has access to those knives."

"I know. There's a hunt out for her. A squad car went to her apartment to pick her up for questioning, but she wasn't there."

"Who found Gunther's body?"

"Reilly. After he talked to us, he did a little more digging and came up with some interesting information about one of the Garden of Eden's new employees."

"Sheila?"

"Yep. She was fired from her job at a bank a month ago because of suspected fraud. What clinched it for Reilly was that the scheme she had used was identical to the one Jack had used on Richard Davis. Then he found out that Jack had been living with her, so he checked—more— found—"

"You're breaking up again, Marco." I waited for the connection to clear up, and when it didn't, I said, "If you can hear me, I'm on my way to Grace's house to watch the video. Keep me posted on developments there. And if you want to come watch the video with us, the address is three two five Greenleaf. It's two blocks north of Lincoln."

I put my phone away and started the engine, thinking back over Sheila's behavior—her helpful information

about Gunther, her drop-in visits, her nosy questions, her
eavesdropping ... When I combined that with her rela-
tionship with Jack, Gunther's death, and now Sheila on
the loose, I got a queasy feeling in the pit of my stomach.
One thing was clear, she was not a stable person. It made
me all the more anxious to find out who those faces were
on the video.

I hit my brakes as an old Buick LeSabre pulled out in
front of me, tires squealing, like teenaged boys out for a
joyride. Then the car dropped down to a speed of fifteen
miles an hour and I caught a glimpse of a bald head on
the driver's side and curly white hair on the passenger
side. Clearly not teenagers. There was no one behind me.
Why hadn't he waited for me to pass? Why did that happen only when I was in a hurry?

At the corner the Buick rolled to a stop, then inched
forward, stopped, then inched some more, as though the
driver expected someone to dart out and hit him. The
problem was, the only other car at the intersection was
me, and I was *behind* him. I ground my teeth as the car
crept along. I could have pushed him faster than he was
going. At the next corner I turned left and took a longer
route, but at least it got me around the snail. I came up to
the stop sign just in time to see him sail past.

What next, a funeral procession?

I finally turned onto Grace's block, then had to hunt for
a parking space. The old homes on her street had one-car
garages that faced an alley, so most people parked at the
curb in front of their homes. I finally squeezed the Vette
into an opening three houses away, then grabbed my
purse and trotted up the sidewalk.

The door was unlocked, so I stepped inside and called,
"Grace, I'm here."

Her office door was shut, but I could hear her moving

around inside. I put my purse on a chair near the door and looked around. There was a tube of clear vinyl lying in front of the TV, so I picked it up, uncurled it like a scroll, and peered through it.

"I see you found the magnifier," I called.

The silence that greeted me lifted the hairs on the back of my neck. "Grace?" I called again. I rolled up the tube and started to lay it on the coffee table—then I froze. Beside a heavy crystal candy dish was a basket of muffins topped with a pink bow.

CHAPTER TWENTY-FIVE

I stared at the basket and my heart began to hammer. Sheila had been there. Sheila, who might have just killed a man.

I glanced at the office door and listened to the stillness behind it. The alarm in my head was so loud I could barely think. Had she done something to Grace?

I moved quietly, heading for the office. Suddenly the old floorboards creaked to my right, and I turned just as Sheila rushed at me, the plaster bust of Elvis raised above her head. There was no time to run, so I braced myself for the attack, and then everything seemed to happen in slow motion. I saw Sheila's mouth open and heard her cry of rage; then her face contorted as she brought the bust down. I scrambled out of her way, watching as the force of her swing pulled her to the carpet.

"You had to keep poking your nose into that murder," she said, panting like an animal. "You had to go talk to that blockhead one last time. You had to make everything good for your precious Grace."

My breath was coming in short bursts. "Sheila, talk to

me," I begged. "Tell me what happened at the banquet center. Did Gunther come after you again?"

"Yeah, thanks to you. But I told you I could take care of myself, didn't I?" She came at me again, swinging the bust like a baseball bat.

I ducked behind the coffee table, flattening myself against the floor, cringing as wood splintered above me. The heavy legs pushed against my side, pinning me against the sofa and sending the basket of muffins and the crystal candy dish skittering off the end.

As she prepared to swing a third time, I shoved the table away and lunged for the dish, then scuttled beneath the tall end table and covered my head. She kicked the table with her foot, trying to tip it over and expose me. I grabbed one of the curved legs and held on tight.

"Sheila, stop!" I yelled as we wrestled for control of the table. "You're only making things worse for yourself." Across the room my cell phone rang, but I couldn't think beyond that moment, beyond keeping myself alive.

With a gut-wrenching roar, Sheila yanked the table out of my hands. As it crashed against the wall I scrambled into the dining room, then sprang to my feet and held the heavy dish in front of me as though it were a shield.

"Never show fear," my father had told me. I tried it now. I was trembling so hard my teeth were chattering, but I managed to bluster, "Sheila, stop this craziness. Calm down and talk to me."

She stood in the doorway between the living and dining rooms, her chest heaving, her lower lip curved down, exposing crooked bottom teeth. "Don't ever call me crazy. That's what Jack called me. 'You're crazy, Sheila. Why would I marry you?'"

"He was a jerk," I blurted, trying to placate her. "A scumbag. You had every right to be angry with him."

"Jack used me. He said we'd go to Mexico together, get married, and make a brand-new life for ourselves. All we needed was money, and that's where I came in." She swiped angry tears from her eyes. "I had a good position at the bank, Jack told me. It'd be a cinch to get money out of people's savings accounts without anyone knowing. I did it, too. I got the money, and then I lost my job and had to take that shit work at the Garden of Eden. But I did everything he asked because I loved him. And then after he had the money, what did he tell me? He didn't need me anymore. He had Melanie. She was gonna help him get all the money he'd ever need."

I started edging toward the doorway. "What happened Monday night? Did you argue with Jack?"

Her upper lip curled back. "I caught him taking one of the waiter's uniforms and I asked him what he wanted it for. He said it was because he wanted to talk to Melanie so they could make arrangements. He had his little plan to meet her in the gazebo." She shook her head. "What a fool I was to think he cared about me."

I tried to shoot a quick glance over my shoulder, to see how much distance was left between me and the front door. My heart sank as I realized I'd barely make it halfway across the living room before she caught me. "No one will blame you for being angry with him, Sheila."

Her face took on a crafty look. "That's right. They won't blame me, because no one's gonna know I talked to him." She lifted the hem of her black T-shirt. Tucked into the waistband of her jeans was the plastic video case. Then she heaved the bust at me and ran for the kitchen, as if she'd decided to flee rather than try to kill me.

I took off after her and grabbed her around the waist just before she reached the back door. We both went down hard on the tile floor, with Sheila shrieking and twisting like a captured animal. I pushed her flat on her stomach and used my weight to hold her down, pressing one knee into her spine between her shoulder blades, twisting one of her arms behind her back, and using my other hand to keep her head turned to the side, her cheek against the tile.

"You killed Jack to keep him from leaving with Melanie, didn't you?" I said, breathing hard, exerting pressure on her arm as she struggling to get loose. "You followed him to the gazebo and hit him." I pushed her arm up farther, making her moan in pain.

"Yes! I hit him," she spat back. "But I didn't mean to kill him. I begged him not to leave with Melanie. I reminded him of our plans, then he laughed and called me crazy. Me! I looked down at my hand and there was that big marble pestle in it, so I hit him. I couldn't help myself."

She slapped a palm against the floor. "He deserved it. The bastard lied through his teeth. He never intended to take me with him. It was her he wanted—that mousy Melanie. He was only using me, just like every man uses me—taking everything I have then spitting me out like a piece of rotten meat."

Huge sobs shook her body. "I didn't want to kill Jack. I loved him. Why didn't he love me back?"

"What happened between you and Gunther today, Sheila?"

She sniffled. "I went out to the center to settle things between us. Like you said, I couldn't let him get away with pushing me around. So I got one of the knives and tucked it in my jeans, then I asked him to step out the back door with me. I told him if he ever touched me again, I'd kill him. He thought that was funny. And then the blockhead shoved me—hard—up against the garbage bin. That's when something clicked in my head, and suddenly the knife was in my hand."

She went limp beneath me, crying hard. "I'm not a murderer. I didn't mean to kill anyone, and I didn't want to hurt you," she wept. "You and Grace and Lottie—you were my friends."

I released her arm and took the plastic case from her waistband. "You have to turn yourself in to the police, Sheila. It will go better for you if you voluntarily give yourself up. I'll even help you find a good lawyer."

She nodded, one cheek against the floor. "Thanks," she said in a whisper.

I waited a moment to make sure the fight had left her, then I stood up and she immediately curled into a fetal position. I was weak from struggling and drained of emotion, but more than that, I was terrified that Sheila had done something to Grace. It was all I could do to make my trembling legs carry me to Grace's office.

Grace was lying on her side on the carpet beside her desk, papers scattered all around her. Her face was a sickly gray, her body too still. Blood trickled down her left temple from a gash in her head. She moaned but seemed unaware of her surroundings. I knelt beside her and felt for a pulse in her neck. It fluttered unsteadily beneath my fingertips.

With my heart in my throat, I reached for her desk phone and pressed 911. Grace moaned again, so I blurted the address, asked for an ambulance, and knelt beside her, whispering a prayer. I blinked tears out of my eyes. Why hadn't I looked in the office right away? What if Grace died because of my delay? "Come on, Grace," I said, rubbing her wrists, patting her face. "Open your eyes. Let me know you're all right. I don't want to lose you. Remember what you always tell me. When the going gets tough, the tough get going."

Her eyes moved beneath crepey lids. I held my breath as her eyelids fluttered, then slowly opened. Her gaze sought mine and her lips tried to form words. I leaned my ear near her mouth.

"Sheila—did it."

"I know, Grace. I know. Help is coming. Just stay with me."

I saw the relief in her eyes and I couldn't help bending to hug her. As I straightened I heard a noise behind me and turned.

Sheila stood above us, her face wet with tears, the little Elvis saber in her hand. She yanked off the sheath, exposing the long, sharp blade. "I can't go to prison," she said in a trembling voice. Then she raised the dagger.

CHAPTER TWENTY-SIX

"No!" I cried as her arm swung down. I had a split second to dodge the blow, but I was afraid it would strike Grace. As the sharp point rushed toward my face, I grabbed Sheila's arm, catching her wrist with both hands. I pulled down on her arm with all my strength, throwing her off balance. She tumbled to the floor and I fell over her, a tangle of arms and legs as we struggled for the dagger.

Her fury gave her greater strength. She sprang to her feet and came at me again, but this time she was too quick for me. This time I could only cross my arms over my head to protect myself.

Suddenly a door crashed open in the outer room. Startled, Sheila swung around, giving me time to pull back my foot and kick her in the knee. As she sagged, Marco charged into the office and grabbed her, pinning her arms down and wrestling the saber out of her hands. Heavy footsteps and more shouts sounded outside, and then Reilly and his squad poured through the doorway.

I could hear Sheila ranting as they led her away, but I

was focused on Grace, who'd lost consciousness again. Marco crouched beside me and we waited anxiously until Reilly came to say the ambulance had arrived.

Marco helped me to my feet so we could get out of their way. I hovered in the doorway, watching the EMTs check her, then followed when they carried her to the ambulance on a stretcher. "I'm going with her," I told Marco and climbed in.

Reilly gave the EMT a nod, letting him know it was okay for me to be there, and then the door was shut behind me. I sat beside Grace, holding her cool hand in mine, telling her she would be all right. At the county hospital she was whisked into the emergency room, leaving me to pace the waiting room alone. Marco arrived within minutes and pressed a cup of coffee in my hand, leading me to a bank of orange chairs.

I sank into the molded plastic seat and held the cup under my nose, breathing in the bittersweet coffee aroma. I took a sip and let it sear down my throat. Marco sat silently beside me, understanding that I needed time to process all that had happened.

"I feel so stupid for letting myself be duped," I said. "I should have sensed something was wrong with Sheila right from the start. She was always so helpful, so forthcoming with information . . . I thought I was smarter than that."

"Sunshine, it happens to the best of us." He put his arm around my shoulders and let me lean against him. "You learn as you go along. And by the way, when you talk to Grace, let her know Richard is out of jail. The Texas case was dismissed and he was cleared of all charges. That should make her feel a whole lot better."

I let out a heavy sigh of relief and closed my eyes. "Have you ever thought you were about to die?"

"Many times."

"You know those words you think of in those dark, scary moments, words you know you should have said but somehow never got around to saying? Then the moment passes and you tuck them away?" I paused, trying not to let him see my chin tremble. "You know what I thought when that blade came down at me? That I should have told Grace what a wonderful friend she'd been to me." My voice caught.

Marco turned me to face him, then brushed a wisp of hair away from my eyes. "You'll have a chance to tell her. She's a strong woman." His eyes searched mine. "So are you."

Reilly came walking up to us and crouched in front of my chair. "Are you doing all right?" At my nod, he rose to his full height and gazed down at me in that superior cop way. "Good."

"Are you about to give me a lecture?" I asked, swiping away a tear.

"Yes."

I settled against Marco's warm shoulder with a contented sigh. "Fire when ready."

He started to shake his finger at me, then stopped. "What's the use? It wouldn't do any good anyway."

"It's taken you a long time to figure that out, Reilly."

Grace was diagnosed with a concussion and admitted to a room to be watched overnight. Within an hour, she was sitting up, talking, and asking for tea. Lottie had come down to the hospital as soon as she heard the news, so I asked Marco to take me home so I could de-stress.

But before I left, I asked for a moment alone with Grace to tell her the news about Richard. Plus, there was something I needed to say to her.

"What is it, dear?" she asked, gazing at me with some concern as I took her hands and held them between mine.

I gave her the wonderful news about Richard, and after she'd absorbed it, I took a deep breath and said, "I want you to know something. You mean a lot to me."

She seemed surprised. "Thank you, Abby. You mean a lot to me, too." She gave my hand a gentle squeeze. "It's been quite a day, hasn't it?"

"That's the understatement of the year. Listen, would you do me one little favor before I leave? Would you give me a quote?" I felt silly asking, like a child needing a bedtime story.

She thought a moment. Then she cleared her throat and said, "As Oscar Wilde wrote, 'One can live for years sometimes without living at all, and then all life comes crowding into one single hour.' I think that's quite fitting, don't you?"

"Perfect."

"Do you still have that bottle of wine I gave you Monday night?" Marco called from the kitchen. "Never mind. I found it."

I had changed into a pair of fresh jeans and a T-shirt, put on a Harry Connick Jr. CD, and was stretched out on the sofa, letting the music float over me. Nikki was at work, and Simon was sitting in my bedroom window watching a gigantic spider spin a web just outside the screen, leaving the apartment to me and Marco, who at that moment came in with two glasses and the chilled bottle, sat down, and put my bare feet on his lap. He poured the wine and handed me a glass, then touched his rim to mine as we toasted life and friendship and good timing.

For a while we just sat there listening to the music and

letting the wine roll over our tongues. I didn't know what he was thinking, but I was thinking how fortunate I was to have him watching my back, and how much I wished it could be like this between us all the time.

As Marco refilled our glasses I said, "Remember what I was telling you in the waiting room, about those things that never get said?"

He put his glass on the coffee table, swung my feet off his lap, and leaned over me, holding me with his enigmatic gaze. "Sometimes they don't need to be said."

He pressed his mouth against mine. A sense of his masculinity curled around me, and my heart thumped as though I was about to leap off a cliff into the dark unknown.

I didn't have a chance to explore that cliff, however, because there was a rap on the door.

My first thought was that Grace had taken a turn for the worse and someone had come to give me the bad news. But surely I would have received a telephone call from the hospital.

"Expecting company?" Marco asked.

"No. I can't imagine who it would be." I glanced at the clock on the bookcase. "It's eight thirty. That's too early for Nikki, and she'd use her key anyway."

"Maybe you should answer it and find out."

Then I remembered I'd forgotten to call my parents to tell them why I hadn't made it to dinner. "Oh, no. It's the SWAT team," I cried, jumping up.

"The SWAT team?" Marco glanced at me like I'd lost my mind.

"Or—even worse—my mother." I smoothed down my hair, straightened my clothing, and hurried toward the door, calling back, "Don't worry. Stay right there. I'll handle everything."

I squinted through the peephole and saw an eyeball peering back at me—a very familiar eyeball.

"Abby?" the muffled voice said through the heavy door.

"Who is it?" Marco asked from the living room.

"No one . . . an apparition . . . It'll disappear any second now. Go away, apparition!"

I looked out the peephole again. The eyeball was still looking back

"Abby, open up!"

This could not be happening.

I opened the door and there stood Jillian, a wide-brimmed straw hat on her head, a black and tan silk outfit on her torso—and a Louis Vuitton suitcase in each hand.

"You are *not* supposed to be here," I whispered viciously. "You're supposed to be in Hawaii. With your husband!" I leaned out the door and took a look down the hallway. No husband. Dear God.

"What did you do with him, Jillian?"

Her chin trembled, then the tremble spread to her face, then she dropped the luggage and threw herself at me, sobbing onto my shoulder. It could mean only one thing: she'd jilted Claymore. At least this time she'd waited until after the wedding.

Marco came up the hallway and mouthed, *"I think I'll go."*

I shook my head wildly and gave him a pleading look that said, *Don't leave me with this crazy woman. Give me ten minutes and I'll have her out of here.*

He wiggled his fingers good-bye, and was gone, shutting the door softly behind him.

I peeled my cousin off my body and held her at arm's length, studying her tear-stained face. "I hope you know you've ruined my romantic evening."

"I'm sorry."

"No, you're not. You're never sorry. Why did you leave Claymore?"

"I didn't." She broke into a fresh round of weeping. "He left *me*."

"That's not possible. You told me he loved you to distraction."

"He lied." Still sniffling, she picked up her bags and headed down the hallway.

"Where are you going?"

"To your room. It's all right if I stay here, isn't it?"

"Wait . . . Jillian . . ."

Too late. She was already unpacking.

Simon skittered around the corner and tried to wedge himself behind the refrigerator.

"I know the feeling," I told him with a sigh.

From the bedroom I heard vinyl clacking against vinyl; then Jillian called, "Do you have any more hangers?"

There was only one thing to do. "Move over, Simon. I'm coming in."

Read on for an excerpt from

another Flower Shop Mystery

by Kate Collins,

SNIPPED IN THE BUD

Available from Signet

I jammed both feet on the brake and brought my old yellow convertible to a screeching halt mere inches from the groin of a dragon. Okay, not a dragon in the fairy tale sense of the word. This dragon was the flesh-and-blood human variety—one Z. Archibald Puffer, a former JAG officer turned law professor who was often referred to as Puffer the Dragon. He was called that not just because of his last name, but also because of his ability to destroy the bravest law student in one fiery blast of fury.

My personal name for him was Snapdragon, because he had a habit of snapping pencils in two and hurling the eraser half at the head of the student whose answer had displeased him. He went through so many pencils that he bought them in bulk, made to his specifications—glossy black barrels with his initials monogrammed in silver to look like bolts of lightning: *Zap*. I had been struck several times and even bore a tiny scar on my forehead from his last attack, which came with his pronouncement that I was never to step foot in his lecture hall again. That was followed in short order by my expulsion from law school, which, in turn, prompted my then fiancé Pryce Osborne to break off our engagement and leave town until his humiliation over my failure had faded. *His* humiliation.

It had occurred to me back then that the old maxim of bad luck coming in threes was actually true. Now, as Puffer glared up the shiny hood of my reconditioned 1960 Corvette with his spiteful, ice blue eyes, and my heart pounded and my clammy hands clasped the steering wheel so hard my knuckles hurt, my gut feeling was that the Rule of Three had begun again. Which meant I still had two to go.

The irony was that the only reason I had come to the law school—a place I tried my best to avoid—was to deliver a lily that Professor Puffer had ordered. However, I didn't think now would be the best time to hand it over: He might snap it off and chuck the vase at me.

"You red-headed fumigant," he jeered, as college students gathered on both sides of the street. "You nearly killed me."

I wasn't sure what a fumigant was, but I knew it wasn't good. "Sorry," I squeaked, slumping down as far as I could. Considering that I was short, it was pretty far.

Was it my fault he hadn't used the crosswalk? Was it my fault he was talking on his cell phone instead of paying attention to traffic? I didn't think so. Had it been anyone else, I would have told him as much. But that steely glare brought back so many bad memories that all I could do was duck.

"Hey, there *is* someone inside," one curious student said, coming up for a look.

I raised my head just enough to peer over the dash. Mercifully, Snapdragon had moved on, but not before stopping at the curb to deliver a parting shot. "Be expecting a call from the police," he sneered, working his cell phone buttons. "I'm turning you in for reckless driving."

Great. Just what I needed to make my morning complete. *Zap.*

I knew what his fury was really about. Puffer was still indignant about the night he'd spent in the slammer over three years ago on a Driving Under the Influence charge. I'd had nothing to do with it, of course—I was still downstate at Indiana University at the time—but that hadn't mattered to Puffer. What had mattered was that the dragon had been publicly disgraced by a Knight—my father, Sgt. Jeffrey Knight, then of the New Chapel PD—and once I stepped foot in his classroom and Puffer made the connection, he never let me forget it.

So it really shouldn't have surprised me that this new trio of unpleasant events would begin with Snapdragon. In fact, my first clue should have been the order I saw when I walked into my flower shop, Bloomers, that morning: one black lily, suitable for funeral display, noon delivery, to Professor Z. Puffer, New Chapel University School of Law. I mean, who would order a single lily for a funeral? Bugs Bunny?

Knowing my history with Puffer, my assistant Lottie had tried to talk me out of making the delivery. But no, I'd decided I needed to face the dragon to conquer those irrational fears I'd held on to way too long. After all, Puffer had no power over me now. I wasn't that frightened first year law student any more. I owned a business, or at least I owned the mortgage for a business. It took courage to run a flower shop at the age of twenty-six. It also took money, which was something I hadn't yet managed to produce in quantity. Which reminded me. I still had to deliver the lily and collect my money.

I glanced over at the dusky purple flower (the closest I

could get to black) in its slender black vase—the entire package wrapped in black-tinted cellophane, tied with a solemn black ribbon and wedged securely in a foam container in front of the passenger seat—and tried to imagine Puffer's reaction when he saw me walk into his office with it. Maybe I should take Lottie up on her offer after all.

Horns honked behind me. I glanced in my rear view mirror and saw a line of cars waiting to turn into the law school's parking lot. I quickly pulled into a visitor's space, shut off the engine, and took long, slow breaths to calm my nerves. What was the big deal anyway? All I had to do was put the pot on Puffer's desk and leave a bill. If I was lucky, he might even be in the cafeteria eating lunch, in which case I could just give everything to his secretary.

A car pulled into the space to my right. I glanced over at the metallic green Mini Cooper and saw Professor Carson Reed at the wheel. Great. Of the hundreds of people I could have seen at the college that day, I had to find the only two on campus who held grudges against me.

From the corner of my eye I watched Reed polish off the last of a burger, crumple the wrapper, check his teeth in his rear view mirror and get out. He eyed my Vette but ignored me as he strode off, briefcase in hand.

I once liked Professor Reed. A tall, vain, handsome, single man in his late thirties, with a reputation on campus of being a playboy, he'd been one of the few professors whose lectures I'd actually understood, even if I hadn't passed his exams. Plus he'd written several papers on the importance of taking a stand against injustice—a subject dear to my heart.

Then Reed became the legal advisor for a cosmetics laboratory that had come to town—a company that I'd recently discovered tested products on animals kept in little wire cages, something I couldn't—make that *wouldn't*—tolerate. Just a week ago, during a demonstration to protest that very fact, Professor Reed had had me arrested for obstruction. Apparently, he hadn't welcomed the picket line I'd organized to block the entrance gate.

As I was being led away in handcuffs, I told him in a loud voice that I'd do it again if it meant saving the lives of innocent creatures, and I'd take on anyone who advocated torturing helpless animals—including him. Then I called him a hypocritical snake-in-the-grass for selling out to corporate greed. The local newspaper even quoted me on that.

Needless to say, Reed was no fan of mine, especially since photos of the protest made the front page of the *New Chapel News,* and the accompanying article painted him in a particularly unflattering light. For a man with Reed's arrogance, I didn't imagine it had been an easy pill to swallow and I was certain the less he saw of me the better. Then again, I wasn't in any rush to see him, either, but since his office was next to Puffer's, the odds of it were high.

I glanced in my rear view mirror and saw a squad car pull up behind me. Puffer had called the cops after all.

"Well, well. Would you look who we have here?" a droll male voice to my left said.

Resigning myself to embarrassment, I got out of the Vette and turned to face Sgt. Sean Reilly, a good-looking, forty-year-old, Irish-American police officer with intelligent brown eyes and a perturbed scowl. "Top o' the lunch hour to you," I said, trying to prompt a smile.

It didn't work. "It's not the top of *my* lunch hour," he grumbled.

"I'd say not, if they have you making routine traffic stops."

My second attempt at humor didn't work either. Reilly planted his hands on his black leather belt. "I don't make routine traffic stops. I heard dispatch read your license plate number and volunteered to take the call as a favor to *you*."

Ouch. And Nikki had laughed when I'd paid extra for a vanity license plate that read: PHLORIST R ME. "Gee, that was really sweet of you, Reilly. Does that mean I can go?"

"No. It means you can tell me why you tried to run down Professor Puffer."

"Let's clear up that misconception right now. I didn't try to run him down. He stepped out in front of me."

"He said you came within an inch of taking his life."

"*Pfft*. It was at least two."

Reilly's scowl deepened.

"He's a drama queen, Reilly. Okay, so maybe I was fiddling with my radio for a second. That's beside the point. The point is, he has it in for me because my father hauled him in on a DUI once."

"Did you, or did you not, almost hit him?"

I scratched the end of my nose, trying to think of a way around the question. Clearly, I should have paid more attention in those law classes. "Yes, I almost hit him but—"

"Uh-uh," he said, wagging a finger at me. "No buts."

"Mitigating circumstances!" I cried. Wow. I *had* remembered something. "Puffer walked out from between two parked cars and was gabbing away on his cell phone. He didn't even look up to see if anyone was coming."

Reilly studied me for a long moment, then finally growled, "All right. Get out of here."

"I'm free to go?"

"On one condition. That I don't get any more calls about your driving. Got it?"

"You bet." I blew him a kiss and watched him pull away. Then I checked the time, saw I had five minutes to get the flower up to Puffer's office, and scrambled for the package.

New Chapel University covered an area of approximately fifteen square blocks, encompassing ten buildings, three dormitories, and a handful of Greek houses. It was a small, private college, but it had an excellent reputation, and its law school held its own with any in the country—not that they could prove it by me. I tucked the flower in the crook of an arm and headed toward the stately two-story brown brick building that housed the law school, pausing at the curb to let a pale blue Jaguar go past. I recognized the car as belonging to Jocelyn Puffer, Snapdragon's wife, a reserved, almost subdued woman who seemed the exact opposite of her husband. It was unusual to see her at the university, not that I blamed her for making herself scarce. I'd want to avoid Puffer, too.

I took a breath and continued on toward the double glass doors. As soon as I stepped into the entrance hall and saw the sights and smelled the smells that had greeted me every day for nine miserable months, I broke out in a cold sweat. *Focus on the flower, Abby. That'a girl.* To my right was a hallway that led to the lecture halls, and to my left was a wide, stone stairway that led up to the professors' offices, the only access other than a private elevator around the corner on the right that was strictly for the staff and the disabled. Beyond the stairway was a law library that didn't get much use now that everything could be found on the Internet.

I turned left and climbed the steps, berating myself for letting my fear of a bully like Puffer get such a grip on me. I was making a delivery, for heaven's sake, not presenting an oral argument. At the top of the staircase I entered the large, central, secretarial pool that served the nine offices around it, three on a side, plus a computer lab and a conference room. The area was empty and quiet now, the secretaries having gone to lunch, except for the one I'd been hoping to find—Beatrice Boyd, whose habit was to eat a tuna salad sandwich at her desk.

Known as Aunt Bea by those of us she'd consoled after we'd limped out of Puffer's inner sanctum emotionally bruised, she was a plain woman with a long, narrow face and graying brown hair that she wore braided and wound on the back of her head, usually with a pencil stuck into it like a hair pick. She used no make up other than lilac lipstick and never wore any jewelry except a slender silver watch. She worked for two of the full-time professors, Puffer and Carson Reed, and as everyone always said, she had the patience of a saint to put up with them.

As I approached, she took her purse out of her desk drawer and straightened, a distracted look on her face. She had on the same navy blue skirt and white blouse that had always been her uniform. "Oh!" she cried when she saw me. "You gave me a start, Abby." She gave me a belated smile that seemed a little on the forced side. "I wish I had time to chat with you, but I have an errand to run."

I held up the wrapped lily. "And I have a delivery for Professor Puffer."

"He's not in," she said, starting for the stairs. "Just set it on his desk."

"Sure." I watched her briefly, wondering what her

hurry was. Then I remembered why I was there and turned to stare at Puffer's closed office door. Okay, I could do this.

Holding the lily in front of me like a shield, I walked toward the dragon's lair, trying to ignore the baseball-size knot of fear in my stomach. As I passed Professor Reed's office I could hear him talking in a sharp, but hushed, voice. No one answered, so I figured he was on the phone. From the sound of it, he wasn't a happy camper.

I stopped at Puffer's door, knocked, and when no one answered, took a deep breath and stepped inside, extremely relieved to find that Beatrice was right. The dragon was gone.

His office was just as I remembered it: a wall of bookshelves with the books arranged not only by color, but also by size; another wall of awards and photos from his JAG days; a Formica topped desk with metal legs; a high-backed leather chair; a door at the back that led to a vestibule with an elevator that went down to the lecture hall; and, finally, the wooden chair upon which I had sat many times, fighting back tears, while he ridiculed my papers.

The memory brought an angry blush to my face, which, on a redhead's fair skin, was bright enough to look feverish. I plunked the cellophane wrapped flower on the desk, next to his computer monitor, propped the bill beside it, and was ready to leave—then I saw the can of glossy black pencils and couldn't resist the temptation. I glanced over my shoulder at the doorway to make sure no one was there, then snatched one of the sleek tools and held it as if I were going to snap it in two, imagining the satisfaction of hurling the eraser end at Puffer.

Suddenly, the door at the rear of his office opened and in charged the dragon in all his intimidating glory—head up, shoulders back, spine stiff and nostrils flaring, as if he were a general in the military embarking on a war campaign.

And there I stood like a deer in the headlights, holding his pencil.